NORMAN'S CONQUEST

Norman's Conquest

A NOVEL

by Don Butler

OTTAWA PRESS
AND PUBLISHING
MYSTERY

OTTAWA PRESS AND PUBLISHING
MYSTERY

Ottawa Press and Publishing

ISBN BOOK: 978-1-990896-18-7
ISBN E-BOOK: 978-1-990896-19-4

Cover design: Joanna D'Angelo
Interior layout: Patti Moran Graphic Design

Printed and bound in Canada

Library and Archives Canada Cataloguing in Publication

Title: Norman's conquest / Don Butler.
Names: Butler, Don (Journalist), author.
Description: Sequel to: A Life of Bliss.
Identifiers: Canadiana (print) 20240346092 | Canadiana (ebook) 20240350804
ISBN 9781990896187 (softcover) | ISBN 9781990896194 (Kindle)
Subjects: LCGFT: Detective and mystery fiction. | LCGFT: Novels.
Classification: LCC PS8603.U8385 N67 2024 | DDC C813/.6—dc23

For Christina Spencer, my wife and creative partner, and in fond memory of the glorious madhouse that was daily newspaper journalism during its heyday.

Part One
Rise and Fall

One

ATHENS, SEPTEMBER 2005

"Christ on a bicycle."

Norman Pugsley hissed the words through clenched teeth. The dull ache in his chest was getting worse and there was no one to complain to about it.

The white-haired Greek man who shared his hospital room was snoring lustily in a nearby bed, deep in the grip of post-operative sedatives. Even if he'd been conscious, he spoke no English, as Pugsley had discovered after a few attempts at conversation.

Pugsley had arrived at the Onassis Cardiac Surgery Centre three days earlier, barely clinging to life after collapsing in his Athens hotel room. In a sense, he was fortunate. The Onassis Centre was Greece's pre-eminent cardiac hospital. If you had a heart problem in Greece, it was the place to be.

Doctors had quickly determined that their new patient, a burly 62-year-old journalist from Canada with thinning grey hair and a bristle moustache, had suffered what they called a STEMI, the most serious type of heart attack, triggered when a coronary artery is completely blocked. They had performed a procedure that saved his life – for now, at least. They ordered him to remain in hospital until they deemed him fit to travel to his home in Ottawa.

The damnable thing was, Pugsley hadn't wanted to be in Greece in the first place. Over his strenuous objections, his newspaper, the Ottawa *Daily Advocate*, had dispatched him to find and retrieve the paper's hapless travel editor, one Bliss Browning, who'd gone rogue, mysteriously travelling to Greece after blowing off his actual assignment to Africa.

The *Advocate*'s editor, Renata Richter, had been talking long-distance to Pugsley on the phone from Ottawa when he'd collapsed. She'd immediately alerted hotel staff. In a very real sense, she'd saved him.

Before his heart attack, Pugsley reflected, he had routinely dismissed Richter, a mid-life recruit from academia, as a "frickin' fruitcake" who had no business running a newspaper. But now, she was at his bedside in Athens and seemed almost heroic – someone who'd acted decisively when it really mattered.

"Renata," he croaked, "I owe you big time." She waved away his gratitude. "Anyone would have done the same thing."

Richter stayed with him for hours, sometimes slipping on glasses to read aloud stories from the *International Herald Tribune*. At times, Richter talked about things that Pugsley deemed nonsensical, like her musings about reducing the *Advocate*'s cops and courts reporting to free up resources for expanded coverage of the arts. But instead of greeting her ideas with derision, as he might have in the past, he quietly asked questions, hoping she'd recognize the impracticality of her notions.

As they became more comfortable with one another, they talked about their childhoods: Richter the only child of Montreal professional parents, a surgeon and a professor of French literature; Pugsley one of five offspring of a small-town carpenter and stay-at-home mom. "Never went to college," he told her. "Marks weren't good enough, and I couldn't afford it anyway. But supposedly one of my ancestors was a famous poet."

"What was his name?" Richter asked.

"Something like … Jesus, what was it again? Coleridge. His last name was Coleridge."

"Not … Samuel Taylor Coleridge?" ventured Richter.

"Yeah, that's it. I looked him up once."

She stared at him. "Holy Hannah, Norman," she exclaimed. "I studied him in university. *The Rime of the Ancient Mariner* is one of my favourite poems. It's long, but once upon a time, I could recite big chunks of it."

"No shit," Pugsley said. He'd been forced to study the epic poem in high school but had flushed it from his memory without regret. Richter shut her eyes and began to utter words strange to Pugsley's ears.

"With sloping masts and dipping prow,
As who pursued with yell and blow
Still treads the shadow of his foe,
And forward bends his head,
The ship drove fast, loud roared the blast,
And southward aye we fled."

She opened her eyes and looked squarely at her bedridden managing editor. "Not bad, considering I haven't recited that poem in nearly 30 years." She studied him closely. "I never would have guessed you had such an illustrious ancestor, Norman," she said.

"Yeah, well, it was a long time ago. Guess I missed out on those genes."

A couple of days after her arrival in Greece, Richter showed up with important news. "Harrison thinks he knows where Bliss has gone." Richter had dispatched Harrison Howard, the paper's books editor and Browning's only true friend, to track down the wayward travel editor while she tended to Pugsley.

"That's amazing," he said. "Where is the bastard?"

Richter ignored the profanity. "He's in the area known as the Mani, it appears. On the trail of that story about the late opera diva Maria Callas he's apparently obsessed with."

"What's the Mani?"

"It's a peninsula of the Peloponnese," Richter said, as if that meant anything to him. "I'm going to fly to Kalamata, link up with Harrison and we'll drive to the Mani to see if we can find Bliss." She gave Pugsley a searching look. "Will you be OK for a few days without me?"

Pugsley wanted to say no. He'd come to depend on Richter's visits to occupy the time and raise his spirits. But he needed to take one for the team. "Sure, sure, I'll be fine."

●●●

The hours passed slowly without Richter's company. His Greek roommate only woke up to eat or when nurses or doctors visited to check on his condition. Pugsley couldn't understand a word they said, so their visits were more disruptive than diverting.

Twice a day, a nurse took Pugsley for a stroll around the hospital. Together, they shuffled down antiseptic corridors and tested his stamina on short staircases. Once, the nurse directed him to a shower stall, where he gratefully washed away days of accumulated grime.

Mostly, though, Pugsley shut his eyes and pondered his life so far. He'd spent the last 37 years at the *Advocate*. There'd been a lot of ups and a few downs, including one big misfortune he tried not to think about. He'd been managing editor for a dozen years but had stalled there. At his age, there wasn't much chance he'd ever be editor-in-chief. And now he'd had a heart attack, in a foreign country to boot.

Norman Pugsley was not an introspective man, but even he recognized he'd reached a fork in the road. Assuming his health bounced back, he could return to his job and play out the string for another two or three years. Or he could heed his heart's not-so-subtle warning and make a change.

Preoccupied by these thoughts, Pugsley was at first only dimly aware of a commotion behind the curtain beside the next bed. Nurses and doctors were bent over the Greek patient, speaking urgently in low tones.

As he watched through a small opening, someone handed a piece of equipment to a doctor, who quickly attached two pads to his neighbour's chest. The doctor stepped back and pushed a button. The man's body convulsed. The doctor pushed the button again. And again. After the sixth attempt, the medical team stopped, shook their heads, and covered his neighbour's body with a white sheet. Orderlies arrived an hour later, placed the body on a gurney and wheeled it away.

In the few days they'd shared the room, Pugsley and the Greek man hadn't exchanged an intelligible word. But now that he was gone – really gone – Pugsley was unaccountably sad. His eyes moistened. "This is ridiculous," he muttered. "Pull yourself together, Norm." But the whispers of mortality were hard to ignore.

•••

Pugsley was starting to feel better. The ache in his chest had subsided and some of his usual energy was beginning to return. Still, his heart skipped a few beats when Bliss Browning, the missing staffer, strode blithely into his hospital room.

To Pugsley, Browning had always been one of the newsroom's most forgettable figures. Now this lacklustre man, whose unfathomable delinquency had forced him to cross an ocean, was standing a few feet from his bed, unflinchingly meeting his gaze. He didn't even have the decency to look embarrassed.

"Jesus, Browning! What are *you* doing here? And what have you done with Renata?" Pugsley demanded. The bastard actually smiled. "She and Harrison have gone home," Browning said, matter-of-factly.

"Whaddaya mean, gone home?"

"They're gone, Norm. On a plane back to Ottawa as we speak. It's just you and me now. I'm going to look after you until you're well enough to travel."

Pugsley's eyelids drooped and closed. *Please, Jesus, let this be a hallucination!* But when he opened his eyes again, Browning was still there.

The pre-coronary Norman had fantasized about the violence he would visit on his wayward employee when he tracked him down. Now they were in the same room, but he found it hard to muster any such aggression.

Browning broke the lengthening silence. "I owe you an apology, Norm. None of this would have happened to you if I'd stuck to the plan and gone to Africa. I'm truly sorry."

Pugsley glowered. "What in the name of tender testicles were you thinking? Was it that bloody Callas story? Is that why you did it?"

"Yes, but it's a long story, Norm. I'll tell you all about it someday."

"Well, did you at least get the damn story?" asked Pugsley, irritated by Browning's evasion.

"I'm not 100 per cent sure. But I think so."

"You're not sure? Bloody hell! Then all of this was for nothing."

"Not nothing," Browning said softly.

"What, then?"

"I ... met someone. Someone very special."

"You *met* someone?"

"Matina. Her name is Matina."

"Mother of suffering Christ, Browning! We're running a newspaper, not a dating service."

"Things don't always happen the way we expect, Norm," Browning replied with a smile. "Sometimes fate writes a different script. I was married once, and it ended badly. I thought I was through with love. But now ..."

To Pugsley's surprise, Browning's words struck a chord. His own marriage had fallen apart years ago. When his wife abruptly told him she wanted out, he was bewildered and aghast. After it became clear her mind was made up, righteous anger incinerated any hope of reconciliation. For a while, things got ugly.

"Look, I've been there," Pugsley said, his tone softening. "My marriage crashed and burned too. But I didn't expect my employer to set me up with a new squeeze."

"Believe me, Norm, I had no idea this would happen. The only woman on my mind was Maria Callas. But Matina might be my best chance ... maybe my only chance ... to find love. There hasn't been much of that so far, and I'm 47. The clock is ticking."

Pugsley gave Browning an appraising look. Perhaps for the first time, he glimpsed the struggling human beneath his bland exterior. "Well," he said at last, "screw all that. So, what's the plan?"

•••

In the days that followed, Browning reliably appeared at Pugsley's bedside bearing pastries he'd purchased from a bakery near his hotel – honey-drenched samades, savory tiropita and sweet and succulent baklava. The treats were unfamiliar, but Pugsley gobbled them greedily.

Between bites, he regaled Browning with tales of his days as a budding reporter at the Minnedosa *Tribune*, the Moose Jaw *Times-Herald* and the Cornwall *Standard-Freeholder* in the 1960s.

"I was 18 when I started at the *Trib*," he recalled. "The editor was a crusty old weasel, Marvin Grundle was his name. I wrote all the stories, took all the pictures. Far as I could tell, Marvin's only job was to give me shit. Got out of there as soon as I could.

"Things were better in Moose Jaw and Cornwall. Learned a lot about newspapering, very quickly. Had no choice if I wanted to survive. But

Peterborough was my favourite stop."

"I didn't know you worked at the *Examiner*," Browning exclaimed. "Was Robertson Davies still around?"

"He hadn't been editor for donkey's years, but he still owned it when I got there. Sold it a few months later. Only met him once. Hell of a beard on that guy – put Santa to shame, it did. Tried to read one of his novels once but couldn't get into it."

"When did you start at the *Advocate*?" asked Browning, who listened politely to these tales. It seemed that Pugsley wanted to talk, *needed* to talk. The act of talking, of remembering, was a sort of therapy, or so it seemed.

"It was 1968," Pugsley said. "The paper wasn't great then, but I was thrilled to land a job on a big-city daily. Never dreamed I'd spend the rest of my career there, though."

"Why'd you stay?"

"I became something of a star, believe it or not. 'Page One Pugsley,' they used to call me. Until … well, let's just say I had a fall from grace. Took me years to recover."

"What happened?" Browning asked.

He didn't answer, and Browning thought for a moment he hadn't heard the question. He was about to repeat it when Pugsley finally spoke. "I don't like to talk about it. It was a painful time." Browning took the hint; he didn't need to know.

One afternoon, a doctor entered the room and listened to Pugsley's heart. "How are you feeling?" he asked in heavily accented English.

"Not too bad, doc," Pugsley said. "When do you think I can get out of this place?"

"I think you're ready. How about tomorrow morning?"

Pugsley brightened. "Shit, yes! Can you get me a flight, Bliss?" he asked, addressing Browning by his given name for the first time.

"I'll see what I can do."

Browning was back early the next morning with good news. "I got you a reservation on an Olympic Airlines flight. It leaves this afternoon for London Heathrow, where you'll catch an Air Canada flight back to Ottawa."

"That's terrific! Jesus, Browning, how'd you manage that?"

Browning grinned. "Well, Norm, I *am* travel editor, after all." He helped Pugsley pack, ordered a cab, and asked the orderlies to fetch a wheelchair. At first Pugsley balked, but relented after Browning told him wheelchairs were standard for discharged patients.

An orderly took them to the hospital entrance, where the cab was already idling. Browning loaded Pugsley's bags into the trunk and the two climbed into the back seat for the drive to El Venizelos, the city's sparkling new international airport.

As usual, traffic was heavy and chaotic, slowing their progress. Browning wasn't concerned; Pugsley's flight wasn't scheduled to leave for five hours. Even so, they narrowly averted disaster when the driver, distracted by his cellphone, had to swerve violently to avoid plowing into the back of a van. "Jesus, man, keep your eyes on the road!" Pugsley admonished the driver, who shrugged, but set his phone down.

When they finally arrived at the main terminal, Browning stacked Pugsley's bags on an airport cart and took him to an area in the terminal where he'd arranged for a wheelchair and an attendant to take Pugsley to his gate.

Pugsley again protested that a wheelchair was unnecessary, but the attendant, a well-spoken young man named Giannis, was solicitous, and he eventually acquiesced, albeit a bit grumpily.

At the security checkpoint, Pugsley turned to Browning. "Guess this is where we say goodbye."

"Guess so."

Pugsley cleared his throat. "I'm not very good at this sort of thing, but I want to thank you for helping me out, Bliss."

"Does that mean I'm forgiven?" Browning asked, smiling.

"Not yet. Maybe later. We'll see," Pugsley replied, suppressing a smile of his own. "When will you be back in Ottawa?"

"Soon. I have some things to take care of here first."

"Matina?"

"Yes."

"Good luck with that."

"Thanks."

Giannis wheeled Pugsley away and joined the lineup at the security checkpoint. Browning watched as his boss stood up, unbuckled his belt, slipped off his brogues and emptied his pockets. He went through the security scanner and raised his arms as a guard used a wand to check for contraband. He collected his belongings, slid on his belt, stepped into his shoes, and settled back into the wheelchair.

Giannis propelled the chair down a corridor leading to departures. Browning was poised to wave, but Pugsley never looked back.

Two

OTTAWA, 1968 (37 YEARS EARLIER)

Norman Pugsley perched on the edge of a straight-backed wooden chair, waiting for his interview with Duncan MacTavish, managing editor of the Ottawa *Daily Advocate.* He'd mailed the newspaper his résumé two weeks earlier and was surprised to receive a prompt response from MacTavish, inviting him to pop by the next time he was in town. "We have no current vacancies," cautioned the letter, "but we get a lot of turnover so we're always eager to meet up-and-coming young journalists like yourself." That was encouragement enough. He'd wasted no time booking the interview.

At 24, Pugsley was already a veteran of journalism's minor leagues. He'd been employed by four small weeklies or dailies. At the Peterborough *Examiner*, where he now worked, he covered city hall, but had earlier reported on the courts, the police beat and general news. Indeed, one of his stories, blowing the whistle on a city manager's sexual harassment of several employees, had won an Ontario Newspaper Award. He had precisely the sort of background big-city dailies were looking for.

Admittedly, it was a mild overstatement to describe the *Advocate* as a big-city newspaper. The capital city only had about 300,000 residents, though another 200,000 or so lived in adjoining suburban municipalities or in Hull and Gatineau across the Ottawa River in Quebec.

Residents seeking fine dining had few choices, and the best were in Hull, where bars also could remain open hours later than those in Ottawa. The city had the dubious distinction of being the world's second-coldest national capital, behind only Ulan Bator in Mongolia. The best thing about Ottawa, people observed derisively, was the highway to Montreal.

None of this mattered to Pugsley. If he could land a job at the *Advocate*, he could bid farewell to small-town journalism. The newspaper might not be in the same league as the big Toronto and Montreal dailies, but it was a giant step up from the Peterborough *Examiner*. Why, there must be 100 journalists working there! It boasted a circulation north of 80,000. The opportunities were endless and, to him, intoxicating.

Pugsley had once been told he resembled a young Lee Marvin, with an angular face more rugged than classically handsome. To ensure he made a favourable impression on this important day, he'd splurged on a new gabardine suit from Peterborough's leading department store. It had set him back $100 – nearly a week's pay – but he fancied that the tightly woven grey fabric gave him a cosmopolitan air. He was clean-shaven (he'd heard that people thought men with facial hair were trying to hide something) and his jet-black hair was neatly trimmed above the collar.

He checked his wristwatch – 2:30, half an hour past his scheduled appointment. It was an unseasonably warm day in late May, and his face glistened with perspiration in the unairconditioned office. He loosened his tie and fanned himself with an *Advocate* section bulging with classified ads. His confidence, rock solid when he'd arrived, was waning fast.

A few minutes later, someone flung open MacTavish's office door, strode out and almost sprinted past him, as if late for an urgent appointment. Pugsley sat for a moment, eyeing the open door, then rose and knocked lightly. A puffy-faced man in his 40s with a shock of red hair and a ragged beard looked up from behind a large wooden desk and waved him in.

"You must be Pugsley," he said, a light Scottish burr colouring his words. He stood and extended a hand. "I'm Duncan MacTavish. Sorry for keepin' ya waitin'. Ya know what this business is like … never know from one moment to the next what'll happen."

Pugsley gripped MacTavish's hand and gave it a firm shake. "Big news story?" he asked.

"Nah. Just the usual shite." MacTavish pointed to a chair. "Have a seat, man."

As both settled into chairs, MacTavish snatched a paper from his desk and scanned it. "It says here you cover city hall for the *Examiner*."

"That's right."

"Important beat," MacTavish said. "Decent paper. Why ya wanna leave?"

"Well, Mr. MacTavish–" Pugsley began.

"Call me Duncan. Mr. MacTavish is my father. Not me," the older man said, with a faint smile.

Pugsley relaxed. "Absolutely. Duncan it is."

"So, ya were sayin'?"

"It's not that I don't like it in Peterborough," Pugsley said. "But I'm ready for a bigger challenge. The *Advocate* is one of Canada's top newspapers–"

"Ya think so?" MacTavish interrupted, raising an eyebrow. "What makes ya say that?"

"Well … Duncan. First of all, it's the biggest paper in the nation's capital–"

"Not by much," MacTavish interjected. "Our circulation's barely ahead of the bloody *Chronicle*."

"Sure," Pugsley acknowledged. "I, ah … you're right. But *you* have the best writers."

"Who, for instance?"

Pugsley wracked his brain for the names he'd recently tried to memorize. "Jake Flaherty, for one. Terrific parliamentary reporter. Henry Ellis. Love his columns. And Joe Flynn is a legendary police reporter."

MacTavish gave Pugsley a skeptical look. "Flaherty's OK. So's Ellis, I suppose. But Flynn's a giant pain in the ass."

"Oh? I didn't know that."

"Yeah, well trust me, buddy – he is. Always making stuff up, just to see if he can get it into the paper."

"You're kidding!" exclaimed Pugsley, genuinely appalled.

"I wish I were." MacTavish let out a weary sigh and refocused on Pugsley. "So anyway, y'actually read the paper, then?"

"I do."

"Then tell me what you *don't* like about it."

Pugsley frowned. This was treacherous terrain. A misstep could snuff out his hopes of a job.

"You have some excellent photographers," he began, "but you don't showcase their work very well."

MacTavish scowled. "Care to elaborate?"

"Well, you need to be bolder. You know – go big."

"*Go big?* That's your advice?" MacTavish snorted. "What else?"

"Well, uh, some of your headlines are weak. They need to be punchier, more to the point."

"I see. Bigger headlines too. I'm seeing a trend here. Ya like things big."

Pugsley said nothing, flummoxed by the combative turn the interview had taken.

"Is that it, then?" asked MacTavish.

"One more thing." Pugsley took a deep breath. "To be honest, Duncan, the paper needs to be more ambitious. It's all well and good to cover the agenda news, but as journalists, we need to dig deeper, tell the stories those in power don't want told."

"Afflict the comfortable and comfort the afflicted?" MacTavish asked, a titch sardonically.

"Something like that."

"So ya're a crusader, then?"

"Not a crusader. But I believe journalists have a social duty. We can make a difference. And we should."

MacTavish studied Pugsley for a moment. "I don't agree with everything ya said. But I'll tell ya this. We're doing a redesign right now to freshen the paper's visual appeal. And we're planning to create a position for a full-time investigative reporter."

"That's terrific!" Pugsley exclaimed. "Makes me all the more eager to work here."

MacTavish's eyes flashed again to Pugsley's résumé. "It doesn't say here if you're married."

"I am. Married a Peterborough girl just over a year ago. Maryanne. We're expecting our first child this fall."

MacTavish squinted at Pugsley. "So ya're a family man … not one of those louts out drinking till all hours? Because, let me tell ya, we've got enough of that sort already."

"I enjoy a drink, like any man," Pugsley replied cautiously. "But no. If anything, I'm almost unreasonably responsible."

"Well, that would be quite a change – though ya might not fit in with the crowd around here," MacTavish said, though the twinkle in his eye betrayed him. "Look, Norman–"

"Call me Norm," Pugsley interjected, breaking into a wide grin.

MacTavish laughed. "OK, Norm. I like the cut of your jib. If I have an opening, I'll certainly consider ya. Something might open up in a week or so, but I won't know till then. Check with me in about 10 days, and we can talk."

•••

Maryanne, a petite blonde with forest-green eyes whose abdomen bore testimony to the developing life within, greeted Pugsley with a hug and kiss when he walked into their rented half-double after making the three-hour drive back to Peterborough from Ottawa.

"How'd it go?" she asked.

"Pretty well, I think. The M.E. and I scrimmaged a bit, but we hit it off in the end. I think he'll hire me if he has an opening. Should know soon."

Maryanne's eyes lit up. "That's wonderful, Norm! What a terrific opportunity for you."

"Terrific for both of us. There's so much more to do in Ottawa – lots of shopping options, national museums, a ton of places that need volunteers." He gently laid a hand on the swell of his wife's belly. "And it's a great place to raise a family."

A wistful look crossed Maryanne's face. "I'd miss Peterborough, though. It's the only place I've ever lived. And it would be harder to see mom and dad."

"Not much harder," Pugsley soothed, secretly relishing the thought of less contact with his in-laws. "Ottawa's close enough that we could easily drive here every month or two. Or your parents could visit us in Ottawa. I'm sure they'd love that."

"Do you know what you'll be doing if they hire you?" Maryanne said.

"We didn't really discuss that. But they're planning to have a full-time investigative reporter." Pugsley's eyes gleamed with barely suppressed excitement. "Imagine if they gave me that job!"

"You'd be great at it," Maryanne agreed.

"There's a ton of hidden stories in a place like Ottawa, just waiting for someone to come along and rip off the lid. I'd really be doing some meaningful journalism. And it would pretty much make my career."

"We should celebrate," Maryanne said suddenly. "Let's open our bottle of Mateus."

"Great idea! I'll fire up the briquets and grill us a few burgers."

Maryanne gazed at her husband.

"We have the best life," she said, patting her belly as she reached for a corkscrew. "I'm so lucky."

"Me too, babe," Pugsley replied happily. "Me too."

•••

Seven excruciating days later, Pugsley could bear it no longer. He grabbed his office phone and dialled the number for Duncan MacTavish.

The managing editor picked up on the second ring. "MacTavish here," he barked.

"Oh, uh, hi … Duncan. It's Norm."

"Norm who?"

"Norm Pugsley. You interviewed me last week."

"Yeah, yeah, I remember. Kinda busy here, Norm. What do ya want?"

"Just wondering if you know yet if you have an opening on staff."

There was a brief silence on the line, as if MacTavish were trying to process the question. "An opening?" he said at last. "Oh, you must mean … no, not yet. We're still thrashing it out. Should know better in a week or so. I'll give you a call. Now I really gotta go. Talk later." The line went dead.

That night, Pugsley told Maryanne what had happened. "It was almost as if he'd forgotten who I was," he said.

As time passed with no word from the *Advocate*, Pugsley began to lose hope. Mentally, he started adjusting to the idea that he'd be staying in Peterborough. He turned his attention back to stories about stop signs and ribbon cuttings.

Then, nearly a month after the interview, his phone rang.

"Norm, it's Duncan here. We've sorted out our issue with one of our reporters. He's gone now. So, we have an opening. Do ya still want the job?"

It took a couple of seconds for Pugsley to understand what was happening. "Absolutely!" he blurted. "I do."

MacTavish chuckled. "We're not getting married, ya know. Ya don't hafta say 'I do.' But I take that as a yes."

"Yes. It's a definite yes."

"Terrific. Couple of things you should know. First, it's a union shop, so you'll have to join up and pay dues."

"That's fine," Pugsley said. He was having trouble drawing a breath.

"Normally, we'd start ya at the one-year rate. But ya've got a fair bit of experience, so I'll bump ya up to the two year. That's $225 a week plus $25 night differential."

"Night differential?" Pugsley said, dismayed. "You mean I'll be working nights?"

"Everyone does at first. You'll work a 6 p.m. to 2 a.m. shift, covering cops, school boards, township council meetings, that sort of nonsense. After a year or two, you'll graduate to days."

Pugsley cleared his throat. "I was kinda hoping you might make me your new investigative reporter."

"Merciful Jesus, man! Ya got balls, I'll give ya that. Look, that's a job for a senior reporter, not a fresh recruit. Work hard and do well, and maybe someday it'll happen."

Pugsley shook off his disappointment. "OK, I'm in. When do you want me to start?"

"Yesterday would have been good. How soon can you be here?"

Pugsley thought for a moment. He should give the *Examiner* two weeks' notice. That would be the honourable thing to do.

"I'll be there Monday," he said.

Three

OTTAWA, AUTUMN 2005

Dr. Beauregard Fisher quietly scanned some charts and papers, then glanced at his patient, concern etched on his florid face. "You've been through quite an ordeal, Norm," he said. "A STEMI heart attack is no joke. They don't call it the widow-maker for nothing. How are you feeling?"

"I've been a hell of a lot better, Beau," Pugsley grumbled, "although I'm sure glad to be back home. Those Greek docs … I'm a lot happier knowing you'll be looking after me now."

The two had first met on a sailboat trip nearly three decades earlier. Fisher was now his family doctor. At 70, he was one of the most prominent family physicians in Ottawa, a past chair of the Canadian Medical Association's board.

"It looks to me like the Greek doctors did a terrific job. They basically saved your life." Fisher studied the papers on his desk. "The good news is the angiogram and echocardiogram we ordered don't show any more serious blockages or damage to your heart."

"That's a relief," Pugsley said.

"But there's some bad news too, I'm afraid," Fisher added. "Your blood pressure's sky-high, your cholesterol levels are elevated, and you have a lot of ceramides in your blood."

"Ceramides? What are those?"

"They've been linked to a buildup of plaque in arteries. You've got them in high concentrations. It means you're at higher risk of cardiovascular disease in the next one to five years."

"Fuck me," Pugsley muttered. His heartbeat had accelerated alarmingly, and he suddenly felt faint. "Please tell me you can do something!"

"Well, together we can. But you won't like it. You're going to have to make some big lifestyle changes."

"Like what?"

"We can put you on a statin to control your cholesterol and a beta-blocker to bring down your blood pressure. But there's no escaping it, Norm. You're going to have to lose some weight. At 220 pounds, you're at least 30 pounds too heavy for your height."

"How am I going to do that?" asked Pugsley, mildly offended. "I can't survive on freakin' lettuce and carrot sticks."

"Obviously, I don't expect that," Fisher replied, "but you do need to eat a healthier diet. More fish, fresh fruits and vegetables and whole grains. And smaller portions."

Pugsley, who lived alone, wasn't much of a cook. Dinner was most often a take-out pizza, a bucket of fried chicken or a frozen grocery-store entrée warmed up in the oven, washed down by a beer or five. Healthy eating was a concept he hadn't explored in years – not since his marriage had broken up.

"You also need some regular exercise," Fisher continued, scrutinizing Pugsley's bulky form. "How much would you say you get in a typical week now?"

Pugsley considered the question. Not much, he had to admit – unless you counted the steps from the couch to the beer fridge.

"I'd say … maybe … a couple of hours a week?" he ventured, making a generous guesstimate.

"That won't cut it, Norm. You need to aim for a minimum of 30 minutes a day, ideally seven times a week. More would be better."

"Look, Beau, I'm pretty set in my ways," Pugsley protested. "There's no friggin' way I'm running marathons at this stage of my life."

"No marathons. But if you want to make it to your 70s, you've got to do *something*. Take brisk walks, swim laps, ride a bicycle, play golf. Anything that raises your heart rate on a regular basis."

"Jesus, Beau, I never knew you were such a hard-ass," Pugsley complained, only half-joking.

Fisher ignored the jibe. "You used to be quite a smoker, Norm. Are you still?"

"Gave cigarettes up ages ago. Those things are coffin nails."

"Well, thank God for that."

"Yeah," Pugsley continued. "I only smoke the occasional stogey now."

Fisher raised an eyebrow. "Define occasional."

"I dunno … maybe a couple a day." There were days when Pugsley chain-smoked cigars, but there was no need to tell his doctor that.

"Two a day is far too many, Norm," Fisher scolded. "You should save them for special occasions. Or better yet, give them up entirely."

Holy Mother of Christ, Pugsley thought. *Next thing you know, he'll tell me to stop drinking.*

"And you're far too fond of the drink," Fisher continued. "No more than a couple a week."

"Fuck me, Beau. I might live a bit longer, but what's the point?"

Fisher didn't crack a smile. "This is no joke, Norm. You've been abusing your body for years. Now the bill has come due. You've got to change your ways."

Pugsley slumped in his chair. He fixed a gimlet eye on his supposed friend, Beauregard Fisher. "Can I still …?"

That earned him a microscopic smile. "Sure, Norm. Believe it or not, regular sex is good for you."

"Well, hallelujah," Pugsley muttered. "Something to live for."

•••

The lobby of the *Daily Advocate* building had an air of decay that reflected the declining fortunes of the newspaper itself. A pair of scuffed black leather armchairs sat disconsolately along one wall while a display on another celebrated the newspaper's three National Newspaper Awards. Tellingly, there had been none since 1996.

Pugsley entered the familiar space and paused to look around, sensing he might be seeing it for the last time. Normally, he'd have taken the stairs to the paper's second-floor newsroom, but a man who'd recently survived a major heart attack should take precautions. He summoned an elevator.

The ancient lift shuddered into motion, taking an unconscionable time to rise a single storey. Pugsley stepped into the newsroom – and was quickly surrounded by solicitous *Advocate* staffers.

"Great to see you back, old buddy!" cried news editor Ryan Young, obsequious as ever. City editor Anita Wilson gave him an awkward hug. Yuri Alexandrov, the paper's foreign editor, abruptly ended his call to Moscow and greeted him with a crushing handshake. "How the fuck *are* you?" demanded sports columnist Flynn Cahill, deploying his favoured expletive. Even surly news desk slug Mick Mulligrew, always eager to avoid actual work, nodded from a distance.

Pugsley, touched by the greetings, assured them he was doing well. But he'd come to see Renata Richter, so after a couple of minutes, he excused himself and headed towards the editor's corner office.

Richter's executive secretary, Judy Rendell, beamed as he approached. "So nice to see you, Norm," she smiled. "We were all very worried about you."

"I appreciate that, Judy. I was a bit worried about me, too," he said. "But as you can see, I'm right as rain."

"So it appears," Rendell said. "Renata's expecting you, but she's on the phone right now. Do you want a coffee or–"

"That's OK," Pugsley said, opening Richter's office door. "I'll just wait inside."

Richter, her thick brown hair slightly more dishevelled than usual, was listening intently to someone on the other end of the line when Pugsley settled into one of the office's lime-green upholstered chairs.

"Norman's arrived," she said into the receiver. "I should go. Can we talk more about this a little later?" She hung up and gave Pugsley an appraising look.

"You certainly look a lot better than the last time I saw you."

"Well, I wasn't at my best then," Pugsley parried. "So how are things around here, Renata? What did I miss?"

Richter's face darkened. "Things aren't great, Norman. I was talking to the publisher when you arrived, and he told me head office is demanding more cuts."

"Jesus. How many?"

"Twenty people out of the newsroom."

Pugsley scowled. "Fucking bloodsuckers. It's death by a thousand cuts. We're already down, what, 50 from our peak?"

"Something like that. It's discouraging. I'm really worried we won't have the resources to publish the special feature sections our readers love so much."

Pugsley bit his tongue. In truth, he didn't think readers would miss Richter's arcane special sections, like the recent one on the roots of unrest in Bolivia. They might even be relieved if they disappeared. But he had no appetite for that discussion. He had more pressing matters on his mind.

"Will they be offering buyouts?" he asked.

"It appears so. But unless enough people come forward, we're likely looking at layoffs."

"I might be able to help you with that."

Richter looked startled. "What do you mean?"

"Look Renata, I've been M.E. here for a dozen years. I'll be 63 next month. I've just had a goddamn heart attack and the docs tell me I'm not in the best of shape, health-wise. I'm thinking maybe I should snag one of those bloody buyouts, coast into retirement and enjoy what's left of my life."

A jumble of emotions flashed across Richter's face: surprise, dismay, empathy. "Oh, Norman. Are you serious? This newspaper has been your life. Wouldn't you miss it terribly?"

"Probably," he allowed. "But to tell you the truth, Renata, I'm not sure my heart's in it anymore. It's been a grand run, but we're taking on water and I don't think I want to be here when the ship goes down."

Richter studied her managing editor for a moment. The professional fit between them had never been easy. Her background was in ideas and academia. Before being named editor of the *Advocate*, she had been researching a book on the Ottoman Empire and the Barbary slave trade. Pugsley was a rough-and-tumble journalist, more of a brawler than a brainiac. She suspected he disparaged her to other managers. A buyout would clear the way for change at the top and perhaps save some newsroom jobs.

That said, she admired his journalistic skills, honed over decades in the newspaper business. He had terrific story ideas, knew just what to do when a big story broke and exuded an intangible newsroom presence she could never hope to emulate. And despite their differences, the two had – dare she think it? – bonded when they were together in Greece. His antagonism to her seemed to have diminished. If he were to resume his duties at the paper, might a better relationship be possible?

"If that's really what you want, Norman, I'll talk to HR and see what we can do. But you would be hard to replace. You have so much experience. And," she added, a strange note in her voice he'd never heard before, "I'd miss your wise counsel."

"Of course you would," Pugsley replied. "You'd be lost without me," he grinned, trying to lighten the sombre tone.

"That might well be true," Richter said with a faint smile of her own. "But seriously, Norman, if you go, I hope we can stay in touch."

"I'm sure I'd be able to fit you into my busy schedule," Pugsley smiled. Somewhat to his surprise, the idea wasn't entirely unappealing.

●●●

A few weeks later, Pugsley was having an afternoon nap in the living room of his suburban bungalow when someone rang the doorbell. He rose groggily from the couch, shuffled a bit unsteadily to the front door and opened it a crack. Bliss Browning, grinning broadly, waggled a hand in greeting.

"Jesus, Browning, you're the last person I expected to see," Pugsley said. "How long have you been in town?"

"Just a couple of days. I went into the office yesterday, and Harrison told me you'd taken a buyout."

"Yeah, the approval came through a few days ago. Guess I'm officially retired now."

"Well, are you going to invite me in?" Browning asked, still smiling. "Or would you rather talk to me through your open door?"

Pugsley looked embarrassed. "Sorry Browning. Sure, come in, come in."

He led his unexpected guest into his living room and invited him to take a seat on the black leather couch. "Care for a beer? Or I could brew some coffee …"

"A beer would be splendid."

While his host fetched the drinks, Browning took in his surroundings. A shiny new LCD television, one of the first of its type, dominated one wall and an imposing stone fireplace partly filled another. A large, framed poster celebrating the Toronto Blue Jays' 1993 World Series victory hung on a third wall, along with a portrait of a pretty teenaged girl. The hardwood floor was unadorned except for a faux bearskin rug in front of the fireplace.

Pugsley reappeared with two frosty bottles of Molson's Export. "Here you go," he said, handing one to Browning.

"So, Norm, I knew you were a Jays fan, but who's the girl on the wall?" asked Browning.

Pugsley took a long swallow of beer. "That's my daughter, Barbara."

Browning looked surprised. "I didn't know you had a daughter."

"Yeah, well, we … don't talk much."

"That's too bad," Browning commiserated. "Is that an old picture of her, then?"

"Yup. She's 37 now … I think." Pugsley abruptly changed the subject. "So, I hear Harrison's replacing me."

Browning nodded. Renata Richter had picked books editor Harrison Howard as her new managing editor. Browning thought it an inspired choice. "I'm sure Harry will do a fine job."

"Yeah, hope so," Pugsley grunted. He'd been gobsmacked by the news that Howard would be his successor, though the choice was in keeping with Richter's erratic judgment. "It's a bit of a gamble. I mean, he's never even been a manager. He's hardly done any real reporting."

"True. There'll be a steep learning curve. But Harry's a smart guy. He'll pick it up quickly. What about you, Norm? How are you doing?"

"As well as can be expected, I guess, considering the state of my ticker." Pugsley massaged the left side of his chest. "My doc thinks I need to change my ways. This beer," he said, waving the bottle, "is supposed to be half of my weekly ration … as if."

"That's hard core," Browning agreed with a sympathetic shake of his head.

"Damn right. No more than a couple of beers a week. Gave up my lovely stogies. Signed up for the rehab program at the heart institute – walking in circles around a track, humping those bloody rowing torture machines. And a nutritionist lady keeps yammering about my diet. I swear I've had more salad in the past couple of weeks than I've eaten in my entire life."

Pugsley drew a breath. "But enough about me. What's happening with you and that girlfriend of yours … Marina?"

"Matina," Browning corrected.

"Whatever. Is it working out or not?"

Browning sighed. "Too soon to say, Norm. I'm hopeful, but there are no guarantees yet."

"What's the issue?"

"For one thing, she lives in a remote region of Greece with her mother. For another, she's a widow who recently lost her young daughter."

Pugsley shook his head. "That's heavy shit."

"No kidding. She's amazingly resilient and I think there's a real connection between us, but she needs time to heal. I understand that. I can wait."

"What'll you do now?" Pugsley asked.

"Well, I've resigned from the *Advocate*, just like you. They probably would have taken me back, but I decided against it. Time to move on and see what happens with Matina. Meanwhile, believe it or not, I'm going to Africa." Browning, who'd always been terrified of travel, lowered his eyes and frowned. "Can't say I'm looking forward to it. Not crazy about sharing my tent with scorpions."

"Or being stalked by lions," Pugsley added, unhelpfully.

"That too."

"So, why're you doing it?"

"Well, as Harry reminded me, I still owe the paper a series of articles on Botswana. I spent the paper's money going to Greece when I was assigned to go to Africa, so I'm going to complete the assignment – assuming I survive." While he was travel editor, Browning, too nervous to actually travel, had spent his whole career sitting at his desk.

Despite himself, Pugsley was impressed. "Honestly, Browning, I didn't think you had it in you."

"I didn't either. But this whole thing in Greece … let's just say it changed me. I'm still scared shitless, but I'm trying."

"We're both trying," Pugsley said.

Browning took a last swallow of beer and rose from the couch. "I should be on my way, Norm. But it was good to catch up."

"Yes, it was. Thanks for stopping by. Good luck with Africa. And with Melinda."

"Matina."

"Yeah. That's who I meant."

•••

Life had settled into an agreeable pattern. Pugsley woke around 8 a.m., fixed himself a simple breakfast of cornflakes and toast, and scanned that day's *Advocate*, trying to ignore the slipshod editing, typos and unfortunate headlines, like the one from the previous week: "Man struck by flying stool."

If the day was pleasant, he'd go for a stroll or do a bit of yard work. If it was rainy, he might drive to a multiplex and take in a matinee. (He was partial to action films and current comedies like *Wedding Crashers, Meet the Fockers* and *The 40-year-old Virgin.*) Most evenings were spent in front of the TV, watching the Blue Jays.

Earlier that month, Pugsley had turned 63. In past years, there would have been cake in the newsroom to mark the occasion, followed by a drink-up at the National Press Club. Not this year. Pugsley bought a take-out pizza, opened a beer, put a candle in a cupcake and celebrated alone. No call from family, not even his daughter – just a quick check-in by Dr. Beauregard Fisher.

If he had a complaint, it was that he felt lonely. He was accustomed to the hubbub of the newsroom, the focused energy generated by a big story, the collegial chatter of men and women with a common purpose. That was gone now, and he missed it.

Whenever he got a call, he hoped it might be a buddy from the *Advocate*. Instead, it was usually duct cleaners peddling their unwanted services or a charity soliciting donations.

One rainy afternoon, as he was preparing to leave for a matinee screening of *Batman Returns*, his phone rang. To his surprise, the caller was the

Advocate's 24-year-old rookie police reporter, Fawzia Hassan. The paper had hired her six months earlier. She hadn't been Pugsley's choice for the job, but Richter had overruled him, declaring that Hassan was brilliant and that the paper needed to diversify its lily-white newsroom staff.

"May I speak to Norman Pugsley?" she asked, lightly accented English hinting at her Somali roots.

"Hi there, Fawzia," Pugsley replied, checking his watch to see how much time he had before the start of the matinee. "I'm on my way out the door. What can I do for you?"

"I'm so glad I caught you, Mr. Pugsley," Hassan began.

"For chrissake, Fawzia, call me Norm."

"Oh, sure, thanks," she said. "I will."

"So … you were saying?"

"Yes. I don't know if you saw it, but I wrote a piece a couple of days ago about an anonymous benefactor posting a $50,000 reward for information leading to an arrest in a 20-year-old murder case."

"Yeah, I saw the headline. Don't think I read the story, though. What's the case?"

"Do you remember a teenaged prostitute, Jenny Birchmount? She was found strangled in a forest outside Ottawa in 1985. No one was ever arrested or charged."

Jenny Birchmount.

Did he remember her? Christ, how could he ever forget her? He felt his heart pounding.

Even now, 20 years later, her name had the power to rattle Pugsley, to trigger a synaptic storm of anxiety. His coverage of the investigation into her murder had nearly wrecked his career and had contributed to the collapse of his marriage. He fervently wished to forget her.

Pugsley said none of this to Hassan. Instead, he feigned nonchalance. "Yeah, rings a bell. I vaguely recall it. It was a long time ago."

"Sure," Hassan said, "but the paper wants to take this on as a bit of a cause, to see if we can do something to help bring her killer to justice. Ryan Young told me you wrote a lot about the case when it happened, and you might be able to help me figure out where to go with this."

Pugsley silently cursed Young. The sonofabitch knew full well how the

Birchmount story had roiled his life.

"I don't know, Fawzia. I doubt there's much I can do to help. Like I said, it was a long time ago. I don't remember much about the case."

"Anything at all would be helpful."

Pugsley checked his watch again. Time was running out if he wanted to catch *Batman Returns*.

"Look Fawzia, I'm sorry, but I gotta go. I'm late for an important appointment. But if I think of anything, I'll let you know."

Four

OTTAWA, OCTOBER 1972

Days before his 29th birthday, Norman Pugsley gathered his daughter Barbara in his arms and gave her a hug.

"It's 7:30," he told the yawning three-year-old. "Do you want me to read you a bedtime story?"

"Yes, Daddy, yes," Barbara squealed. "*Goodnight Moon*!"

Pugsley suppressed a sigh. The classic Margaret Wise Brown picture book was Barbara's favourite. He must have read it to her 100 times by now. He was thoroughly sick of it, but it made his daughter happy, so he smiled and said, "Good choice."

In truth, Pugsley didn't really object to the repetitive readings. He was just glad he was able to put his little girl to bed. That hadn't been possible when he was a night-shift reporter at the *Advocate*, working 6 p.m. to 2 a.m. He couldn't even eat dinner with his family, let alone read bedtime stories.

The night shift wasn't very rewarding. It involved interminable telephone cop checks that rarely yielded anything newsworthy, filling gaps in news stories started by dayside reporters and covering tedious meetings of school boards and obscure municipal councils.

Every now and then, something out of the ordinary would happen: a murder, perhaps, or a fatal car accident. That got his adrenaline pumping, but it also meant he had to seek comment from bereaved families and ask for pictures of the unfortunate victims. He didn't shy away from the grim task, but intruding on a family's grief always made him queasy.

At times, it felt like he'd be stuck working nights forever. Then one night he wrote a story that changed things.

One of his regular duties was covering the monthly council meetings in Gloucester Township, a suburban municipality outside Ottawa. The councillors were an old-boys club of like-minded men who thrashed out their decisions in private, emerging only to ratify them without debate at a brief public meeting.

This secretive process irritated Pugsley, who believed public bodies should be open and transparent. After he wrote about the council's practices, the provincial government promised reforms to ensure greater openness. A few days later, managing editor Duncan MacTavish called Pugsley into his office. "Great work on that Gloucester story, laddie," he said. "I think ya've earned a move to days."

He now worked a very civilized 9-to-5 shift, was home in time for dinner with Maryanne most nights and could put his daughter to bed.

Pugsley retrieved the paperback copy of *Goodnight Moon*, already worn from repeated readings. He tucked his daughter into bed, propped himself up on a couple of pillows, and began to read words he could almost recite from memory.

In the great green room
There was a telephone
And a red balloon
And a picture of–
The cow jumping over the moon ...

Before he'd read even half the book, Barbara's eyes fluttered and closed and her breathing became slow and regular. He read a few more pages to make sure she was asleep, then closed the book, gently kissed his daughter's forehead, and crept from the room, shutting the door behind him.

•••

Pugsley was working on a story about Ottawa's oldest resident – a 106-year-old matriarch named Sophie Biddle – when city editor Malachi Thompson tapped him on the shoulder.

"Do you have a minute?"

"For you, Malachi, I have *five* minutes," Pugsley smiled. Thompson, a short, intense man in his mid-30s with a reflexively bellicose temperament, didn't return the smile, but Pugsley wasn't fazed. He admired his boss's no-nonsense style. And he was impressed by his keen news instincts.

He followed Thompson to his small, cluttered office adjacent to the newsroom, shut the door and settled into a chair. "What's up?" he asked.

"Joe Flynn is retiring," Thompson said, getting straight to the point. "I'd like you to take over the police beat."

Flynn had covered cops for the *Advocate* for nearly two decades. He was an old-school reporter who'd entered the business long before journalism schools sanded off the rough edges. His police contacts were legendary, lubricated by innumerable booze-soaked sessions with constables and desk sergeants. He'd been off his game for a while, though. His productivity had dropped noticeably, and he frequently showed up for work with alcohol on his breath.

"It's hard to imagine the *Advocate* without Joe," Pugsley said. "He's an institution around here."

Thompson eyed him shrewdly. "He's certainly been here for donkey's years," he acknowledged "But he's well past his best-before date. His retirement gives us a chance to reset our police coverage. Are you up to it?"

Since moving to days, Pugsley had been working general assignment, writing stories about unusually hot, cold, wet or windy weather, covering service club luncheon speeches and interviewing oddballs, like the 65-year-old man riding a unicycle across Canada for no discernible reason.

Front page stories were as rare as bikinis in winter. One he was particularly proud of recounted the dramatic rescue of a five-year-old child named Jenny Birchmount from the Ottawa River. She'd strayed into deeper water while at a beach and might have drowned if not for the quick action of a teenaged swimmer. He'd landed great interviews with the teenager and several witnesses.

Mostly, though, he was biding his time for the opportunity to take on a beat. Now, one had fallen into his lap. An important one, at that: crime coverage was one of the *Advocate*'s top priorities.

"Is the Pope Catholic?" he asked Thompson. "Of course I'm up to it. When do I start?"

"Flynn retires in two weeks. Until then, I want you to work with him. Get him to introduce you to his sources, learn whatever's useful from him. And don't fall for any of his bullshit."

Pugsley offered a mock salute. "Aye-aye, boss. And thanks for the opportunity."

"Just don't fuck up," Thompson said coldly.

That evening over a festive dinner of fish sticks and fries, Pugsley told Maryanne about his new assignment. "It's a great chance to show the paper what I can do," he enthused.

His wife furrowed her brow. "But what about your hours of work, Norm? It's been lovely having you home for dinner for the past few months. Will you still be able to do that?"

"I'll still be on the day shift. But you're right, I can't control when news happens. If there's a murder or some other major crime, I'll have to work whatever hours are required. Goes with the territory."

Maryanne gloomily impaled a fish stick with her fork. "Guess we'll just have to hope criminals like being home for supper, too," she said.

●●●

Joe Flynn was 45 minutes late for lunch. Flynn had suggested he and Pugsley meet at noon at the Cornwallis, a popular and long-established bar known for its pizza and meatball sandwiches. But he was nowhere to be seen.

In truth, Pugsley wasn't expecting much from their meeting. He and Flynn had gotten off on the wrong foot four years ago. As a rookie reporter, Pugsley had scored an interview with the wife of a high-profile Ottawa gangster on the lam. His subsequent story delighted his editors. But Flynn only saw a presumptuous youngster who'd scooped him on his own beat. He made his displeasure clear.

Pugsley sipped his draft beer and glanced at his watch. He hailed a waiter and ordered a pizza with pepperoni and pineapple. He'd eaten most of it when a sudden commotion announced Flynn's arrival. A bald, corpulent man with beady eyes and a roadmap of burst capillaries on his snout, Flynn bellowed greetings to the bar's servers, all of whom appeared to know him personally.

Eventually, he spotted Pugsley and shambled unsteadily in his direction. He was wearing a tie tucked into his shirt below the second button, but no jacket.

"Hey, Pugs, you didn't wait for me?" he complained, eyeing the remnants of the pizza.

"Well Jesus Joe, I wasn't sure you were even coming."

Flynn squinted at his watch. "Shit, I *am* a bit late. Lost track of time, I guess. Sorry about that." He settled heavily into a chair opposite Pugsley. "Christ, I need a beer," he wheezed, signalling to a nearby waiter. "Hank, bring me a pitcher of Red Cap – the large one."

Pugsley swallowed his exasperation. He'd already spent 10 days trailing after Flynn, hoping to pick up at least a few useful tips. But aside from some cursory introductions at police headquarters on Waller Street, he hadn't learned much of value. With his retirement only days away, Flynn appeared to have embarked on a well-lubricated farewell tour.

The server appeared with a prodigious pitcher. "Ah, that's better," Flynn exclaimed, pouring some of the frosty brew into a tall glass. He took a long swig, then looked at Pugsley. "Need a top-up?"

Pugsley's beer glass was less than half full, but he wanted to keep a clear head.

"No thanks, Joe. Look, I was hoping you might give me a few tips–"

"Hey Hank!" Flynn bawled, turning in the server's direction. "Meatball sandwich, OK?" He glanced at Pugsley. "Sorry, but I'm fucking famished here."

Pugsley gritted his teeth. "Yeah, sure Joe. Get your order in and we'll talk."

"Done!" Flynn announced, then struggled to his feet. "Just a minute while I take a piss."

Pugsley rolled his eyes but said nothing. Fifteen minutes passed with no sign of Flynn, though his meatball sandwich arrived, its saucy solitary presence mocking him. He finished the last of his pizza and was on the verge of paying his bill when Flynn lurched into view.

"Ah, that's better," he exhaled, taking a seat.

"Must have been a helluva piss," Pugsley muttered.

"It was. Damn prostate's acting up again today. Nearly didn't make it. And you won't believe it, but I knew the guy at the next urinal. Ex-cop. Haven't seen him in years, but we're all caught up now."

"That's terrific, Joe," Pugsley said, barely disguising his irritation. "Can we please talk now?"

"Of course," Flynn replied, picking up the sandwich and ripping off a giant bite. "Fire away."

"Look, Joe, you've been on the cop beat for years."

"Decades," Flynn corrected.

"OK, decades. So, what's your advice? What should I be doing?"

"Well, obviously, get to know the guys down at the cop shop. Hang out with them, get pissed with them, go whoring with them."

Pugsley's eyes narrowed. "Whoring?"

"Sure. Cops enjoy sex as much as the next fella. And a lot of them are divorced. They've gotta get it somewhere."

"But … prostitution is illegal."

"No, it's not. Soliciting is illegal. As long as the lady is over 18, paying for sex is A-OK."

"That may be true, but cops are supposed to enforce prostitution laws. It's not a good look if they're customers."

Flynn took another bite of his sandwich and shook his head sadly. "My God you're naïve. If you only knew who sees prostitutes in this town – politicians, doctors, lawyers, judges, cops … the fucking cream of society!"

Pugsley stared at Flynn. "That's unbelievable."

"Believe it, buddy."

"Well, I won't be joining them," Pugsley said, making little effort to conceal his disgust. "I'm a happily married man."

"What's that got to do with anything?" Flynn asked.

"For one thing, I love my wife."

"And I love mine, bud. It's not like I discuss it with her, for fuck's sake. What she don't know can't hurt her, right? Right?"

Pugsley took a deep breath. Flynn was testing his patience and he was eager to wrap up this troublesome meeting.

"OK, Joe, thanks for your help. I think we're done here."

"Whatever you say, Pugsley," Flynn said blandly, ingesting more of his sandwich. "But I haven't told you the best part."

"What's that, Joe?" Pugsley said wearily.

"Zotique Laframboise."

"Who?"

"He's a cop. Sometimes even a fire chief."

"What are you talking about?"

Flynn took another swallow of beer. "You disappoint me, Pugsley. You obviously don't read my stories. If you did, you wouldn't ask that question."

"I do read your damn stories … sometimes," Pugsley shot back, suddenly on the defensive.

"And yet you've never heard of Zotique Laframboise. Listen to me, Pugs, because this might be the best advice I give you today."

"Go on."

"Let's say you're covering a breaking story … a shooting, a fire, a murder … and you've got 10 minutes to file before deadline. But the bloody cops won't tell you diddly-squat." Flynn paused and smiled triumphantly. "That's when I call my friend Zotique!"

"Who the hell *is* he?" Pugsley asked.

"He's nobody. He's a made-up cop or fire chief. And he's always good for a juicy quote."

Pugsley was aghast. "You … make shit up!?!"

"Sure. Just slip in a quote like, 'We believe foul play is involved and we're continuing our investigation,' said Sgt. Zotique Laframboise. Or if it's a fire you can write, 'It looks like arson, but we won't know for sure until the inspector finishes his work,' Fire Chief Zotique Laframboise said."

Pugsley was aghast. "That's the most unprofessional, unethical, inappropriate thing I've ever heard," he sputtered. "You should be ashamed of yourself!"

"Oh, get the pickle out of your arse, Pugsley. It's a lark. Where's the harm?"

Pugsley laid ten dollars on the table, enough to cover his bill with a generous tip. "Happy retirement, Joe," he barked. "You're an asshole."

"Screw you, Pugsley. And good luck. You'll need it with that attitude."

Five

OTTAWA, WINTER/SPRING 2006

It was a typical late-January day in Canada's capital. The daytime high was forecast to reach -21 Celsius but feel like -32 with the wind chill. The sun rose at 7:30 a.m. and would be gone by 5 p.m. None of that was surprising.

What *was* surprising were the results of the previous day's federal election. The Conservatives, led by Stephen Harper, had defeated Paul Martin's Liberal government, abruptly ending 13 years of Liberal rule.

Norman Pugsley had stayed up late watching the election results, managing to limit himself to only two beers over the course of the evening. Though it would be an exaggeration to call him a political junkie, he'd had a lively interest in politics ever since his days in the parliamentary press gallery in the 1980s.

He was gathering the resolve to start his day when the phone rang. Still naked, Pugsley staggered from his bed and lumbered to the phone, answering on the fourth ring.

"H'lo?" he croaked, voice not quite ready for the demands of speech.

"Oh Norman. Is that you? Is this Norman Pugsley?"

Pugsley suppressed a groan. "Yeah, it's me, Renata. Jesus, what time is it?"

"It's 7:30. I hope I didn't wake you," Richter said. "I'm just so upset. That appalling man is going to be our prime minister!"

The remnants of sleep still clogged Pugsley's brain. "Whoa, Renata. Calm down. What appalling man?"

"Stephen Harper!" The agitated editor almost spat. "I can't believe our country chose a reactionary like him to lead our government."

"Hold on, Renata. I wouldn't call Harper a reactionary." Pugsley suddenly realized he was debating politics with his former boss while stark naked. He scoured the room for his bathrobe and slipped it on.

"Perhaps reactionary is too strong a word," Richter allowed, "but he's just so … so … conservative! He wants to take us back to the 1950s, when sexism was rampant."

Pugsley debated whether to confess he'd voted for Harper's Conservatives but decided it would be unwise.

"Let's give the guy a chance. He probably won't be as bad as you think."

"I do hope you're right, Norman. But I'm inclined to doubt it." There was a brief silence on the line, as if Richter were steadying herself.

"How are things at the *Advocate*?" Pugsley asked, seizing his opportunity to change the subject.

"Oh, you know … not great. Taking 20 bodies out of the newsroom really hurt. Enough people asked for buyouts, so we avoided layoffs, which is good, I suppose." There was a tremor in Richter's normally confident voice. "But another way to look at it is that 20 people didn't want to be there anymore. That's really depressing."

Pugsley wasn't a particularly empathetic man, but even he recognized his former boss's morose mood.

"I'm sorry I'm not there to give you a hand," he blurted, rather rashly.

"Me too. Harrison is terrific, but you were always so steady. I could count on you when things went sideways. You never let me down."

That wasn't quite the way Pugsley recalled their working relationship, but Richter's praise pleased him. Which probably explained what he said next.

"Look, Renata, did you mean it when you said we should keep in touch? Because if you did, I'm up for a coffee or a lunch sometime."

"Oh Norman!" Richter gushed. "That would be marvellous. Let me check my calendar … it looks as if I'm free for lunch Thursday. I've heard great things about that little Ethiopian place in the market. I'm told they make a terrific wat, served on amazing injera. I've been dying to try it. I'll make a reservation for noon and send you the details."

"Um, sure Renata, sounds great," Pugsley said limply. He hurriedly hung up, as if the phone were radioactive.

Wat? Injera?

My God ... Wat have I done?

•••

"I see you survived," Norman Pugsley said with a smirk as Bliss Browning slid into an empty seat at the Peloponnese Bar in Ottawa's east end.

"It was touch-and-go there for a while," Browning replied, brushing the snow off his hiking boots. "Out of Africa has a whole new meaning for me now."

At managing editor Harrison Howard's request, Browning had returned to Ottawa a few days earlier while his eight-part opus on Botswana was being edited at the *Daily Advocate*. He'd written the enormous series, running to more than 30,000 words, from his new temporary home in the Greek region known as the Mani.

"I have to admit I was surprised when you wanted to see me again, Browning," Pugsley said, sipping on Moosehead lager. "It's not like we're friends or anything."

"True. But I felt I owed you a report on my expedition to Africa after all you went through trying to find me in Greece. I still feel responsible for your heart attack."

"Can't argue with that," Pugsley said. "Let's get you a beer and you can tell me all about it."

"I'd rather have an ouzo. I've become rather fond of the stuff."

Pugsley's eyes widened at the mention of the potent Greek liqueur. Ouzo overindulgence had incapacitated him in Athens, making him an easy mark for a prostitute bent on robbery. And that was before his heart attack. But those weren't memories he was eager to revisit. "Suit yourself," he said, signalling to a waiter. "An orzo for my friend here," he said, mangling the beverage's name in classic Pugsley fashion.

"Can you bring some mezedes with that?" Browning asked, looking apologetically at his companion. "Haven't eaten yet today," he explained, "and it's never a good idea to drink ouzo on an empty stomach."

"Let's move on," Pugsley barked hastily. "Tell me about goddamn Africa."

"Well, first of all, Botswana isn't easy to get to. It's mostly desert – barely two million people live there. My safari started just across the border with Zimbabwe in Victoria Falls. I hooked up with the operator there and met my fellow adventurers."

Browning popped a stuffed vine leaf in his mouth, chasing it with a sip of ouzo. "Please, help yourself," he said, pushing the plate of mezedes towards Pugsley, who waved them off. "Not fond of that stuff," he muttered.

Browning pulled the plate back. "I'm not going to lie, Norm. I was beyond anxious. The first night after we set up camp in Chobe National Park, I could hear lions roaring when I turned in for the night. Had a ferocious need to pee around 3 a.m., but no way was I leaving that tent."

"Good call," Pugsley said, taking a slug of Moosehead. "No piss is worth fucking with lions."

"I got a bit more comfortable after a few game drives," Browning continued. "The best ones were right at dawn. Lots of wildlife visible then – impala, wildebeest, buffalo and of course, lion. Best of all, though, were the elephants. Awesome creatures. We'd sit in our safari vehicle and watch them at water holes for hours. One evening, just before dusk, three walked right past my tent, not 20 feet away. Incredibly, given their size, they made almost no noise."

"Jesus, Browning, weren't you worried?"

"Not really. Entranced, mesmerized, spellbound? You bet. It was magical."

Pugsley shook his head. "Not sure I'd want a bunch of wild elephants that close to me. Wouldn't take much for them to stomp you and your flimsy little tent."

"I suppose you're right, Norm. But somehow, when I was sitting there watching them, that didn't occur to me. All I felt was gratitude."

Browning popped a piece of goat feta into his mouth and bit into a Kalamata olive before continuing his tale. "The food was memorable, too," he said. "One night, our cook served us crocodile tail. It was surprisingly good if you could forget where it came from. Tasted a lot like chicken."

Pugsley shuddered, briefly rendered speechless by the notion of ingesting a carnivorous reptile.

"After we left Chobe," Browning went on, "we headed for Maun, a city in the northern Kalahari that's a jumping off point for the Okavango Delta, a huge swampy inland river delta that floods every year. We flew to a camp on a small charter plane." Browning grimaced. "I'm a nervous flyer, so I just closed my eyes and prayed for it to be over.

"But the Okavango itself was spectacular. It's home to an incredible variety of wildlife – leopard, lion, rhino, elephant, giraffe, zebra, hyena, crocodile. But for me, the hippos were the most frightening. They're the most ornery, aggressive creatures in Africa.

"One morning, our guides loaded us into dugout canoes and took us out on the water. It wasn't long before a hippo surfaced, not 15 feet from our canoe. He clearly wasn't happy to see us. Our guide poled us out of there ASAP. It took a while for my heart rate to return to normal, I can tell you."

Pugsley drained his Moosehead. He wanted to order another but, mindful that his doctor would disapprove, asked for a glass of water instead. "Bugger me, Browning, you've had a real adventure. Now I want to read your damn newspaper series."

"Well, Norm, it won't all be so adventurous. There are also pieces about the history and culture of Botswana, desertification in the Kalahari Desert, Botswana's Bushmen, known as the San, and other topics near and dear to Renata Richter's heart."

"Yeah, Renata's a piece of work," Pugsley allowed. "We're having lunch later this week. I think we're becoming friends. How crazy is that?"

Browning laughed. "Pretty damn crazy."

"What about that Greek girl of yours, Browning? Anything to report?"

"We're taking it slow and steady. I've rented a house in the Mani, not far from where she lives with her mother. We're not exactly courting, but we do see each almost every day."

"That's promising," said Pugsley. "What's her name again … Margarita?"

"It's Matina."

"Good name. Give her my regards, willya?"

●●●

Renata Richter was already perusing the menu at the Amazing Addis Bistro when Pugsley arrived, 15 minutes late. Though flustered and full of apologies for his tardiness, he looked sharp. His hair and moustache were neatly trimmed, and his weight had shrunk to 205 pounds, largely thanks to his new exercise regimen and the sharp decline in alcohol consumption ordered by Dr. Beauregard Fisher. He was wearing a smart burgundy turtleneck sweater and dark, freshly pressed pants.

Richter beamed as her former managing editor took a seat opposite her in the tiny restaurant. Pugsley couldn't help noticing that she was sporting a stylish hairdo and a lightly patterned blouse of blue silk, open at the neck to the third button.

"Great to see you, Norman," she said. "You're looking terrific!"

"Thanks Renata. It's good to see you, too." He studied her briefly. "You've done something with your hair."

Richter appeared to blush. "Yes. My stylist calls it a side-parted lob. I was tired of looking like a well-used mop. I wanted something sleeker and more polished."

"Well, it works for me," Pugsley said, earning a warm smile from Richter.

"How is retirement so far?" she asked. "It must feel strange after such a busy working life."

"No, it's good," Pugsley said. "I miss the gang at the *Advocate*, but now I have time to do all the things I never could do when I was working."

"Like what? Travelling the world? Taking some courses? Learning a new language?"

"Nothing like that," Pugsley said. "Catching matinees at the Cineplex. Watching a lot of sports …"

Richter's smile dimmed imperceptibly. "When I was doing post-doc work at Oxford in 1979, I got tickets to the women's final at Wimbledon. Martina Navratilova beat Chris Evert in straight sets. My fondest sports memory – not that I have many."

"Yeah, tennis is OK," Pugsley allowed. "But baseball's my real passion. Maybe I could take you to a game sometime," he said, a bit rashly. "I'm sure you'd like it."

Richter winced and glanced at her watch. "Oh dear, look at the time. I guess we should order. I'm due back at the office at 2."

"Why don't you pick something for us, Renata?" Pugsley said, quietly relieved that she hadn't accepted his baseball offer. "I know diddly-squat about Ethiopian food."

"Sure," she said. "I can recommend a few things. We definitely need some wat. Would you prefer beef, goat or chicken?"

Pugsley was innocent of wat's provenance, but whatever it was, he wanted to avoid the goat. "Let's stick with beef," he said.

"Or maybe the chicken?" Richter suggested. "It's the most popular choice in Ethiopia."

"OK then, the chicken."

"We should also get some bayaynetu," Richter continued. "That will let us sample a variety of vegetables, curries and lentil stews. And it's so colourful. You'll love it."

"Whatever you say."

"What about some dulet?" Richter suggested. "Perhaps I should tell you, though, it's offal."

"Awful?"

"No, offal – minced tripe with liver and lean beef, fried in butter with onions and spices."

Pugsley blanched, his worst fears about foreign cuisine realized. "You have it if you like, but I'll pass."

Richter frowned. "All right, ixnay on the uletday."

"Pardon?"

"Sorry, Norman. Just lapsing into Pig Latin. I used to speak it quite fluently when I was a girl."

"Never took Latin," said Pugsley, who was unaware of the porcine variant. "Wasn't much good at languages other than English."

"Oh, that's too bad. I love languages." Richter blinked. "I speak four, you know – not counting Pig Latin."

Pugsley was getting hungry. "Are we ready to order?"

"Almost. But would you like to try some kitfo? It's delicious."

"Sure," he said. Whatever kitfo was, he reasoned, it had to be better than entrails.

Richter summoned a waiter and gave him their order. "Would you like something to drink, Norman?" she asked. He'd kill for a beer, he thought, but his doctor would disapprove.

"Do they drink anything non-alcoholic in Ethiopia?" he asked instead.

"Of course. They have wonderful juices. Avocado juice, perhaps?"

Pugsley was beyond caring. "Why not?"

As they waited for their order, Richter told him how the latest round of buyouts had sapped newsroom morale, with new managing editor Harrison Howard doing his best to keep the survivors focused and productive.

"And Bliss did amazing work on his Botswana assignment, once he finally got there," she said. "I think it could be an award-winner." Pugsley, remembering the Bliss Browning who once cowered in a corner of the newsroom, chuckled.

Richter gave him a casual look. "We've also been working on that unsolved Jenny Birchmount murder case Fawzia discussed with you a few weeks ago."

"Uhum," Pugsley choked.

"We haven't been making much progress. Fawzia doesn't have a lot of police contacts yet. She hasn't been able to find out much."

To Pugsley's relief, a waiter arrived and placed their order on the table – colourful mounds of food arrayed atop what appeared to be a spongy flatbread.

"Wow! That looks amazing," Richter exclaimed. The waiter smiled, placed two glasses of avocado juice on the table and turned to leave.

"Just a second, buddy," Pugsley called out. "We haven't got any damn cutlery here."

"Oh Norman," Richter said, laughing. "That's a good one." She tore off a piece of the flatbread, used it to scoop up food from one of the mounds and popped the works into her mouth as Pugsley gaped in astonishment.

"We, uh … eat with our hands?" he asked.

"Of course," Richter said. "Use the injera like a spoon to scoop up whatever you want to eat."

"So that flat thing's the, um, injuria?"

"Injera. Yes. It's a sourdough flatbread."

Pugsley tentatively tore off a piece. "Which one's the wat?"

Richter pointed to a red mound of chicken stew. Pugsley scraped up a bit and cautiously tasted it. It was surprisingly good. "Humph," he exhaled. "Will wonders never cease."

Emboldened, Pugsley sampled other mounds of food. None were quite as tasty as the wat, but at least they were edible. He began to relax.

"You haven't tried the kitfo yet," Richter noted. "Have it with some gomen and fresh cheese. The tartare will melt in your mouth."

"Tartare?" Pugsley said quizzically, scooping up some kitfo and raising it toward his mouth.

"You know … ground raw beef. Ethiopians mix it with niter kibbe, a spiced clarified butter."

The progress of Pugsley's right hand to his mouth abruptly ceased.

"Ground raw beef? You're kidding, right?"

"Not at all, Norman. It's a real delicacy."

Pugsley set the scoop of kitfo down on the remaining injera. "You know what?" he said, patting his belly. "I think I'm done."

"You're full? Well, I'll ask them to put the kitfo in a doggy bag for you. You really don't want to miss it."

Pugsley knew when he was beaten. "Fine. I'll take it home," he said, reckoning that it would be easy enough to dispose of the repellent dish once he and Richter had parted.

"Good," Richter said. "Now we must have coffee. Ethiopia produces the best in the world." Pugsley happily agreed. Coffee, surely, held no hidden terrors.

Two steaming mugs of dark brew duly appeared, and as Pugsley was taking a tentative sip, Richter suddenly straightened in her chair and rapped her forehead with her right hand.

"I wanted to talk to you about the Birchmount murder case, but I got sidetracked by the food," she said.

Shit! Pugsley made a show of checking his watch. "Jesus, Renata, I'd love to talk about it, but we're out of time. You're supposed to be back in the office in 10 minutes."

Richter frowned. "Damn. You're right … I have that meeting." She brightened. "But I can cancel it. This is too important." Pugsley started to object, but Richter had already pulled her phone from her purse and was making a call.

"Hello Judy? It's … you know who this is. Look, can you reschedule the meeting about the special section on Bulgaria? I know it's short notice, but I'm having an important discussion with Norman … yes, Norman Pugsley … and I can't get away. Next Tuesday at 2? Great, thanks."

She slipped her phone back into her purse and smiled at Pugsley. "There. Now we have all the time in the world."

"What is it you want to know?" Pugsley asked, struggling with rising panic.

"It's just that Fawzia really needs your help," Richter explained. "She's a young, inexperienced reporter. You're a veteran journalist with a lot of savvy. And I'm told you covered the murder back in 1985. I know you said you couldn't help when she called a few weeks ago. But I'm hoping you have more time now to give her a hand."

Pugsley held Richter's gaze for a few silent seconds, lowered his eyes and sighed before speaking. "I've been trying to forget about Jenny Birchmount for the past 20 years," he said at last, "but it seems she haunts me still."

"Norman! What do you mean?"

"I really don't want to get into the details, Renata. Let's just say that story wasn't my finest hour." He looked down at his coffee and spoke slowly. "Mistakes were made, and it caused me a lot of misery."

"I didn't know that," Richter said gently. "Obviously you've got some unresolved issues with this case. But sometimes we need to face up to the things that unsettle us to deal with them. Maybe this is your golden opportunity."

Pugsley scowled. "All I know is I'd be thrilled if I never heard Jenny Birchmount's name again."

Richter reached across the table and lightly touched Pugsley's hand. "I realize this is hard, Norman. But Fawzia won't be able to pull this off without your help. I'm asking that you do this, as a favour to me."

Pugsley gazed at Richter's hand on his, her soft touch stirring something unfamiliar in his long-dormant heart. He should say no to this. He should run away.

"Christ on a bicycle," he muttered. "You win. Have Fawzia give me a call."

Six

INSIDE PASSAGE, BRITISH COLUMBIA, 1977

Norman Pugsley stood on the deck of the *Aquaholic*, drinking in the stunning scenery of Rescue Bay. He'd boarded the 70-foot ketch earlier that day after a short flight from Bella Bella on an amphibious Beaver airplane.

He found it hard to believe he was there, about to embark on an eight-day exploration of British Columbia's Inside Passage. He'd dreamed of such a trip since he was a teenager, and now, just days after his 35th birthday, it was happening.

Christ, he'd certainly earned it. He'd spent nearly half his life in the newspaper business – the last five as a star police reporter for the Ottawa *Daily Advocate*, chasing down murders, reporting on bad cops, having beers with the good ones. This vacation was his first real splurge.

He wished Maryanne and Barbara were there to share the experience, but the itinerary included close encounters with grizzlies and black bears, and Maryanne – terrified of anything ursine – wanted no part of that. And Barbara was still a bit too young. So here he was, batching it.

His first impressions of the *Aquaholic* were positive. The gleaming white sailboat could accommodate up to 10 passengers in five cabins below deck. Those on board gathered for meals and conversation in the large main cabin, accented in mahogany, with fresh food prepared in an adjacent galley kitchen. The skipper piloted the boat from a central cockpit on the spacious deck.

"So, what do you think?"

The question from Hank Johannsen broke Pugsley's deck-top reverie. He turned and faced the skipper.

"It's bloody magnificent. Everything I hoped it would be."

A wide grin creased Johannsen's weather-beaten features. "That it is. And the great thing is, it only gets better. You're going to see things that will amaze you."

"When do we start?"

"We're just waiting for the last three passengers to arrive … Say, you're from Ottawa, aren't you?"

Pugsley nodded.

"Then you'll have company. The passengers we're waiting for are all from Ottawa – a couple and a single guy." Johannsen flashed another smile. "It'll be a reunion of sorts!"

Before long, the drone of an incoming Beaver shattered the silence of Rescue Bay. The passengers emerged and transferred to the *Aquaholic* in an inflatable Zodiac.

Pugsley hailed the trio. "I'm from Ottawa, too."

"You don't say," replied one of the newcomers, a lean, fit man who looked to be in his early 40s. "That makes four of us. What are the odds? I'm Beauregard Fisher and this lovely lady is my wife, Deirdre." The attractive blonde by Fisher's side, a few years younger than him, smiled.

"And this lively fellow," Fisher continued, gesturing in the direction of a generously proportioned man approaching from the rear, "is Jackson Clifford."

"Call me Jack," Clifford roared, giving Pugsley's right hand a vigorous squeeze. "You're Pugsley, right? We're gonna be roommates."

Pugsley knew he'd be sharing a cabin – just not with whom. "Then I'm especially pleased to meet you, Jack. I look forward to getting to know you."

"Yeah, me too," Clifford said, then added, "You should know I snore like a buzz saw. Fart a lot, too. Hope you're OK with that."

Pugsley was struggling with how to respond when Clifford guffawed and clapped him on the back. "Aw, I'm just fuckin' with ya," he bellowed. "You didn't think I was serious, didya?" He grinned and shook his head. "I'd be the roommate from hell, wouldn't I? Christ on a bicycle!"

Pugsley managed a weak smile. "You surely would." *Christ on a bicycle. Good expression*, he thought.

Clifford laughed delightedly at his younger companion. "We're gonna have a blast, you and me!"

•••

After breakfast the next morning, Johannsen set sail for Mussel Inlet, at the head of a long fiord known as Mathieson Channel. "We're gonna find us some bears," he promised.

Along the way they passed a splendid alpine waterfall, the first of dozens they'd see on the trip. Mussel Inlet was more spectacular still, framed by sheer granite cliffs rising hundreds of metres. Soon, grizzlies began emerging from the forest in numbers, looking to feed on the estuary's salmon. Pugsley and his companions piled into the Zodiac for a closer look, Johannsen edging the craft to within a few dozen metres of the majestic beasts, most of whom ostentatiously ignored them.

They watched as two young siblings retreated, woofing and puffing in alarm, when a massive alpha male sauntered into view. A mother and two cubs ambled past along a rocky ledge, the two youngsters gamboling at the water's edge.

"Jesus," Pugsley whispered. "This is awesome. I've lost count of how many grizzlies we've seen today."

"At least a dozen for sure," Beauregard Fisher offered.

"That's the bear minimum," cracked Clifford, to muted groans from his companions.

That evening, over a meal of freshly caught Dungeness crab, the party toasted their good fortune. "That's one of the best bear-viewing days I've ever had," said Johannsen. "And I've been doing this for nearly 20 years." He cocked an eyebrow. "Maybe we should have people from Ottawa on board more often!"

"Fine by me," Fisher said.

"Me too," Pugsley chimed in.

"More women next time!" cried Clifford, grinning at Pugsley. "No offence, Pugs, but I'd rather share my cabin with someone with a pussy."

Pugsley repressed a smile at the crude humour. He'd heard a lot worse as a police reporter. There was no hint of amusement from Deirdre, though.

She gave Clifford a frosty stare. "You're actually quite the jerk, aren't you?" she observed.

Belatedly recognizing his wife's indignation, Fisher intervened. "That remark's really not appropriate, Jackson," he scolded. "There are ladies present."

"Yeah," Clifford replied, unrepentant. "Just not enough of them."

"There's one too many troglodytes, though," Deirdre said, rising to her feet, "I'm outta here." She strode off in the direction of her cabin.

"What did I say?" Clifford protested, wide-eyed with feigned innocence.

"You'll have to excuse my wife," Fisher said. "She volunteers at a shelter for sexually abused women. She doesn't have much tolerance for people who make crude jokes." He looked pointedly at Clifford. "Nor do I, for that matter."

"What a humourless pair you are," Clifford snorted. "Life's too short. You should both loosen up."

Fisher stared for a moment then rose from his chair. "I need to get some air," he said.

"I'll go with you," Pugsley chimed in.

Pointedly not inviting Clifford to join them, the two men scooped up their drinks and left. Once above decks, Fisher turned to Pugsley. "I feel sorry for you, having to share a cabin with that asshole."

"We're getting along OK. He's got a twisted sense of humour, though. It can get a little tiresome."

"No kidding," said Fisher. "He told me he owns a company in Ottawa called Clifford Construction. Ever heard of it?"

"Can't say that I have. But I don't write for the business section, so that's not surprising."

"You're a writer?"

"Yup. For the *Advocate*."

"What do you cover?"

"The police beat. It keeps me hopping."

Fisher peered at Pugsley, as if seeing him for the first time. "Norman Pugsley … yeah, I've seen your name in the paper. You're good."

"Thanks," Pugsley said, pleased by the praise. "What about you, Beauregard? What do you do for a living?"

"Please, call me Beau. Nothing nearly as interesting, I'm afraid. I'm a doctor."

"No shit! That's impressive. What's your specialty?"

"People, I suppose. I'm a general practitioner."

"Really?" Pugsley hesitated before continuing. "My family doc just retired and I'm looking for a new one."

"Good luck with that," Fisher said, offering a sympathetic smile but nothing more.

"So, how'd you meet Deirdre?" Pugsley asked.

"She's a nurse. We met at the hospital. Kind of a whirlwind romance. Six months later, we were hitched."

"You did well," Pugsley said. "She's a real beauty."

"Thanks. I know I'm lucky. Do you have a family, Norman?"

"Call me Norm," Pugsley said, grinning. "Maryanne and I have been married for 10 years. We have a nine-year-old daughter, Barbara."

"Just the one?"

"So far. We're hoping for more, but …"

"I get it," Fisher commiserated. "We've been trying for three years. No luck yet. Can't complain about the effort, though," he laughed.

"It's nasty work, but somebody has to do it," Pugsley agreed with a smile.

"Speaking of which … I should go. Deirdre will be wondering where I am. And I can guarantee she'll still be fuming about Clifford."

Pugsley remained on deck for a few minutes, transfixed by the tranquility of his surroundings and the vermillion sky's fading light. He felt a profound sense of peace, as if the burdens of his regular life had magically evaporated.

Reluctantly, he rose and headed to his cabin. Clifford was propped up on his bed, reading a book. He looked up when Pugsley entered.

"Look Pugs," he said, a chastened expression on his face, "I'd like to apologize. I was a little over the line with that remark at dinner." He grimaced. "Sometimes things come out of my mouth before my brain can process them."

"Don't apologize to me, Jack," Pugsley said. "Tell Deirdre you're sorry for what you said."

"I will."

"Good," Pugsley said. "What are you reading?"

"It's called *Delta of Venus*. A bunch of short stories by someone named Anaïs Nin. One of the guys at work thought I'd like it. Only read a couple so far, but they're pretty hot. I guess you'd call it erotica."

Pugsley frowned. "Can't say I've heard of it. Not that I read much erotica."

"Neither do I. But it's kind of a turn-on, to be honest." Clifford gave his roommate a sly look. "I could lend it to you when I'm done."

"Doesn't sound like my cup of tea," Pugsley demurred, with a shake of his head. "I'm partial to thrillers and mysteries, myself. But thanks anyway."

"No problem, Pugs. To each his own."

•••

The trip passed with the timelessness of a dream. For hours, the *Aquaholic* tracked the misty shoreline of uninhabited Princess Royal Island, the largest on British Columbia's north coast – a remote place teeming with bears, including the fabled white spirit bear.

More than once, Pugsley and his mates witnessed whales breaching and blowing in the surrounding waters – most memorably when a pair of humpbacks spouted within metres of the sailboat. As the cetacean air wafted over the boat, the passengers on deck gagged and pinched their noses.

"Jesus! What's that smell?" Clifford groaned.

"Whale bad breath," Johannsen replied. "It's really quite foul."

"That's unbelievable," said Pugsley, fanning the air with a hand.

"You could say they've got a whale of a problem," Clifford ventured. His fellow passengers, all too familiar by now with his bad puns, said nothing, not wishing to encourage him.

At last they arrived at Gribbell Island, said to boast the highest concentration of spirit bears on the coast. Johannsen introduced them to Marven George, an Indigenous guide from Hartley Bay, whose job it was to show them one of the rare white bears. He led the party along an overgrown former logging road to a viewing platform on Riorden Creek, a fast-flowing stream about 10 metres wide.

"Now, we wait," George said.

The hours ticked by. At first, Pugsley and the others filled the time by quizzing George about the spirit bears, more formally known as Kermode bears. "They're a subspecies of black bears," he told them. "Most Kermodes actually are black. Only about 400 are white. "

"So, they're albinos?" Deirdre asked.

"Not albinos," George corrected. "The white ones have mutant genes. Their white fur helps them catch more salmon than the black bears. The fish have trouble seeing them."

After an hour or so, the questions petered out. Deirdre pulled a copy of Maclean's magazine out of her backpack and leafed through it. Pugsley whistled tunelessly off and on. Clifford tried to sleep but was regularly startled into wakefulness by his own snores. Beau Fisher twiddled his thumbs and emitted periodic sighs. A light rain began to fall.

After five hours on the viewing platform, Pugsley was ready to give up when George stiffened, peered upstream and hissed, "White bear!"

The electric words were an adrenal jolt, the torpor of the interminable wait transformed in an instant into alert watchfulness. Necks craning and cameras at the ready, Pugsley's posse waited breathlessly for the spirit bear to appear.

Then there he was, ambling regally down the creek, white fur gleaming as an emergent sun filled the rain forest with light.

"He's a bruiser," whispered George. "A good 200 kilos, I'd say."

As the bear drew nearer, it became apparent that his fur wasn't pure white, but rather mellowed to amber on his back and neck. "Oh my God, oh my God," Deirdre whispered, transfixed. Even Clifford was struck dumb.

The bear, unperturbed by the clatter of clicking shutters, sauntered within a dozen feet of the viewing platform, searching fruitlessly for an errant salmon, and eventually disappeared around a bend.

Later, back on the *Aquaholic*, Pugsley and his mates gathered for one last shipboard supper, buoyed by the euphoria of their sighting. Johannsen filled glasses with Sauvignon Blanc. "White wine for a white bear," he said, raising his glass. "To the bear!"

"To the bear!" echoed the others.

"Well," said Fisher, turning toward Pugsley with a grin, "how was that for a day?"

"Best ever. I've done canoe trips in Algonquin Park and seen animals along the way – moose, wolves, black bear. But never anything as magnificent as that white creature."

Pugsley paused to sip some wine. It was the first time he'd tried Sauvignon Blanc, and he wasn't sure he liked it. But nothing was going to taint his pleasure.

"Y'know," he mused, "I think I'll write a piece for the newspaper's travel section about this trip. People need to know about this place."

Clifford, who'd been scribbling something on his napkin, rose and called for silence. "I've written a poem about our bear," he announced. He held up his napkin and began to recite.

Here's to the glorious white bear,
Who's mostly an out-of-sight bear,
He's a bear of great Spirit,
But there's no need to fear it,
He loves salmon, though humans he might share.

His very bad limerick drew laughter and applause from the assembled, their appreciation clearly fuelled by the wine.

"Christ on a bicycle, Jack!" belted out Pugsley, deploying Clifford's own catchphrase. "That's really good. And no bad jokes!"

Clifford beamed. "Ah, Pugs. What would be the pun in that?"

Seven

OTTAWA, SPRING 2006

It was Fawzia Hassan's idea to meet at the Jolly Cow in Sandy Hill, the sort of chichi counterculture emporium Pugsley normally shunned. But Hassan, not far removed from her student days, didn't own a car and shared a nearby apartment, so it was a convenient choice for their rendezvous.

Convenient for her, at least. For Pugsley, it meant trekking downtown from his redoubt in the suburbs – an expedition he'd largely avoided since his retirement six months earlier. The excursion was especially galling given that he'd only agreed to meet the *Advocate*'s young police reporter as a favour to his former boss, Renata Richter.

Pugsley took a tentative sip of his latte, as if it were something faintly menacing. Hassan had urged him to order it after he confessed that he had no idea what a latte was. "It's delicious," she promised.

"So," Hassan asked brightly, "your first latte. What do you think?"

"Too much milk and not enough coffee," replied Pugsley, whose idea of a good brew was a double-double from Tim Hortons. "But overall, not bad."

Hassan giggled and swiped a hand across her upper lip. "You've got a …"

"Got a what?"

"Latte moustache!"

Pugsley grabbed a napkin and wiped the offending whiskers.

"Better?"

"Much better."

He scrutinized the young woman across the table. She was perhaps 25 –

the same age he'd been when first hired by the *Advocate* – and reported on crime and the police, a beat he'd once covered with distinction. But they had nothing else in common, he thought to himself.

She was gorgeous, with flawless ochre skin and a mop of artfully frizzed black hair. Despite his recent weight loss, he was pudgy, white and balding. She was an immigrant whose refugee family had come to Canada when she was five. One of his distant ancestors, Horace Pugsley, was a United Empire Loyalist who arrived in 1784, long before Canada was a country. She was just beginning her professional life. His was over.

"So, Fawzia," Pugsley said, turning to the reason for their meeting, "tell me where you're at with this, ah, Birchmount murder case. What have you found out so far?"

"Not a lot, unfortunately. From what the police tell me, there hasn't been much response to the reward offer. A few tips but nothing terribly helpful so far."

"Any word on who put up the reward?"

"Afraid not. The person apparently wanted to remain anonymous."

"Who are your sources?" Pugsley asked.

"That's the problem. I'm new on the beat, and I haven't yet been able to cultivate many reliable sources. Most of my information is coming from police media staff."

"Well, that's no good," Pugsley said, frowning. "The media mouthpieces never tell you a goddamn thing that's useful."

"What about you, Mr. Pugsley? Do you still have sources that could be helpful?"

"If we're going to work together, you've got to stop with the 'Mr. Pugsley' crap. Makes me feel like a fossil. Call me Norm, for chrissake."

"Sorry. In my culture, we respect our elders. Somehow, calling you by your first name seems too chummy. But I'll try."

"Good. Now, sources. It's been more than 20 years since Jenny's murder. Most of my police sources are either retired or dead. But I'll check and see who's still out there. Maybe they've heard something."

"Terrific. What do you remember about the case … Norm?" she asked.

Pugsley paused to collect his thoughts. For two decades, he'd diligently tried to banish all memories of the Birchmount murder. Now Fawzia wanted him to summon them up – and relive a painful episode of his own history. *Be careful Norm. Proceed with caution.*

"I think you know most of it," he began. "Jenny was 19 when she was killed. She'd had a rough life … abused sexually and physically by her father. She left home when she was 16 and had to turn to prostitution to survive. She did well enough for a while – guys who use hookers like them young and fresh-faced, and Jenny was all of that."

Hassan flinched. "Something wrong?" Pugsley asked.

"We don't call them hookers anymore, Norm," she said. "They're sex workers."

"Why does your generation need to change all our words?" Pugsley growled.

"Just trying to haul you into the 21st century," she replied.

"Well, don't. So far, I'm not fond of this century," Pugsley said grumpily. "Now you've made me lose my train of thought. Where was I?"

"You were saying men like sex workers young," Hassan told him.

"Yeah, not quite. But anyway, Jenny's luck ran out on a cold November night in 1985. Her frozen body was found a few days later in a woodlot in the Greenbelt. She'd been strangled.

"There weren't a lot of clues. The night she was murdered, one of her fellow … oh, Christ … sex workers saw her get into a luxury car – likely a Cadillac, BMW or Mercedes – with a man who looked to be in his late 40s. The police checked out hundreds of men who fit the profile – guys that age who owned black luxury cars. They identified a few suspects, but there was never enough evidence to bring charges."

"Were you still on the police beat?" Hassan asked.

"No. I'd been on Parliament Hill during the final years of the Trudeau government, and the paper had named me its investigative reporter about six months earlier." Pugsley got a wistful expression on his face. "That had long been an ambition of mine."

"Why were you covering the story?"

"I volunteered. My daughter, Barbara, was only a couple of years younger than Jenny, so her murder really hit close to home. I remember thinking, 'What if that were Barbara? How awful would that be?'

"One other thing. When Jenny was five years old, she almost drowned and I wrote a front-page story about her rescue. I felt a real connection to her – it really shook me up when she was killed. I wanted to catch the guy who did it."

"I get that," Hassan said. "Since I started on this story, I've become a bit obsessed, to be honest. Some young Somalis join criminal gangs because they don't fit in. The discrimination can be tough to handle. Believe me, I've faced it." Hassan wiped her eyes with the back of a hand and took a deep breath before continuing. "Jenny's challenges were different, but her life was just as hard. If the two of us can find justice for her, that would be something special, wouldn't it?"

Oddly, Pugsley felt moved by Hassan's words. "It sure would." The ghost of Jenny Birchmount hovered, but to his surprise, he now felt more willing to open a long-locked door, even if only a crack. "Let's get to work, my young apprentice!" They tapped their lattes in an informal toast.

•••

Other than bills and advertising flyers, Norman Pugsley didn't receive a lot of mail. So, he was intrigued when the postman delivered a letter – bearing an exotic stamp and a Greek postmark – from his former employee and one-time nemesis, Bliss Browning. He tore it open and began to read.

March 22, 2006
Areopoli, Greece

Dear Norm:

Please forgive my primitive recourse to snail mail. Internet access is hit-and-miss here in the Mani, so I thought an old-fashioned letter was best.

I hope you're doing well and are now fully recovered from your unfortunate heart attack. Harrison tells me you're helping Fawzia Hassan with an investigative story on a cold-case murder. Good for you. Fawzia is talented, but she's very junior. She will benefit greatly from your years of experience and deep police contacts. Plus, I'm told you covered the murder when it happened, so you bring that knowledge to the story as well.

It will also be good for you too, I suspect. It must have been traumatic to walk away so abruptly from your journalism career after so many years and accomplishments. Working with Fawzia lets you ease back into the game. Who knows where that might lead? You're still relatively young, Norm. Your best years may still be ahead of you!

One thing I've learned is that life is unpredictable. A year ago, I was working in a dead-end job, captive to my fears and insecurities. No one at the newspaper respected me. I knew that. I had no prospects, professionally or personally. The only thing that made life tolerable to me was the music of the legendary Greek opera diva, Maria Callas. I was existing, not really living.

Now, I've broken free of those constraints. I left my safe but soulless job, travelled places I'd never imagined, met someone who inspires and amazes me. My life has changed so much in the space of a few months. Perhaps yours will, too.

Norm, I've never really explained why I went to Greece last year instead of Africa. I'm not sure you'll understand, but you deserve an explanation.

Remember those panic attacks I had last summer? They were triggered by someone who wanted me to do something unthinkable – at least for me. This source told me that, in the 1960s, Callas secretly gave birth to a child. She hid the pregnancy from the father, the Greek tycoon Aristotle Onassis, because she feared he'd end their relationship if he found out. Callas supposedly gave her child up for adoption right after birth. She never laid eyes on the baby but was told it was a healthy boy.

The source who told me this wanted me to travel to Greece, find Callas's lost son, and let him know who his parents really were. Naturally, I doubted this story at first. And to be honest, the idea of travelling to Greece terrified me.

But my informant persisted and in the end, I chose to believe. I feel confident that I've solved the mystery and maybe found a life with the special woman I told you about, Matina. She isn't yet ready to love, but I'm hopeful.

I live in a little blue-and-white house, a five-minute walk from Matina and her mother. Almost every day, we take long, invigorating hikes in the countryside, slowly cementing the bond between us. We're really getting to know one another, Norm. I think she likes what she sees. I know I do.

Meanwhile, I'm beavering away on my travel stories. I've lined up a few American and British newspapers that are interested in travel pieces from Greece. There are so many amazing places here, Norm. I had no idea.

Best regards,
Bliss Browning

p.s. I don't know if you read my series on Botswana (I can't believe many people got through all eight parts) but Renata and Harrison were very pleased. They plan to enter it in an international travel writing competition. Just imagine!

Pugsley put the letter down. He couldn't help smiling. If Bliss Browning, once the most timid mouse in the newsroom, could find a new life, maybe he could too. Maybe one day he'd be reconciled with his daughter, Barbara, or even find love again. Maybe one day, he'd get justice for Jenny Birchmount.

•••

Dr. Beauregard Fisher held a stethoscope to Norman Pugsley's chest. "Deep breath," he intoned. He listened, then moved the chest piece to a different spot. "Another deep breath … aaaaand another."

Fisher straightened up, slipped the stethoscope out of his ears and smiled. "Everything sounds normal, Norm. You're making an excellent recovery."

"That's terrific, Beau," Pugsley said. It had been seven months since his last checkup, and those were the words he'd hoped to hear. "I've been following your bloody instructions to the letter."

Fisher arched an eyebrow skeptically. "Really? You've even cut down on the booze?"

"You don't believe me? I'm hurt!" Pugsley said with mock indignation. "I'll have you know a six-pack of beer lasts me two weeks these days."

There was no need to tell his doctor he usually followed the beer with a whisky chaser.

"It does look as if you've dropped some weight, Norm. Step on the scale and we'll see where you're at." Fisher shifted some weights on the mechanical scale, then let out a low whistle. "199.5 pounds. Good work."

"Really? I broke 200? I haven't been that low in 20 years. Worth a celebration, don't you think?"

Fisher spotted the twinkle in Pugsley's eye. "A little one … sure. Just don't undo all your hard work. You still have a way to go before you're at your best weight."

"Slavedriver," Pugsley complained.

"What about your family, Norm? Have you heard from your daughter recently?"

Pugsley's face darkened. "Not a word. She lives in Richmond Hill these days, so it's not like she can just drop in. But a phone call every now and then would be nice."

"What happened there, Norm? You and she were so close when she was younger."

"Barbara didn't handle my divorce from her mother well. She blamed me, I guess. She was in touch after the heart attack, but once it was clear I was going to pull through, I didn't hear from her again."

"That's too bad," Fisher said. "It's important for cardiac patients to get emotional support. They can easily slip into depression otherwise."

"I'm fine, Beau. Been on my own for years now. I'm used to it."

"Sure. But didn't you like to get together with your newspaper buddies before you retired?"

"Yeah, we had some laughs. Of course, we usually were pissed," Pugsley added with a brief chuckle. "I'm not allowed to do that anymore, because of you!"

"Not because of me, Norm," said Fisher. "Because of your heart attack. I'm just the messenger. Please, don't shoot me. Do you still see your office mates?"

"Not a lot. I guess they're busy. Or maybe they just don't need me anymore now that I'm not their boss."

Fisher frowned. "That's a bit cynical. I'm sure your work buddies genuinely enjoyed your company."

"Perhaps. Some of them were probably sucking up to me because they thought it would be good for their careers." *After all,* Pugsley thought, *that's what I did when my career was in the toilet.*

"Isn't there anyone you're in touch with from the office?"

"As a matter of fact, there is. You know the editor, Renata Richter? I've told you about her."

"The crazy lady?"

"That's her. We've been getting together for meals now and then."

"Well, that's a surprise. Given everything you've told me about her, she's the last person I'd expect you to see."

"Me too," Pugsley said. "She's still bat-shit crazy when it comes to journalism, but if you can get past that, she's OK."

Fisher gave Pugsley a long look. "Why, you sly bastard! You're sweet on her, aren't you?"

"No, no. That's insane. Not at all. No way. No chance."

"Methinks you doth protest too much, my friend," Fisher said with a smile.

Is he right? Am I falling for Renata? Christ on a bicycle!

"No, Beau. She only wanted to persuade me to work with one of the paper's reporters on a cold-case murder."

"Oh? Which one?"

"The Jenny Birchmount case. It's been more than 20 years. You probably don't remember. She was a teenaged, um, sex worker – that's what they call them these days, or so I'm told – who was murdered in the mid-80s."

"They never found the killer?"

"No. He's still out there somewhere. Assuming he's still alive."

"So, what does the paper want you to do?"

"I'm working with the *Advocate*'s police reporter, a sweet young thing named Fawzia Hassan. Someone offered a $50,000 reward for information leading to the arrest of the killer. We're doing some digging to see what we can turn up."

"Sounds stressful," Fisher observed, furrowing his brow. "You're still recovering from a very serious coronary, Norm. You stepped down from your job to take better care of yourself, which was smart. Jumping back into some big murder story might not be wise."

Pugsley nodded slowly. "Truth be told that case brings back a lot of bad memories. I'm not all that eager to revisit it."

"That's another reason to be cautious, then," Fisher said. "Stress can be a killer, especially for people with heart problems."

"So as my doctor, you're advising me not to do this?"

"If you're sure you can handle it, go ahead. But it might not be the best idea."

"Thanks Beau. Once was more than enough. I'll tell Fawzia I'm out … on doctor's orders."

Eight

NORTHWEST TERRITORIES, AUGUST 1979

Pierre Trudeau dunked the plastic plate in the chill waters of the Hanbury River, scouring it vigorously with a scrub brush. Once satisfied that all food remnants had been dislodged, he handed the dripping dish to Norman Pugsley, who patted it dry with a small camp towel and set it on a nearby flat rock.

It still seemed surreal to the 35-year-old Pugsley that he was helping the former prime minister of Canada wash dishes in the northern wilderness. Only a week earlier, he'd received an unexpected call from Beauregard Fisher, inviting him to join Trudeau and six others on a two-week canoe trek down the Hanbury and Thelon rivers.

"One of the guys had to drop out at the last minute – a death in the family," Fisher explained. "We need an eighth person, so naturally I thought of you. You *are* an experienced canoeist, aren't you?"

Pugsley was, though most of his canoeing had been on flat water in Algonquin Park. The Hanbury and Thelon featured plenty of challenging white water, and he was less familiar with that. But the chance to be part of such a memorable expedition was irresistible.

"Of course, Beau. I've been canoeing since I was a boy."

A few days later, Pugsley was in a Twin Otter seaplane soaring over Great Slave Lake in the Northwest Territories with Trudeau, Fisher and five others, en route to their starting point at Sifton Lake.

The other expedition members included two of Trudeau's former bodyguards – known only as Barry and Gary – Liberal Senator James Brody and Jean LaRoche, a long-time friend of Trudeau's. One surprise participant, at least to Pugsley, was Jack Clifford, his roommate during the sailboat tour of British Columbia's Inside Passage two years earlier.

"Who invited him?" Pugsley whispered to Fisher, rolling his eyes.

"Yeah, I know. Turns out his company was involved in building Trudeau's famous swimming pool at 24 Sussex, so .... I hope it doesn't put you off," Fisher added apologetically.

"Don't worry. I can put up with him for a couple of weeks," Pugsley said, secretly dismayed.

For his part, Clifford greeted Pugsley effusively. "Christ on a cloud! If it isn't that skinny reporter I met in B.C. Not quite so skinny now, though," he added, with an appraising look.

After the plane disappeared, the group quickly set up camp and divided the tasks. Brody and Clifford claimed to have some culinary skills and were designated the cooks. The others acted as sous chefs or handled dish-washing duties.

Clifford summoned the group to dinner on their first day. The menu included succulent tenderloin steaks, which had been preserved on dry ice, washed down by fine French wine transferred into plastic bottles for easier transport.

Trudeau, who hadn't said much to that point, spoke up. "This is truly delicious, Jack. You've set a high bar. I hope you can keep it up."

"Well ... just watch me!" Clifford shot back with a grin, eliciting a weary smile from the former PM.

Early the next morning, the group loaded their canoes and began paddling, soon reaching the Hanbury River. The river narrowed and Pugsley and his companions found themselves navigating a series of shallow, rocky rapids.

The river bottom, often only inches beneath their canoes, was littered with boulders, requiring constant vigilance and frequent back-paddling to keep speed in check. More than once, the adventurers had to line their canoes through shallow sets of rapids before reaching calmer waters.

"The blackflies aren't as bad as I expected," Pugsley observed from the stern of the craft he shared with Fisher on a more languid stretch of the river.

"That's because it's cold and windy," Fisher hollered from the bow, half-turning his head. "If the winds drop and it warms up, you'll be begging for mercy."

"At least I've got my trusty bug hat," Pugsley said.

"You're going to need it. Did you bring a bug suit too?"

"I thought the hat and some insect repellent would be enough."

Fisher snorted. "I'll pray for you."

•••

As they travelled past the tundra's rocky hills, swamps and sand dunes, the group fell into something of a routine. They rose early in the perpetual light of the barren lands, had a quick breakfast and were often on the water by 6 a.m.

At times they traversed remote lakes along the Hanbury route. On the river proper, they regularly encountered unrunnable sections, like the double set of Grove Rapids, requiring long and arduous portages. Even at age 59, Trudeau proved as adept at flipping a canoe on his shoulders as Pugsley, more than two decades his junior.

The former PM seemed to relish the rhythm of their journey, paddling in quiet contemplation much of the time. His tenure as prime minister had ended with his election defeat three months earlier, and it struck Pugsley that he might be relieved by the respite from the public spotlight he'd been under for a dozen years.

On the lakes, the weather dictated their progress. If the wind was with them, they made good time, but unfavourable winds required maximum effort for minimal gain. If a thunderstorm approached, they hunkered down and rode it out in their tents.

By late afternoon, they would set up camp, often on a glacial esker or sandy beach. Happy Hour was declared, and Trudeau mixed over-proof rum daiquiris, to hallelujahs from his appreciative companions. The dinners that followed were no longer gourmet feasts; the disappearance of their dry ice had seen to that. Most often, dinner was pasta and sauce, mac and cheese or lentil chili. But when they were able to hook grayling, trout or Arctic char in the northern waters, they ate royally.

During their dinners together, Pugsley studied his companions. Brody, an athletic man in his early 40s with the noble face and bearing of a patrician, was a Liberal party fundraiser who'd been rewarded for his efforts with a Senate appointment two years earlier. He had a reputation as a bon vivant and exuded a seductive charm that Pugsley, as a journalist, instinctively resisted.

LaRoche, compact and intense with a shock of greying hair, had been a classmate of Trudeau's at Collège Jean-de-Brébeuf, the secondary school of choice for Quebec's francophone elite. He was a partner in a Montreal law firm and someone Trudeau turned to for advice from time to time.

Barry and Gary were well-muscled clones who rarely spoke, though they hung on Trudeau's every word, nodding vigorously whenever he spoke and guffawing at his occasional wry remarks.

It was after a less-than-memorable chili repast that Pugsley found himself washing dishes with Trudeau. A bit intimidated, he hadn't said much to the former PM so far. It didn't help that for some reason, Trudeau thought his name was Gordon. But you can't wash dishes with someone in silence, even if they get your name wrong.

"So, Pierre … can I call you Pierre?" Pugsley asked.

"Of course, Gordon," Trudeau replied, with a tiny smile. "After all, it would no longer be accurate to call me Mr. Prime Minister, would it?"

Gordon! Jesus! Why does he keep calling me Gordon!

"Yeah, that's true, I guess. Did you like being prime minister, Pierre?"

Trudeau didn't immediately respond, and Pugsley briefly wondered whether the question had offended him. "There were certainly times when I didn't." Trudeau paused again, almost visibly collecting his thoughts. "But most of the time I enjoyed being prime minister. Very much."

"What was the best part, if you don't mind me asking?" Pugsley said.

"The power! I loved the power!" Trudeau declared, before giving the jest away with a slight smile.

"Seriously, it gave me a purpose. I suppose I was searching for one for a long time. Something where I could make a real difference," he mused. "I believe in justice and fairness, and I want a strong Canada, including Quebec. I think I had some success. If I had the chance, I'd do more." Though a famously private man, he seemed to be speaking freely, perhaps because everyone had agreed that anything said on the canoe trip stayed on the canoe trip.

"Well, if that's what you want, you couldn't do much better than being prime minister," Pugsley ventured. "It must have been tough to lose that job."

Trudeau handed Pugsley a plate. "Yes and no. Maybe it was time to move on. I'm feeling quite liberated now. A trip like this would have been difficult if I were still prime minister. What about you, Gordon? I'm told you're a journalist. What sort of things do you cover?"

"It's Norman."

"Pardon?"

"My name. It's Norman."

Trudeau stared at him, seemingly mortified. "I do apologize, Norman. That's unforgiveable."

"Hey, don't worry about it … Pete!"

Trudeau laughed and for the first time, Pugsley relaxed. "As a matter of fact," he said, returning to Trudeau's question, "I cover the police beat for the *Advocate*."

"And you … like that?" Trudeau asked, a note of disbelief in his voice.

"I do. It's real life, you know. The seamy side, for sure, but it's real."

"I suppose."

"Don't get me wrong. It's not always fun. Terrible things happen to good people and it's my job to tell those stories. Nobody looks forward to the death knock."

"The death knock?"

"That's when you have to contact the dead person's next of kin to get their comments and a picture. People are usually in shock. Sometimes they're cooperative, but often they slam the door in your face."

Trudeau handed Pugsley another dish but said nothing.

"Sometimes I even feel sorry for the criminals," Pugsley continued. "Most have had tough lives. They've made some bad choices, but they're not all terrible people."

"Haven't you written about anything else?" Trudeau asked, though he appeared to be losing interest and was only being polite.

Pugsley considered Trudeau's question. "A couple of years ago I wrote a piece about a sailboat trip I took off the coast of B.C. We saw one of those spirit bears – the white bears that live in that area. They're threatened by hunting and habitat loss caused by logging and pipelines. My story brought that to people's attention. It caused a bit of a stir."

Trudeau's eyes widened. "You wrote that? I remember the story. We talked about it at a cabinet meeting."

"No shit!" Pugsley's face reddened. "Oops. Sorry, prime minister … I mean, Pierre."

Trudeau appeared unfazed by Pugsley's vulgarity. "One of my ministers from B.C. thought we should do something to protect those bears – push for a protected sanctuary, perhaps. We needed the cooperation of the provincial government and the premier just wasn't interested. But I'm sure it will happen someday. Still, Norman," Trudeau said, reappraising his dishwashing companion, "you've made a difference!"

Pugsley grinned. "I guess that makes two of us, eh Pierre?"

•••

On the sixth day, the winds dropped and daytime temperatures soared to 28 degrees Celsius. Blackflies pounced in numbers that beggared belief.

Everyone donned full bug suits except Pugsley, who had only his head net. While that protected him from the neck up, the ravenous insects infiltrated every opening in his clothing and had their way with his tender flesh.

Even their tents offered only limited refuge. Whenever anyone entered, hundreds of marauding blackflies buzzed in with them. It took an hour of focused swatting to reduce their numbers to tolerable levels.

"Christ, Beau!" groused Pugsley as he squashed a dozen dive-bombing blackflies inside the tent the two shared. "These bugs are fucking relentless."

"Oh, come on, Norm. Admit it – you're having a good time. I mean, you and Pierre are pals now."

"I wouldn't say that. He shut me down right quick when I tried to ask him about those movie star women he used to date."

"You asked him about that? What were you thinking?"

"I'm a journalist, Beau. It's what we do."

"Sure, but you should know that Trudeau never talks about his personal life – especially with journalists. You'd have more luck asking Brody about his female admirers. I hear he's quite the rover."

Pugsley bashed a battalion of blackflies assaulting his lower leg. "My chats with Pierre have done one thing, though: made me interested in political reporting. That was never one of my ambitions, but meeting Trudeau has changed that."

"Too bad he's planning to leave politics," Fisher said. "It would be very useful as a journalist to have a personal connection with the prime minister."

A wistful expression flitted over Pugsley's features. "That would be amazing. But … ain't happening, I guess."

"By the way," Fisher said. "I meant to ask. Did you ever find a new family doctor?"

"Not yet," Pugsley said, surprised that Fisher had remembered a conversation from two years ago. "Seems they're scarce as hen's teeth."

Fisher smiled. "Call my office when we're back."

That night, the party of adventurers huddled in their dining tent, confined to quarters by the merciless blackfly hordes.

"Dammit, I say we all need a drink," exclaimed Brody, stripping off his protective layer of bug armour.

"Seconded," concurred Clifford, adding with a grin: "I hear alcohol kills flying insects."

"I declare the motion passed," said Fisher. By popular demand, Trudeau mixed eight rum daquiris and distributed them to his companions, who made short work of them.

"Another round?" asked Trudeau, amiably.

"Just one?" replied Brody, grinning but not truly joking. It wasn't just women he liked; he'd been open about his fondness for alcohol from day one of the trip.

The daquiris did the trick, loosening tongues and sweeping away all concern about the swarming bugs. The 43-year-old Brody, who'd guzzled his cocktails, was especially garrulous.

"Being a senator … it's … a great gig!" he gushed, his accustomed eloquence deserting him. "Decent pay, fabulous pension, guaranteed job till you're 75. And respect! People are impressed when I tell them I'm a senator." Brody leaned forward and whispered conspiratorially. "And there are some real beauties in the Senate's page program, lemme tell ya."

Fisher chuckled, but Trudeau, whose own taste for younger women had been no secret, frowned. "I do hope you behave appropriately around those pages, James. After all, you're old enough to be their father."

"Of course," sputtered Brody. "I'm a model of decorum. I look, but don't touch … usually."

"Usually?" Trudeau said, his tone suddenly no-nonsense.

Brody winked but said nothing.

"Let's talk about something else," interjected Pugsley.

"Good idea," said LaRoche.

"*Great* idea," amended Trudeau.

•••

After an hour's paddle the following day, the river abruptly narrowed and the current accelerated.

"It's Dickson Canyon!" Fisher bellowed, striving to be heard over the roaring waters. "Get ready for one bastard of a portage." The infamous Dickson Canyon portage, a five-kilometre slog over ridges, bogs, tundra and small forests of spruce, was the longest and most gruelling on the route. But travellers had no choice: the river here was a roiling cauldron of white water punctuated by heart-stopping waterfalls.

The portage took them well out of sight of the river. The route was unclear, with only a few cairns to guide them, and progress was slow. The blackflies were ferocious under the intense Arctic sun, and Pugsley's companions sweltered in their full bug suits. Lacking a bug suit of his own, Pugsley was marginally cooler but infinitely more attractive to the rapacious insects.

It took three trips and nine hours, with frequent stops to wolf down handfuls of the abundant cloud berries and huckleberries growing along the portage route, to transport their canoes, supplies and gear past Dickson Canyon, even with the two muscular bodyguards.

"Jaysus!" wheezed Clifford, shrugging off his bulging pack when they were finally through. "That was hell on a pogo stick. Damn near killed me."

"Really? I feel fresh as a daisy," teased Trudeau, who somehow looked it. Clifford, for once at a loss for words, frowned.

With another portage looming at Ford Falls, the weary voyageurs set up camp on a massive white sand esker flanked by black spruce and meadows of tundra. Another round of Trudeau's rum daiquiris, a pasta dinner, and Pugsley and his companions, exhausted by the day's travails, retreated to their tents. Within minutes, a chorus of thunderous snores rattled the wilderness silence.

•••

After portaging past Ford Falls, Pugsley's party paddled downriver for 90 minutes and set up camp at Helen Falls, a dramatic waterfall in a canyon section of the river. At a viewpoint overlooking the falls, they found a logbook stored in a dry box inside a cairn.

"Why don't you write something, Norm?" Fisher said.

"Yeah, you're supposed to be the wordsmith," chimed in Clifford. "And this trip is historic, in a way. Write something for posterity."

A bit flustered, Pugsley retrieved a pen, thought for a moment and began to inscribe an entry in the logbook.

We arrived at Helen Falls in late August 1979 after a week's paddle from Sifton Lake. Our group of eight includes a doctor, a lawyer, a Canadian senator, a businessman, a journalist and oh yes ... Pierre Trudeau, the 15th prime minister of Canada, and two of his bodyguards. We have wined and dined our way down the Hanbury, provided nourishment for untold biting insects, conquered portages that would defeat lesser men. Tonight, we'll toast our achievements over dinner with the last of our wine. Life is tough. Tomorrow, we hope to complete the Hanbury River section of our trip and begin our journey through the area known as the Thelon Oasis. Blackflies aside, it has been a spectacular experience. We wish safe passage to all who read this.

"Let me see what you wrote," Clifford demanded when Pugsley was finished. He read the words twice, then turned to Pugsley.

"It ain't poetry, but it'll do, I guess," he said.

"Thanks Jack," Pugsley said. "I'll try not to let your praise go to my head."

"Would have liked it better if you'd mentioned my name," Clifford grumbled.

"Oh, you and Trudeau? You want equal billing?"

"Well ... I *did* build his damn pool. And you know what they say," Clifford cackled. "A pool and his money are soon parted."

•••

Below Helen Falls, the Hanbury River runs fast and rough for about a kilometre. Clifford, mildly stung by Trudeau's jibe after the Dickson Canyon portage, saw an opportunity for payback.

"Hey Pierre," he called. "Bet you can't run these rapids solo."

Trudeau smiled and waved an arm in invitation. "After you, Jack."

Clifford turned, studied the river for a few minutes and launched his canoe, handling the serpentine rapids if not with ease, at least successfully. Then it was Trudeau's turn. With the thoroughness that had marked his years as prime minister, he walked the shoreline, making mental notes of the river's eddies, twists and turns.

While Fisher, Brody and LaRoche watched from a clifftop, Pugsley, Barry and Gary took up positions along the foot of the bluff, ready to intervene should disaster strike.

At first, Trudeau and his craft made good progress, slipping past submerged rocks. Then suddenly, his canoe veered, seemingly with a will of its own despite his expert paddling. Another moment and it had crashed into the cliff wall, dumping him into the turbulent waters. Barry reached out desperately but Trudeau was swept past him.

Pugsley didn't stop to think. He jumped into the chilly waist-deep water, steadied himself against the powerful current, snagged Trudeau's life jacket with both hands and, grunting with effort, hauled his spluttering companion to safety. The canoe was swept downriver by the current, coming to rest in stiller waters.

When the group reassembled below the rapids, Clifford was grinning. "Well, Pierre," he gloated, "guess I won that round." Trudeau, still catching his breath, acknowledged him with a half-hearted wave of his hand. Before the group pushed off, though, he took Pugsley aside and thanked him for the rescue.

"I might have been able to ride it out," he said quietly, "but maybe not. I'm in your debt, Norman."

"Forget it." Sensing the older man's chagrin, Pugsley joked: "Saving political leaders is my specialty. If you really want to repay me, run again and win the next election, so I can cover your government."

Trudeau gazed at Pugsley thoughtfully. "I might just do that," he said, a gleam in his eye. "Everyone deserves a shot at redemption."

Nine

OTTAWA, JUNE 2006

Fawzia Hassan could barely contain herself, even on the phone. "Mr. Pugsley," she exclaimed before quickly correcting herself. "I mean, Norm. I'm so glad I finally got you. I have some terrific news!"

Pugsley was dismayed to hear Hassan's voice. He'd been avoiding her since promising Dr. Beauregard Fisher he'd withdraw his offer to help search for Jenny Birchmount's killer. He'd been dreading this conversation with Hassan and had already ignored several phone messages from her.

"Oh, hello Fawzia. Good to hear from you," he lied. "Sorry for not getting back to you. I've been, um, crazy busy."

"No need to apologize, Norm. I'm sure there are a lot of demands on your time. But I think I'm finally starting to get somewhere on our Jenny Birchmount story."

"Oh?" Pugsley brightened. This could be good news, he thought. *Maybe she doesn't need me after all.*

"Bernard Lachance, one of the detectives who worked the case in 1985, has agreed to talk to us. He's tied up for a few days in a court case, but he's promised to get together with us as soon as he's free."

"That's terrific, Fawzia. I knew you could do it." *This is your chance, Norm. Tell her you're out.*

"Well, I couldn't have done it without you, Norm," Hassan continued.

"What … what do you mean?" Pugsley asked with a sinking heart.

"The detective wasn't going to meet with me until I told him you were working with me on the story. It seems that, even after all these years, some people still hold you in high regard at police headquarters."

"I doubt that, Fawzia," Pugsley said slowly, struggling to suppress rising feelings of doom. "Most of them probably don't even remember me."

Hassan's emphatic head shake was almost audible over the phone. "You're being way too modest. From what I've heard, you're legendary in cop circles. They think you were the best police reporter the *Advocate* ever had. I'm *so* glad we're working together."

"You know, Fawzia, I was talking to my doctor recently …"

"Oh dear," she interrupted in alarm, "I hope you're OK?"

"Sure, sure. I'm fine. Just a routine follow-up after my heart attack last year."

"Thank God. So all is well?"

"My doctor did wonder if it was a good idea for me to tackle a stressful story like this while I'm still recovering."

Hassan chuckled. "He mustn't know you very well. From everything I've heard, you love a challenge. The tougher the better, right?"

"Right," Pugsley agreed, without conviction. "I did think about it, though. He *is* my doctor, after all."

"But … we're still good?"

Pugsley swallowed a sigh of resignation.

"Of course." He paused. "We're still good."

●●●

Renata Richter took a sip of Grüner Veltliner and smiled contentedly at her former managing editor. "What a lovely evening," she gushed. "This was an inspired idea, Norm."

"I'm glad you approve." Pugsley smiled, suppressing a belch after an overly ambitious swig of draft beer.

The two were dining alongside the Rideau Canal on the patio of the National Arts Centre's swanky restaurant on a comfortable evening in late June. It was the latest of several meals they'd shared in recent weeks – most, at Richter's suggestion, in casual places serving ethnic food. So far, they'd sampled Ethiopian, Japanese, Korean and Indian cuisine. All were well outside Pugsley's comfort zone, so in desperation he'd suggested the more conventional restaurant at the arts centre. At least he could get a steak.

Surprisingly, Pugsley had come to relish his meals with Richter. They weren't dates exactly, he told himself – both paid for their own meals – but they were a welcome break from the isolation of retirement. Richter also kept him apprised of developments at the *Advocate* and shared her hare-brained schemes for the floundering newspaper, the latest being her idea of dressing reporters in period costume to re-enact key events in Canadian history on the streets of Ottawa. Mercifully, Pugsley had been able to talk her out of it.

He had to admit she was looking good. She was wearing a stylish teal sharkskin jacket and matching skirt, floral silk blouse and a pair of stiletto leather pumps that, he noted with surprise, showcased her well-toned legs to good advantage.

He wasn't sure what was in it for her, but her engaged and animated expression suggested she was enjoying his company too.

Richter studied her former managing editor's face. He looked younger than when he'd worked at the *Advocate*, she thought, thanks perhaps to his weight loss. You wouldn't call him handsome, but he had an interesting face, a face with character. She liked it.

He'd even dressed up for the occasion. Nothing too formal – a grey herringbone blazer and black turtleneck – but unusually presentable by Pugsley's standards. He'd trimmed his moustache and excised the tufts of hair that normally sprouted from his nose and ears.

Richter had another sip of wine. "Fawzia tells me you're making progress on the Jenny Birchmount story," she ventured.

"Perhaps," Pugsley said, shifting uncomfortably. "I don't want to get your hopes up, but Fawzia seems pleased."

"I'm just grateful she's got you in her corner," Richter said. *Time to change the subject*, Pugsley thought.

"Had a letter from our old travel editor, Bliss Browning, recently. He says you're planning to enter his Botswana series in a contest."

"We've already entered it in *National Geographic*'s annual competition," Richter confirmed. "He'll be up against the best travel writing in the world, but I think he has a chance. It was absolutely stellar work. What did you think of it, Norm?"

"Um, yeah, it was pretty good, I guess." The truth was Pugsley had read only one of the eight articles in Browning's series, but it would be impolitic to admit that to Richter.

"Better than pretty good, I thought. It was terrific. I learned so much about Botswana. And the writing! It was …" Richter wracked her brain for the right superlative.

"Indescribable?" Pugsley suggested.

"That's not it. Sublime! It was sublime!"

A waiter arrived bearing their meals.

"Who's having the guinea fowl?" he asked. Richter raised her hand.

"And the steak must be for you, sir," he said, placing a plate in front of Pugsley.

"Well done as I ordered?"

"Yes sir. As you ordered."

Richter looked dubiously at the hockey puck of meat. "You know, Norm, I think you need to widen your horizons. I have an idea how we might do that."

"What do you mean?" asked Pugsley. He carved off a piece of overcooked beef and popped it in his mouth, chewing vigorously.

"It's just that I've noticed you're a bit set in your ways," Richter explained gently. "That's not a moral failing or anything. But it means you're missing out on a lot of wonderful experiences. You need to loosen up, try new things … taste new things."

Pugsley scowled. "I think I've been trying a lot of new things with you. You tried to feed me raw ground beef, remember."

Richter looked blank. "Raw ground beef?"

"Yeah, in that African place you took me to. Crapto or something."

"You mean kitfo?"

"Whatever. Who eats stuff like that?"

"Well, it's a delicacy in Ethiopia. But Norm, millions of people love steak tartare."

"Sure. I love steak too if it's cooked right."

Richter stared for a moment, then sighed. "This is what I was talking about. There's a whole world of pleasure out there that has passed you by.

I'd love to introduce you to it if you'll let me."

Pugsley suppressed a cough. *Did Renata just say she wants to introduce me to a world of pleasure?*

"Tell me more," he prompted, a bit hoarsely.

"Well, one of my favourite places in the world is the Apotheosis, a terrific boutique hotel in Mont-Tremblant. The food is amazing, they have a spectacular spa and there's an infinity pool that overlooks the lake." Richter reached across the table and touched Pugsley's right hand lightly. "Will you go there with me? Separate rooms, of course."

Pugsley hadn't seen this coming, though the idea of a getaway with Richter was unexpectedly appealing.

"As long as you don't feed me anything too weird," he said after a pause. "Sure. I'm up for it – on one condition."

Richter raised an eyebrow.

"If you want to show me your world," Pugsley began, "I want to show you mine."

"I don't know, Norm. I'm not really into baseball and beer …"

"Renata, I'm hurt. There's a lot more to me than that. One of *my* favourite things is canoe camping in Algonquin Park. If you'll do that with me, I'll go to your fancy-ass hotel with you."

"Camping? In tents?"

"Those are my terms. Separate tents, of course."

"But I've never been camping," Richter protested.

"That's great. Something I know that you don't." Pugsley offered a mischievous grin. "Think of it this way. It will … widen your horizons."

"Touché. You drive a hard bargain, Norman Pugsley." This time, Richter squeezed his hand, beaming. "I may live to regret this, but yes, I will go camping with you this summer. Maybe I'll get a special eight-part series out of it for the *Advocate*."

Lord preserve me, he groaned to himself.

Ten

OTTAWA, NOVEMBER 1985

Jenny Birchmount stepped out of the shower and reached for a pink towel hanging on a hook. She tackled her dripping hair first, wringing as much moisture as possible from her shoulder-length auburn locks, then moved with brisk efficiency to dry her arms, torso, buttocks, legs and feet.

She paused to examine her body in the bathroom mirror. At 19, it was well-proportioned, her breasts pleasing if modest in size, her waist narrow, her hips agreeably rounded, her legs sleek and slender. A butterfly tattoo graced her lower back and her private parts were carefully shaved.

She wasn't pleased with her face. Her nose was too big, she thought, her eyes an insipid shade of hazel. There was a small scar on her forehead, mostly healed, the residue of a bad date a couple of months earlier. But perhaps she was being too hard on herself. After all, men seemed to like her face well enough. She'd even been called beautiful.

And there'd been plenty of men in the three years she'd been selling her body on the streets of Ottawa. She hadn't had much choice. She was in her early teens when her mother died of cancer, leaving her in her father's care, though "care" wasn't the right word. Grieving the loss of his wife, he had turned to whisky for comfort and channelled his drunken rage at Jenny, his only child.

She put up with his verbal and physical abuse for a time. But as her body developed, her father's attentions took a sinister turn. The breaking point came when he entered her room while she slept and tried to force himself on her. She kicked him off and fled the house, calculating she was safer living on the street.

She was 16 and on her own. She needed money for rent, food, clothes and other necessities. She was able to land a couple of minimum-wage jobs, working days as a clerk in a discount store and evenings cold-calling potential customers on behalf of a lawn-care company.

Between the two jobs, she was surviving, but only barely. Then one night in a bar, she met a greasy young man who gave her crack cocaine and showed her how to smoke it. "No charge," he said.

She soon became addicted, but the drugs were no longer free. Instead, the pusher became her pimp, forcing her into prostitution and taking her earnings in exchange for a steady supply of crack.

For two years, that was her life. An endless cycle of mercantile sex, drugs and debasement. So many men.

Then she met Joe.

Joe wasn't his real name, of course. In her world, people didn't use real names. But it was the name he provided.

Their first encounter had been nine months ago. He was cruising through the ByWard Market one evening in his sleek late-model car, lots of tinted glass, when he pulled over and lowered his window.

"Hello gorgeous," he smiled.

"Would you like a date?" she responded, trying not to roll her eyes.

He nodded. "Hop in."

He appeared to be in his late 40s – old enough to be her father, though nothing like him physically. She'd had many men of that age. At least he was reasonably attractive, for an older man. Clean-shaven, a sprinkle of silver in his hair. Carrying a few extra pounds but not enough to turn her off.

"What would you like to do?" she asked.

"Just talk, for now."

"OK," she said. She'd heard that before, too. "But you're gonna have to pay either way."

"That's fine."

So, they talked. She told him a bit about herself. Not the full story – irrelevant, she thought – but he appeared interested. He didn't talk about himself. At all. He seemed decent enough. He could make her laugh. She didn't meet many like him.

When they parted, he gave her a fleeting kiss, just the briefest brush of his lips on hers. He pulled out his wallet. "Thanks for your time," he said. "Is $100 enough?" *Perhaps he hasn't done this very often,* she thought. She said it was. More than enough, but she didn't tell him that.

"Can I see you again?" he asked.

"Sure. When?"

"How about same time next week?"

"You know where to find me."

"You never told me your name," he pointed out.

"You can call me Tess," she said. She'd adopted the name as her street handle after seeing Roman Polanski's film version of the novel *Tess of the D'Urbervilles*, whose titular 16-year-old heroine is raped.

Their chaste trysts continued, always inside his car. She told him more of her story. Her drug addiction. Her controlling pimp. Her dream to leave the life and study to become a massage therapist at Ottawa's community college. He was a good listener. It made her want to be better. For him. To please him.

He didn't ask for sex. But as her comfort with him grew, she seized the initiative.

"I'd like to make you happy," she told him on their fifth "date."

She unzipped his fly, liberated his stiffening penis and pleasured him. His moans, and other responses, confirmed her success. "Christ," he murmured.

After that, sex was a regular part of their liaisons. They still talked first – Joe wanted to hear her latest news and was quick to offer advice – but their sessions always ended with heavy breathing in the commodious backseat of his sedan.

He was tentative at first, anxiously checking in with her as they coupled.

"Is that OK, Tess?"

"I'm not hurting you, am I?"

Over time, Joe's jitters gradually abated, replaced by unfettered passion and a growing appetite for experimentation.

One day he asked her, "Will you show me some of your tricks?"

"Tricks?"

"You know … the kinky things you do with other clients."

She wasn't crazy about that. She didn't want to tarnish what she had with

Joe, whatever it was, exactly. But she trusted him. Perhaps, she thought, she even loved him. After all, he'd encouraged her to get off the drugs and break free of her pimp. If that's what he wanted, who was she to refuse?

It began with mutual spankings and dirty talk. On one occasion she stripped down to a pair of stockings and invited him to penetrate her. That clearly turned him on. There was role-playing, with each taking turns as dominant and submissive. A bit of bondage.

They still talked, though less and less. Sex occupied more of their time together. But Joe was generous. He usually gave her $200 – more than double her normal rate. Sometimes, if he was especially pleased with her, he bumped it up to $300.

Tonight she would see him again. She smiled as she styled her hair with a blow dryer, anticipating their time together. She slipped on thong underwear and a push-up bra and picked out the clothes she would wear. A form-fitting red cotton top that showed off her cleavage. A tight black leather skirt that ended mid-thigh. A pair of high-heel pumps.

It was a brisk evening in mid-November, temperature hovering near zero Celsius and a hint of snow in the air. She slipped on her winter jacket, zipped it up and walked to their rendezvous point on York Street, a few blocks from her apartment.

He was punctual, as ever. She opened the car door, settled into the passenger seat and gave him a quick but ardent kiss.

"Where are we going tonight, Joe?" she asked as he pulled into traffic. He liked to drive while they talked until they reached a secluded spot where they were unlikely to be interrupted.

"I've got a good place in mind," he replied. "It should be deserted at this time of night."

"I hope so," she said, with a suggestive smile.

Joe returned her smile. "Have you been a good girl, Tess?"

"Of course."

"Are you staying off the crack?"

"Yes … most of the time."

"What about that pimp? Is he out of the picture?"

"He still bothers me now and then. But I think he knows the score."

She suddenly remembered she had news.

"Guess what, Joe? I got my application in to the college this week. I should hear whether I've been accepted in the next month or so."

"That's terrific, Tess. I want to be your first customer when you become a massage therapist," he added with a lascivious side-glance.

After a 20-minute drive, Joe turned onto a dirt lane in the Greenbelt, the natural area that encircles Ottawa. As he'd predicted, they were alone. There were no lights. For all practical purposes, they were invisible.

"Can you leave the heater on while we do it?" she asked. "I don't want to be cold."

"If that's what you want. But don't worry," he assured her with a smile. "You're too hot to be cold."

They stepped out of the car and slipped into the back seat. She shucked off her jacket, tossed it in the front seat, and wriggled out of her skirt.

"Ta-da!" she exclaimed, presenting herself for his approval.

"Awesome," he exclaimed.

He laid her down on the seat and buried his face in the musky warmth of her groin, eliciting squeals and moans of delight.

After a few minutes, he raised his head and looked at her. "I'd like to try something new, if you're game."

"Sure. What is it?"

"It's called breath play. Basically, you cut off your partner's air supply for a short time while you're doing it. It's supposed to be a real turn-on."

She frowned. "I've heard of it. Some of my clients ask for it. But I always refuse. It's dangerous, Joe."

"If you don't know what you're doing, I agree, it's dangerous." He paused. "But I've been reading up on it. And you'll be doing it to me. Not the other way around."

"I don't know Joe. I'm up for most things, but I'm not comfortable with breath play."

"Do you trust me?"

"Yes. Of course I trust you."

They fell silent for a moment. Then Joe had a suggestion. "How about if I show you how to choke me safely?"

She considered Joe's idea. He seemed so eager, and she hated to disappoint him.

"You really know what you're doing?" she demanded.

"Of course."

"All right, Joe. Show me."

"I'll lie down and you get on top of me. Once we start humping, put both your hands around my neck, but don't squeeze my windpipe. Press the sides of my neck instead. Not for too long. Twenty seconds at most. Then relax your grip and ask if I'm still OK. If I say yes, choke me again. Rinse and repeat until I give you the signal to stop."

"What's the signal?"

"I'll raise my right hand."

"OK," she said dubiously. "Let's give it a go."

She climbed on top of Joe, guided him inside her, then put her hands lightly around his neck, positioning them as he'd instructed.

"Good," he said. "Now squeeze."

She tightened her hold but released it 10 seconds later.

"Are you all right?" she asked in a quavering voice.

"I'm fine. You need to choke me longer for this to work."

"Sorry. I'll try again."

This time she maintained the chokehold for about 20 seconds before releasing it.

"That was much better," Joe said. "Now do it again."

When he raised his hand to end the encounter, he was glassy-eyed and panting. "That was incredible," he said, when he'd recovered. "It gave me an amazing high … almost hallucinogenic. And so fucking erotic. It was like being in an Anaïs Nin story or something."

Joe sat up and faced her. "Your turn?"

She gave a start. But the effect on him had been undeniable.

"You know I'd never hurt you," he reassured her.

"I know," she said, reclining onto the seat. "But please, Joe. Be careful."

"I will."

They switched positions and coupled. He placed both hands around her neck and began to squeeze. Twenty seconds later, he eased his grip.

"Still OK?"

Feeling woozy, she gasped for air then nodded. He applied pressure a second time. Twenty seconds. Twenty-five.

In his excitement, he shifted, inadvertently trapping her right arm under his leg. She tried to raise her arm to stop him, but it was pinioned. She tried harder. She just couldn't. She couldn't speak. She couldn't breathe. Her eyes widened in panic, but he mistook it as arousal.

Thirty seconds. Forty.

She saw explosions of light. Her mother's face. A favourite childhood doll. And then she was gone.

Eleven

OTTAWA, DECEMBER 1985

Norman Pugsley tossed the City section of the *Advocate* aside, rose from his chair and strode purposefully across the newsroom to city editor Morgan J. Peck's office. He didn't have a lot of time for Peck, who'd come to the *Advocate* after failing his probation at the *Globe and Mail*, a fact Peck had neglected to mention when he applied to the *Advocate*. The Ottawa newspaper's editors, giddy at snagging a recruit from the prestigious Toronto newspaper, hadn't bothered to ask for references.

"Got a minute, Morgan J.?" Pugsley began. Peck preferred to be known by his full name, including middle initial. Privately, though, female journalists at the paper called him Morgan the Muppet while their male colleagues favoured Little Pecker.

Peck glanced up from the story he was editing. Though reporters had been writing on computers for years, he preferred to do his edits by pen on printouts. He told himself it was easier to spot typos and flabby writing that way.

"What's up, Norm?"

"I was just reading our latest story about the Birchmount homicide," Pugsley began.

"Awful case," Peck said, shaking his head.

"Yes, it is. Body found in a woodlot in the Greenbelt. It's been more than a month, and the cops don't seem to have the first fucking clue who did it."

"So it appears."

Pugsley frowned. "I know she was a whore, and most people don't give a damn when bad things happen to them. But Jesus, Morgan J., she was 19 years old! She had her whole life ahead of her. She turned to prostitution because her so-called father was abusing her. And now she's dead. Strangled and dumped in the bush like garbage by some sick psychopath."

"A sad story," Peck agreed.

Pugsley drew several slow, measured breaths. "When Jenny started selling her body, she was about the same age as my daughter Barbara is now," he said. "I can't help thinking how I'd feel if something like this happened to her."

Morgan J. Peck waited patiently for Pugsley to get to the point. He'd only been supervising him since March, when Pugsley had been appointed the paper's investigative reporter after a stellar stint on Parliament Hill covering the Trudeau government's final term.

He hadn't yet developed any chemistry with Pugsley. Found him to be an irritating know-it-all, truth be told. But he'd learned that Pugsley liked to talk things through before committing to a course of action.

"Her death feels personal to me," Pugsley continued. "I'd like to get involved in the story. I still have great contacts from my days on the police beat. And I'm our investigative reporter now. This story could use some investigation. I have the skills to do that."

Peck hesitated. The newspaper already had two solid reporters assigned to the police beat. One of them, Jake Berger, had been working nearly full-time on the Birchmount murder story. Not that he was getting anywhere. And Pugsley had only just started work on an exposé of auto garages that were allegedly overcharging customers for repairs.

"I don't know, Norm. Jake's been working the story pretty hard. I'm not sure he'd appreciate being bigfooted by you."

"I wouldn't do that," said Pugsley. "We'd be a team. We'd work on it together."

"What about your investigation into the crooked garages?"

"I can still dig into that as well." He gave Peck a tight smile. "You know, Morgan J., I can walk and chew gum at the same time."

Peck could see Pugsley's mind was made up. There would be no dissuading him.

"Fine, Norm. Give it your best shot. But we need a quick win. If you don't turn something up soon, I'm taking you off the story."

Pugsley grinned. "Thanks boss. You won't regret it."

•••

Jake Berger had mixed feelings when the city editor told him Norman Pugsley would be working on the dead hooker story with him.

After all, Pugsley was one of the paper's hotshot reporters. His stories landed on the front page with such regularity that newsroom staffers, with mock reverence, called him Page One Pugsley. Not only had he aced the parliamentary beat, regularly breaking exclusive stories with the help of impeccable sources in the Prime Minister's Office, he'd been a legendary police reporter for the *Advocate* in the 1970s.

Berger, by contrast, was a relatively callow journalist with just four years of experience, the last two on the police beat. In many ways, he was still finding his feet. He had little to show for all his hard work on the Birchmount murder beyond a rather pedestrian profile of the unfortunate victim's short, tragic life.

Berger told himself he should welcome the opportunity to work with a journalist of Pugsley's stature. He would surely learn a lot. But the role of second banana wasn't appealing, and Berger feared his own modest skills would be overshadowed by the journalistic supernova that was Norman Pugsley. So when Pugsley ambled over for a chat, Berger was more than a little wary.

"Hi Jake," Pugsley said amiably. "I guess you've heard we'll be working together on the Birchmount story."

"Ah, yeah, um, sure," Berger mumbled. "The, um, city editor …" Inexplicably, he couldn't seem to recall his boss's name.

"Morgan J. Peck?" Pugsley prompted, with a smile.

"Yes, Morgan … J.," Berger said, adding the initial after an awkward pause. "He mentioned it to me yesterday."

"Is it OK with you?"

"Sure. Why wouldn't it be?"

"No reason as far as I'm concerned," Pugsley replied. "But some people are possessive about their stories."

"Oh well," Berger said, avoiding eye contact. "Not a problem for me."

"Right, then," Pugsley said. "Let's get right to it. What have you found out so far about poor Jenny's killing?"

For a few long seconds, Berger, eyes downcast, said nothing. Pugsley thought perhaps the young reporter hadn't heard his question when Berger glanced up and sighed.

"Not much," he admitted. "The cops are still trying to identify the driver of the black luxury car Jenny apparently got into before she was killed, but if they've got any strong leads, they aren't telling me."

Pugsley frowned.

"Nothing?"

"Nada."

"Who have you been talking to at the cop shop?"

"I've tried to chat up most of the cops working the case. The lead detective is Callum Stewart –"

"Arseling," Pugsley muttered.

Berger blinked. "Pardon?"

"You know, an ass."

"Oh. Right. He is. Anyway, so far, he's given me nothing. There's a new detective, a fellow named Bernie Lachance, also working the case. He's been a bit more helpful. He's the one who told me they haven't ID'd the driver yet."

"Did he say whether they've narrowed the list of suspects at all?"

"Only indirectly. He told me they've eliminated a lot of possible suspects, so I guess that means there are a smaller number still under investigation."

Pugsley furrowed his brow, deep in thought.

"It's curious," he said at last, breaking his brief silence. "Usually, the police would be more forthcoming than that. They'd be issuing updates on the investigation and appealing to the public for information. That hasn't happened this time. My gut tells me they're hiding something."

"Really?" said Berger. "Why would they do that?"

"Good question," Pugsley said. "Maybe they're protecting someone."

Berger's eyes widened. "You think Jenny's killer is some sort of big shot?"

"We have no evidence of that. But we shouldn't rule it out." His mind flashed back to something former police reporter Joe Flynn told him years ago about powerful people seeing prostitutes. He had a low opinion of Flynn, but even a clock is right twice a day, he thought.

"I'm still in touch with some of my sources from my days on the police beat," he said. "Let me bounce it off a few and see if anyone salutes."

Despite himself, Berger was impressed. Pugsley was as advertised, dammit: resourceful, creative and decisive.

"What should *I* do?" he asked plaintively.

"Just keep your powder dry until I can poke around and see what turns up," Pugsley said. "I'll let you know what I find out and we'll take it from there."

•••

"Hello, Tony," said the disembodied voice on the phone. "It's Norman."

Ottawa Police Staff Sgt. Anthony Weaver broke into a broad smile. "Norman? Norman Pugsley?"

"Guilty."

"Wow. Talk about a blast from the past! How the hell are you, Norm?"

"Not bad, Tony. And you?"

"Up to my ass in alligators, as usual."

"Hope I'm not interrupting."

"You are. But fuck, Norm, you know I'll always make time for you. What's up?"

"I'm hoping you can give me a hand," Pugsley began. "I've been assigned to see what I can find out about the Jenny Birchmount murder investigation."

"Oh," said Weaver, uncertainly. "I'm not really involved in that."

"I know, Tony. But you hear things, right?"

"I suppose. A few things."

"You lads are being pretty tight-lipped about the status of the investigation. That has me thinking there's something sensitive about it, something awkward."

"You figured that out all by yourself?"

"It's just a theory. But I'm hoping you can tell me if I'm on the right track."

Weaver lowered his voice to a whisper. "Like I said, I'm not involved in the investigation. But from what I hear, at least a few of the remaining suspects are so-called respectable people."

"Can you tell me who?" Pugsley asked.

"You know I can't, Norm. The chief would have my ass on a platter if he ever found out."

"Look," Pugsley said, "you've helped me in the past, and I've never given you up. There's no chance I'd burn you now. You can trust me."

"It's not that I don't trust you, Norm. It's just that … well, this is a sensitive case. It could easily blow up in our faces if we're not careful."

Pugsley remained silent, waiting to see if Weaver had anything to add.

He did.

"I don't know who all the suspects are. I've heard one might be a politician."

"His name?"

"You'll have to find that out from somebody else. Perhaps someone in the Prime Minister's Office might know. I think you have some friends there."

"Well, I did," Pugsley said, "when Trudeau was still PM. But he's gone now, and I'm not sure how much the new Tory gang would tell me."

"Too bad. But I can't do *all* your work for you."

"I know. Can't blame me for trying, though."

"Nope."

"OK, thanks Tony. You've been very helpful."

•••

Fred Wright was having yet another dreadful day. Barely 16 months after his boss, Brian Mulroney, had won a smashing majority in the 1984 federal election, his Progressive Conservative government was mired in a seemingly endless string of minor scandals.

The latest was known as Tunagate. One of Mulroney's cabinet ministers had overruled federal inspectors and allowed the sale of a large quantity of tuna even though it had been declared unfit for human consumption. Wright, a senior aide in the Prime Minister's Office, had been in full damage control mode for days, but the story wasn't going away. Journalists were circling like sharks.

So when he got a message that reporter Norman Pugsley wanted to talk to him, Wright's instinct was to blow him off. He didn't know Pugsley well, but he knew he'd been close to former prime minister Pierre Trudeau.

"What does he want?" Wright snapped at his administrative assistant, Jim Dunning. "If it's about the damn tuna, forget it."

"He didn't offer any details," said Dunning, "but he said it had to do with a politician who might be under investigation. Maybe a Liberal."

Wright brightened. A Liberal in trouble? Just what the Mulroney government needed to shift media attention from its own self-inflicted wounds.

"In that case, yes, I'll talk to him," Wright said. And for the first time in weeks, he smiled.

Wright returned Pugsley's call later that day, after enduring another tainted tuna-dominated question period in the House of Commons.

"Norm, it's Fred Wright."

"Thanks for returning my call, Fred. I know you're crazy busy these days."

"Not sure I'll ever be able to eat a tuna sandwich again, and they used to be my favourites. What can I do you for?"

Pugsley cleared his throat. "I'm wondering if you've heard anything about an MP or Senator who's being investigated by Ottawa Police?"

"I, uh …"

"A police source told me one of the top suspects in the murder of a young prostitute earlier this year might be a politician. Have you heard anything?"

Wright hadn't, but he didn't want to admit that to Pugsley. The words *prostitute* and *murder* danced in his brain like a Broadway chorus line. He just needed to connect them to the word "Liberal."

"It … rings a bell," Wright said, stalling for time. "Let me talk to a few folks here and get back to you … on the Q.T."

"Thanks Fred. Much appreciated."

Wright convened an urgent meeting of Conservative backroom operatives to discuss Pugsley's startling and potentially invaluable query. "Does anyone know anything about this? If it's true and if it's a Liberal, it would totally change the narrative. It might even convince me there is a God and he's a Conservative."

That got a laugh but to Wright's chagrin, nobody had heard anything useful. "Dammit," he fumed. "We've got to come up with a name for my friend Pugsley." He fell silent for a few seconds, pondering what to do.

"If a Liberal *were* under investigation for killing a prostitute," he mused, "who would it be?"

"So many candidates," muttered one of the assembled, to titters.

Wright frowned. "Seriously. Who's the most likely Liberal?"

One of the aides, a brash young man named Cooper Horton, raised his hand.

"I don't know if he's the guy," Horton began, "but Senator James Brody is a notorious muff-diver. He's always hitting on the young Senate pages. It wouldn't surprise me if he employed the services of prostitutes from time to time."

"That's good," Wright said, nodding. "As I recall, he has some sort of friendship with Trudeau – canoe buddies or something. But could he kill a woman?"

"Who knows?" said Horton. "Maybe if someone was blackmailing him, threatening to go public …"

Wright summed up the discussion. "I think we have a plausible candidate in Senator Brody. I'll put a bug in Pugsley's ear. He can investigate and see where it leads. All off the record, of course … not for attribution.

"Gentlemen," he said, dismissing the operatives, "I think I see a light at the end of our current tunnel to tuna hell."

Twelve

OTTAWA, JANUARY 1986

City editor Morgan J. Peck glanced impatiently at his watch. "Where the hell *is* he?" he asked Jake Berger, who shrugged. "Who knows? Norm marches to his own drummer."

Pugsley was late for the meeting he'd requested. He hadn't said exactly why he wanted to meet but intimated he had new information about the Birchmount murder investigation.

Peck scowled. "Well, he'd better show up soon. I have better things to do than sit around waiting for Norman fucking Pugsley to grace us with his august presence."

Berger was surprised, though not dismayed, by Peck's evident distaste for one of the newsroom's stars. He'd assumed that Pugsley was beloved and admired by his bosses, but Peck's petty outburst told a different story and made him wonder if others felt the same sense of inadequacy around the star reporter that he did.

Five minutes later, Pugsley walked briskly into the city editor's office. He grunted hello and took a seat. Not a word of apology for his tardiness.

"Nice of you to show up, Norm," Peck said.

"You'll be happier once I tell you what I've learned," Pugsley replied.

"We'll see," Peck grumbled. "What you got?"

Pugsley pulled out his note pad. "I've been chasing down a tip from one of my police sources that one of the leading suspects in the Birchmount murder is a politician," he began.

"Mother of Jesus!" Peck exclaimed. "Is it true?"

"Far too soon to say," Pugsley replied, "but a senior aide in the Prime Minister's Office told me he's heard stories about prostitutes and James

Brody, the Liberal senator. He had no real evidence, so it could all be bullshit, but according to my source, Brody's name is out there in political circles."

He flipped through his notebook until he found what he was looking for. "Here's a direct quote from my PMO source: 'James Brody has a well-earned reputation for inappropriate sexual conduct. There have long been rumours that he sees prostitutes. Jenny Birchmount might have been one of them.' "

"That doesn't sound like very solid information," Peck said, a bit deflated.

Pugsley closed his notebook. "You're right. It isn't. But there's something else. Six years ago, I was on a canoe trip in the far north with Pierre Trudeau and a bunch of other guys. Brody was part of the expedition. One night, he got drunk and said some pretty inappropriate things about the female pages in the Senate. So, it's possible. He's not the type to hold back with women."

"Christ!" Peck muttered. "What a scandal! What a story!"

"Only if it's true," Pugsley interjected. "We're a long way from that. My source is a Conservative, so he has reason to smear a Liberal. And none of my Liberal sources claim to know anything about it."

"Well," Peck observed, "you'd expect that. This would be devastating for the Libs, so they're not likely to discuss such a damaging rumour. What about Brody? Have you asked him what he was up to the night this Birchmount girl died?"

"Unfortunately, he's in the Philippines. Part of a parliamentary delegation attending a conference there. I haven't been able to reach him yet, but he's due back in the next few days. I'll try him then."

"Can we afford to wait that long?" Peck paced excitedly. "If Brody's name is circulating, the CBC or the *Globe* or someone is bound to hear it. We don't want to lose the scoop here, Norm."

"You don't have to tell me, Morgan J.," Pugsley said. "I'll go back to the police and see if anyone will confirm that Brody's a suspect. We'd still need to talk to the senator himself, of course."

"Good idea. Meanwhile, write up what you know so we'll be ready to publish as soon as we get confirmation."

Pugsley frowned. "That's not a good idea. It's bad to have an unverified half-story sitting in the computer system. What if it gets published by accident or leaked to someone?"

"How the hell could that happen?" Peck snapped. "Only Jake and I would even know it existed, and I certainly wouldn't publish it until it's confirmed."

"I'd be more comfortable if we just left out Brody's name for now," Pugsley said.

"Fine, fine," Peck grumbled, irritated by the reporter's caution. This was the kind of story that could burnish an editor's reputation, and Morgan J. Peck was nothing if not eager for some burnishing. "Write a draft that includes everything we know except his name, then."

"What do you want *me* to do?" Berger asked.

"Work your own sources, Jake," Peck said. "We need a full-court press on this. We have to move fast. If we break this story, there could be a National Newspaper Award in it for both of you." And maybe a big promotion for me, he thought but didn't say.

•••

A couple of days later, Berger stuck his head into Peck's office. "Got a minute, Morgan J.?" he asked. "There's someone here you should talk to."

Peck looked up peevishly from the story he'd been editing. He hated being interrupted in the middle of an edit. "I'm kind of busy, Jake. Can it wait?"

"I suppose. But I *really* think you need to hear this. It's about Senator Brody."

Peck set his pencil down. "Why didn't you say so? Come on in, then.' "

Berger signalled to someone behind him, entered the office and took a seat, followed a moment later by the shambling figure of Joe Flynn, the *Advocate*'s long-retired former police reporter.

"Jesus, Joe!" exclaimed Peck, who'd shared beers with Flynn a couple of times since landing at the *Advocate*. "This is a surprise."

The years hadn't been kind to Flynn. Never svelte, he seemed to have expanded to the point that he waddled rather than walked. With each laborious step, he defied gravity. He fell heavily into an office chair, which wobbled alarmingly.

Flynn panted, trying to catch his breath after the exertions of ambulation. “Good to see you too, Morgan. You’ve risen quickly at the paper. City editor now. Imagine.” Was there a touch of incredulity in Flynn’s voice? It sounded that way to Peck.

“Yes, well, these are different times, Joe. It’s been what, 12 or 13 years since you last worked here?”

“Something like that,” Flynn replied, glancing around. “Place hasn’t changed much. Still kind of a dump.”

Peck drew a deep breath. “To what do I owe the pleasure of this visit?” he asked.

Berger jumped in before Flynn could answer. “When we talked a couple of days ago,” he told his boss, “you said I should work my sources on the Birchmount story. But the cops weren’t talking. So I thought, ‘Why not call Joe?’ He had a lot of success when he was our police reporter. Maybe he’d heard something.”

“And had he?” Peck asked, cocking a quizzical eyebrow.

“Not when we first spoke,” Berger said. “But he said he’d make a few inquiries and get back to me.” Berger glanced at Flynn. “Maybe I should let Joe take it from here.”

Flynn cleared his throat with a mighty harrumph.

“I might be retired,” he began, “but I still talk to a lot of cops. Kinda the circle I move in. So when the boy here got in touch,” he said, motioning in Berger’s direction, “I put his question to the guys I talk to on the force.”

“And?” prompted Peck.

“And whaddya know, a couple of them had heard Brady’s name.”

“Brody,” corrected Berger. “It’s Senator Brody.”

“Yeah, whatever,” Flynn said.

“So let me be clear,” Peck said. “These cops you talk to … they told you Liberal Senator James Brody is under investigation for the murder of the prostitute Jenny Birchmount?”

“Bingo,” said Flynn.

“So that’s a yes?”

“Fuckin’ A.”

Peck studied Flynn's florid face for a long moment. "Who told you this?"

Flynn snorted. "You know that's not how this works, Morton."

"It's Morgan," Peck corrected. "Morgan J. Peck."

"The point is cops tell you these things off the record. The deal is I don't reveal my sources. That's the only way they'll talk to you about shit like this."

"I get that," Peck snapped. "But how can we be sure these cops know what they're talking about?"

"Oh, they know. Let's just say … they're involved."

"They're investigating the case?" Peck asked.

Flynn nodded, his jowls jiggling. "Like I said, they're involved."

"And based on what they've told you, there's no doubt in your mind that Senator James Brody is one of the suspects?"

"Bingo."

"If we reported that, there's no chance it would blow up in our faces?"

"No chance."

"None at all?"

"None at all."

Peck turned toward Berger. "What does Norm think?"

Berger squirmed in his seat. "Well, I haven't told him about this yet."

"Why not?"

"He's off doing his own thing. Haven't seen him or spoken to him since we talked in your office two days ago. Maybe his phone's out of order or something."

"Norm?" interjected Flynn. "Norman Pugsley? I don't think he's ever going to get *this* story. Most of the cops I talk to think he's a fuckin' prima donna."

"Be that as it may, Joe, we shouldn't go with the story until we've spoken to Norm," Peck said.

"Suit yourself," said Flynn. "If you don't want it, I'm pretty sure I could interest the *Globe* or CBC."

"Don't even think that Joe," cried Peck, aghast. "Where's your loyalty to the *Advocate*?"

"You mean the newspaper that gave me a lousy $341-a-month pension after I sweated blood for them for decades? That newspaper?" Flynn spat into a wastebasket. "I don't owe them jack shit."

"For what it's worth, boss," said Berger, "I think we should go with the story. Norm already wrote a draft version. It's just awaiting confirmation. I think Joe just got that for us."

"So, we'd say something like, 'police sources say Senator Brody is under investigation for murder'?" Peck said.

"Sure. It's true. So why not?"

Peck frowned. "What about Brody? Can we get a comment from him?"

"He's still out of the country and can't be reached," said Berger.

"Well, can we at least get a comment from the Liberal party on his behalf? Surely they can reach him in Timbuktu or wherever the hell he is."

"Sure. I'll give it a shot."

"OK then. Let's get a comment and plan the story for tomorrow's paper."

"Terrific," Berger said. "I think that's the right call, Morgan J."

"Joint byline with you and Norm?" asked Peck.

"Norm got the tip about Brody, and he effectively wrote the story. He really deserves the byline," Berger said. "Maybe just a "files from" for me."

"Try to reach Norm," Peck told Berger. "But yeah, that's what we'll do."

"And keep my name out of it," added Flynn. "Don't want this to fuck up my relationship with the cops."

•••

A furious Norman Pugsley stormed into Morgan J. Peck's office early the following morning clutching a copy of that morning's edition of the *Advocate*.

"What the hell is *this*?" he thundered, slamming the newspaper on Peck's desk. A two-line, six-column headline across Page One shouted, in 100-point type, "Police target Grit senator in murder probe."

The accompanying story, credited to investigative reporter Norman Pugsley, asserted that police sources had confirmed that Liberal Senator

James Brody was a prime suspect in the unsolved killing of Ottawa prostitute Jenny Birchmount.

Lurid details of the murder followed. It wasn't until the story's turn on page A7 that readers encountered a Liberal party spokesman's denial. "There's not a scintilla of truth to this," Bill Watson, an aide to Liberal leader John Turner, was quoted as saying. "We spoke to Senator Brody in Manila, where he's attending a conference on the future of the pineapple trade, and he knows nothing about any such investigation. Nor did he ever meet the young woman in question."

"How did this get into the paper?" Pugsley demanded. "And under my byline to boot!"

Peck, taken aback by his reporter's outrage, tried his best to calm the waters.

"I'm sorry you weren't consulted, Norm," he said. "But Jake said he couldn't reach you and police sources confirmed the story."

"Not to me," Pugsley shot back.

"Not to you, perhaps, but Joe Flynn got a thumbs up from his police buddies."

Pugsley blinked. "Joe Flynn! That sorry old drunkard? He's barely drawn a sober breath for the past 20 years. You printed a story like *this* on the say-so of that bloody arse?"

Morgan J. Peck didn't like the way the conversation was going. "Now Norm," he said, "no need to be abusive. Joe Flynn is a legend in this newsroom. He's got a lot of credibility with me."

"Really? Then why didn't you put *his* byline on the damn story?"

"Well, he didn't want a credit. Besides, you wrote it, Norm."

"I didn't write *this*," Pugsley retorted, wagging a finger at the front-page story. "I didn't write that police said they were investigating Brody."

"No, but you were the one who told us you'd heard they were."

"Christ on a bicycle!" Pugsley roared. "That was unconfirmed rumour. I made that clear. And by the way, I was home all evening last night. If Jake wanted to run this past me, all he had to do was pick up the fucking phone."

"Your phone wasn't … out of order?"

"Of course not. Why would you think that?"

Peck and Pugsley stared blankly at one another, each seemingly at a loss for words. The jangling ring of Peck's own telephone shattered the brief silence.

The city editor grabbed the receiver. "Yes, what is it?" he barked. His tone abruptly changed when he realized the caller was *Advocate* publisher Clark Sherman.

"Yes sir, my apologies. What can I do for you?" he said meekly. Pugsley could hear only Peck's end of the conversation, but whatever Sherman was saying, it clearly wasn't congratulatory.

Peck listened intently to Sherman, saying little beyond "yes sir" or "I agree" or at his most verbose, "you're right, you're right." When the publisher's tirade finally ended, Peck said, "I'll find out and get back to you, sir." He slowly set the receiver down, slumped forward in his chair and emitted a long, shuddering sigh.

Then he glanced at Pugsley, seemingly remembering that his furious star reporter was still in his office.

"That was our publisher," he began. "He's not a happy man. Had a call this morning from Liberal leader John Turner personally. Seems Turner called the chief of police, who told him our story wasn't true. Senator Brody isn't a suspect. He's demanding a front-page retraction and apology. And a personal apology from you to the senator. Oh yes, and we'll likely be sued for libel."

"Jesus!" said Pugsley, wide-eyed. "What a cluster-fuck!"

"A career-ender," Morgan J. Peck agreed gloomily. He didn't say whose career he had in mind.

•••

Later that day, Ottawa police issued a terse but devastating news release.

A front-page story in today's Ottawa Advocate *newspaper said police sources had confirmed that Senator James Brody is being investigated for the murder of Jennifer Birchmount, 19, of Ottawa. Senator Brody is not a suspect. The police have made no such statement. The murder investi-*

gation continues but no charges are imminent. We continue to investigate this case.

Within minutes, publisher Clark Sherman had convened a crisis meeting in his office. Called to attend were editor-in-chief Gordon Davis, city editor Morgan J. Peck and police reporter Jake Berger. Norman Pugsley had also been summoned, but was at the police station, trying to sort out what went wrong. They weren't waiting for his return.

To say Sherman was upset badly understates the ferocity of his fury. "This is the sort of unimaginable blunder that destroys our credibility," he raged. "Not to mention the money we'll have to shell out for defaming Brody." He glared at the cowering journalists. "How the fuck did this happen?"

Davis cleared his throat. "I approved the story, Clark, after Morgan told me we had police confirmation." He shook his head sorrowfully. "It appears that was bad information."

Sherman fixed a steely gaze on Peck. "Who told you police had confirmed the story?"

Peck shifted uncomfortably. "It was Norm Pugsley who first said Brody was a suspect. Then Joe Flynn told us his police sources said it was true."

"Joe Flynn!" Sherman exclaimed, his face darkening to an alarming shade of magenta. "How did that burnt-out old reprobate get involved in the story?"

"Jake approached him to see if he'd heard anything," Peck replied. "He made a few inquiries and claimed the cops had confirmed Brody was under investigation."

"Unbe-fucking-lievable!" Sherman cried. "We ran with a sensitive story like that based on Flynn's say-so?"

"I didn't know that when I signed off or we never would have done it," said editor-in-chief Davis. "Morgan said he had solid confirmation and assured me the story had been vetted by our lawyers." Peck winced. Though he'd told his boss he'd run the story past the paper's lawyers, he hadn't actually done so, unwisely judging it unnecessary.

"But look," Davis continued, "this whole thing went off the rails because of Pugsley. If he hadn't raised Brody's name–"

"It came from someone in the PM's office," Peck interjected. "Norm even wrote up a draft story," he said, neglecting to mention that Pugsley hadn't wanted to do so and had urged caution as they tried to confirm the rumour.

"And he thought that was a credible source?" Sherman said. "Any idiot would question information like that coming from a political opponent. And why in the name of God would Pugsley believe *anything* Joe Flynn said?"

Peck briefly considered telling Sherman that Pugsley hadn't known about Flynn's involvement. But a self-preservation instinct led him to hold his tongue. And Berger, taking his lead from his boss, kept his mouth shut as well.

"OK gentlemen," Sherman said, "we need to fix this. We'll run a retraction and apology on A1 tomorrow. Get Pugsley to send a personal written apology to Brody. If we're very lucky, that might spare us from having to pay a shitload of money, though I doubt it."

Sherman glowered at his assembled minions. "And tell Pugsley I want to see him asap. There will be consequences for a screwup like this."

Thirteen

OTTAWA, SUMMER 2006

Detective Bernard Lachance ushered Pugsley and his young sidekick, Fawzia Hassan, into the rumpled living room of his split-level home in the Ottawa suburb of Orléans.

"Sorry about the mess," he said, gesturing at the stacks of documents and newspapers strewn across the room's hardwood floor. "I'm not much of a housekeeper. That used to be my wife's job, but we broke up a couple of years ago." He grimaced. "We weren't getting along, but at least she kept the place tidy."

Lachance was a heavyset man in his early 50s. French was his first language, but he spoke English fluently with a light accent. It was his idea to meet at his home instead of police headquarters. "I'm not sure my bosses would be happy if they knew I was talking to you about the Birchmount case."

"Oh?" Pugsley said quizzically. "Why is that?"

"You know, police departments never like to talk about unsolved murders. Makes them look bad."

"So, why'd you agree to talk to us?"

Lachance paused for a moment to gather his thoughts. "The Birchmount murder was the first big case I worked on after I was promoted to detective. I worked hard on that case. The whole department did. We had a few leads, but never enough evidence to lay charges. Our failure – my failure – has haunted me ever since."

He glanced at Pugsley. "I know you had your own issues with that story, Norm. When Fawzia here said you were working on the case with her, I thought … maybe we both have a shot at getting this right."

Pugsley said nothing. He wasn't yet ready to discuss with Hassan the whole sordid tale of his experience with Jenny Birchmount's story. But Lachance's words resonated. God knows, he'd felt the same emotions often enough.

"Well, detective," Hassan said, evidently willing to hold her questions for the moment, "we're happy you're willing to share what you know with us. What can you tell us?"

Lachance cleared his throat. "Let me start by saying I know who posted the reward for information in the Birchmount case, but I can't share that with you. The person who posted it demanded full confidentiality, and I have to respect that."

"Understood, detective," Pugsley said. "But whoever it was must be quite wealthy to offer a reward of that size."

"That's a fair assumption," Lachance acknowledged.

Pugsley prodded further. "What's their connection to the case?"

"No obvious connection," Lachance said. "Not a family member or anything like that. Just a citizen who'd like to help us solve this terrible crime and find justice for Jenny, it seems."

"Admirable," murmured Pugsley, a note of skepticism in his voice.

"So that's what you *can't* tell us," interjected Hassan. "What *can* you tell us?"

Lachance blinked. "For one thing, it's likely that Jenny's killer was a regular customer. When we spoke to the sex workers in the market, they said a man in a black luxury car picked her up on York Street that night. They'd seen Jenny get into that car several times before."

"Did they describe what he looked like?" Hassan asked.

"They didn't get a good look at him. All that tinted glass. But a few who caught a glimpse thought he was white, in his 40s or 50s."

"Did Jenny ever say anything about her john to the other, um, sex workers?" Pugsley said, glancing at Hassan.

"She didn't really share much with them," said Lachance. "But she did tell one of them he was a gentleman who treated her well."

Pugsley snorted. "A gentleman strangler! That's rich. Did this guy ever approach any of the other girls?"

"It appears not. None reported having him as a client," Lachance replied. "He seems to have been … a one-woman man, so to speak."

"Did anyone spot him after Jenny was killed?"

"No. After that, he was never seen again. It was as if he never existed."

"That adds up," Pugsley said. "Unless he was a psychopath, the killer would want to lie low. It doesn't seem that we're dealing with a serial killer here," he continued, thinking out loud.

"No," said Lachance. "A handful of other sex workers have been killed since Jenny died, but we arrested the perps. None fit the profile of Jenny's murderer. And none admitted to it, obviously."

"You said earlier you had a few leads during your investigation. Can you tell us about those?" Hassan prompted.

"We checked out hundreds of men in their 40s or 50s who owned black luxury cars. Almost all of them had strong alibis. We narrowed it down to four suspects, but that was as far as we got. There wasn't enough evidence to charge any of them."

"Do you still have that list?" Hassan asked.

"As a matter of fact," said Lachance, with a tight smile, "I do." He picked up a file from the floor, opened it, extracted a single sheet of paper, and passed it to Pugsley.

He began scanning the list, then abruptly stopped at the third name.

Jack Clifford.

Pugsley stared and passed Hassan the list.

"Christ on a bicycle," he whispered.

•••

Pugsley was silent as he and Hassan drove away from their meeting with Lachance, but his mind was whirling.

"Well, that was useful, I think," Hassan offered, settling into the spacious passenger seat of Pugsley's Ford Explorer. "I mean, we found out Jenny's killer was likely a regular customer who drove a black luxury car. More important, we got the police suspect list. A pretty successful day's work if you ask me."

She glanced at Pugsley, who hadn't responded. "Norm? Are you OK?"

Lost in thought, Pugsley had been only half-listening. "Sorry, Fawzia," he said. "I'm a little shaken up." He pulled over to the side of the road, put the vehicle into park and gave her an apologetic look. "I need a minute."

"What's up?" she asked, slightly alarmed. "Your heart?"

Pugsley shook his head, then took a deep breath. "I never would have guessed," he began before his voice faltered.

"Never would have guessed what?" Hassan prompted.

"That Jack Clifford – *Jack Clifford!* – could have murdered Jenny. I mean, I know the guy. Been on a couple of adventure trips with him – even roomed with him once." He shook his head. "He's an asshole. A womanizer. Crude. But a murderer?" He shook his head again. "Never would have guessed."

"All right," Hassan said slowly. "I'm at a bit of a disadvantage here. The name rings a bell, but who exactly is Jack Clifford?"

"When I first met him, he owned a construction company. His big claim to fame was that he was involved in the contract to build Pierre Trudeau's swimming pool at 24 Sussex Drive in the 1970s. He was always well connected politically. For the last decade or so, he's been one of the city's most active developers – condos, office towers, that sort of thing."

Hassan let out a low whistle. "Ah yes, I *have* heard of him. A bigshot, then."

"You could say that."

"It won't be easy to bring a guy like that down," Hassan ventured.

"*If* he's even the perp," Pugsley said quickly. "Just because he's on the list doesn't mean he did it."

"No, I guess not," Hassan agreed. "So, what's our next move?"

"I'm not sure. But we have to be careful we don't jump to conclusions." Pugsley grimaced. "Believe me, you don't want to do that. And let's not drop his name to your editor."

"But you know this Clifford guy, right?" Hassan said. "Maybe you could get together with him – for drinks or something – and ask him a few questions."

"Like 'Did you kill Jenny Birchmount, Jack?' That sort of question?" Pugsley said.

"Of course not," Hassan snapped. "But what if you casually mentioned that you're working on a story about a cold case murder? He'd probably ask you which one. The way he reacts when you tell him it's the Birchmount case could be revealing."

Pugsley considered Hassan's idea, surprised by her savvy. "Not bad," he said. "It's certainly worth a try. I could tell him we know the killer drove a black luxury car and was in his 40s or 50s. If he's our guy, that might shake him up a bit, too."

"Then there's our ace in the hole," added Hassan, smiling triumphantly. "The police thought he was a prime suspect. You could tell him that."

A slow smile spread across Pugsley's face. "I'm sure he knows he was a suspect at the time – he would have been interviewed by the cops. But it might shake him up to learn we know that too."

"So," Hassan summarized, "I think we've just figured out our next move."

Pugsley nodded, feeling a little of the old adrenaline coursing through his veins. "I'll call him today," he said.

•••

"Norm Pugsley! F-u-u-u-cking long time, no see!" Jack Clifford rose to his feet in the pub and pumped Pugsley's right hand with what appeared to be genuine enthusiasm. "What's it been, 15 years? Twenty?"

"Longer," Pugsley replied. They'd crossed paths a handful of times over the years when Pugsley was a reporter but hadn't exchanged more than quick greetings. "Last time we spent any time together we were in canoes, fighting off the blackflies in the Northwest Territories. And before that, bears in B.C."

"Christ, has it really been that long?" Clifford shook his head. "Where does the time go?"

"Tell me about it."

Clifford studied Pugsley for a moment. He had to admit Pugsley wasn't looking half bad. How old was he now? At least in his 60s for sure. He was carrying a few extra pounds, but who the hell wasn't these days? And there was something about him – he couldn't quite put his finger on it – an energy or something.

"I have to tell ya, Pugs, I was more than a little surprised when you called out of the blue to suggest we get together. It's not like we've kept in touch."

Pugsley acknowledged Clifford's comment with a brief nod. "True that. We've both added some mileage since we were last together."

"So," Clifford asked, narrowing his eyes, "why the call? You need my company to build you a chalet or something?"

"I dunno, Jack. I'm retired now and that means I've got time to think about things I've done in my life. Those trips we took together, through the Inside Passage and in the North, those are a couple of my fondest memories. You were part of both, and I guess I just wanted to compare notes on what life's done to us since."

"That's it?" said Clifford. "You just want to shoot the shit with me? Not trying to probe into city construction contracts or anything?"

"Not just that," Pugsley said with a slow smile. "I want to have a beer with you too!"

Clifford flashed a wolfish grin. "I can get behind that, Pugs." He raised an arm, attracting the attention of a server.

"What can I get you gentlemen?"

"What do you think? Couple of IPAs?"

"Actually, Jack, I'm more of a lager man myself."

"That's OK. Some of my best friends are lager drinkers," Clifford laughed. "I don't hold it against them. Not worth being at loggerheads over." He glanced at Pugsley. "Loggerheads, get it? Lager-heads!"

The Jack Clifford siting across the table was recognizably the same man Pugsley had met nearly three decades earlier. Still a larger-than-life font of groan-worthy puns. Inevitably, though, time had left its mark. His beard, once jet black and untamed, was Santa white and neatly trimmed now, his hairline receding and thinning. And there was an unmistakeable aura of prosperity to his bulky frame, affirmed by his dark grey bespoke suit.

"You know, Jack, we may not have kept in touch, but I've been following your career from a distance for years. You've done very well for yourself."

"I'm not one for false modesty, Pugs." Clifford puffed out his chest. "Truth is, I've done fucking fabulously. My company is worth more than a billion dollars and I own most of the shares. So yeah, I don't have to worry where my next meal's coming from."

"I guess not. What about family, Jack? You were single when I last saw you. Did you ever marry?"

"Three times!" Clifford smiled ruefully. "I can be a bit of a slow learner. I've sworn off that shit now."

"That … shit?"

"You know. Marriage."

"Ah. Any kids?"

"A couple. They live with their mother. I guess I'm a lousy dad. Too damn busy with my company to give them much attention. But enough about me. How's your life been, Pugs? Did you ever move on from that crappy newspaper?"

Pugsley suppressed his irritation at Clifford's disparaging dismissal of his journalistic life's work. *Keep your eye on the ball*, he told himself. *Remember why you're here.*

"No, Jack, I stayed at the *Advocate* until my retirement last year. Spent the last dozen or so years as managing editor, in fact."

"Managing editor, huh?" Clifford said, with a twinkle in his eye. "That's the second banana, right? What's the problem – couldn't quite make it to the top?"

"Close, but no cigar," Pugsley agreed through clenched teeth.

"That's a pity. Never cared much for your newspaper," Clifford grumbled, his face darkening like a mid-summer thundercloud. "Always seemed anti-developer to me. Can't tell you how much grief that rag has caused me over the years. Couldn't have been any worse, I guess, if you'd been in charge."

"That's quite an endorsement, Jack," Pugsley said with a grimace. "Thanks."

"You're welcome," said Clifford, oblivious as usual to his own offensiveness. "Say Pugs. Do you ever see that doctor who was on the trips with us? What's his name again?"

"You mean Beauregard Fisher?"

"That's him."

"He's my family doctor."

"No kidding. Hope he's keeping you healthy."

"As a matter of fact, I had a heart attack last year. A big one. In Greece. Almost bought the farm."

"Geez Pugs, sorry to hear that. But you're OK now?"

"Knock on wood," Pugsley said, rapping lightly on his noggin.

Clifford patted his ample belly. "My doc keeps telling me I should lose weight," he said, "but Jesus, you only live once, right? What's the point of life if you can't enjoy it?"

"Yeah, well, Beau told me I needed to make some changes if I wanted to enjoy my life much longer."

Clifford snorted derisively. "Is he still married to that humourless bitch?"

Pugsley winced. "Yes, he and Deirdre are still together," he replied. "More than I can say for me and Maryanne. We divorced in 1988."

Clifford shook his head. "Women."

"I guess. But if I'm being honest, the problem was more me than her."

"How so?"

Pugsley hesitated. Even after all these years, his breakup with Maryanne was painful to think about, let alone discuss.

"I had a setback at work a couple of decades ago," he began. "Let's just say I wasn't the same guy after that. Maryanne tried to be supportive at first, but she didn't like the person I was becoming. Hell, I didn't like the person I was becoming. But I couldn't seem to pull out of it. Finally, she'd had enough and left."

For once, Clifford was at a loss for words. Jokes and puns were clearly inappropriate. "Didn't you have a daughter?" he said at last.

"Barbara. She's turning 38 later this year." Pugsley gave Clifford a sorrowful look. "We talk occasionally on the phone, but I haven't seen her in five years."

"What's the problem?"

Pugsley shrugged. "Hard to say. We were happy as clams when she was growing up. I think she blamed me for the marriage breakup and has never really forgiven me. I mean, she invited me to her wedding, but she wanted her mother to give her away, not her rotten old dad."

"That's tough, Pugs. But here's the way I see it. You can't control what other people think. If your daughter – Belinda, is it?"

"Barbara."

"Right. Barbara. If Barbara can't get past the fact that her parents split up, there's not a lot you can do. It's her problem and her loss, not yours."

Pugsley managed a sad smile. "My loss too, Jack. My grandkids are 10 and eight, and I barely know them."

"Well, fuck. That ain't right," Clifford declared. "I've got three grandkids and they practically live at my chalet on Baptiste Lake in the summer." That lupine grin again. "I'm happy to avoid my ex-wives, but don't you dare try to keep me away from my grandkids."

"You're lucky," Pugsley said, genuinely envious. "But aren't you a bit lonely without a mate? I know I am, at times."

"Nah. I don't lack for female company. That's never a problem if you're a man with money. But that's all it is – company. And a bit of the old in-and-out from time to time," Clifford added, with a cackle. "What about you, Pugs? Good-looking guy like you must have a lady or two."

"Not really. Though strangely enough, I do seem to be drifting into something or other with my former boss, the *Advocate*'s editor."

"Why's that strange?"

"It's strange because I couldn't stand her when I was working for her. Thought she was a complete flake."

"What's changed?"

"Not sure. But we've had a few meals together, and we seemed to hit it off." Pugsley glanced at Clifford, a bit surprised at how much he was talking about himself. "I'm even taking her camping in a couple of weeks in Algonquin Park. And she's never camped before."

"No shit! Should be … interesting," Clifford said, wide-eyed. "Can you get her to take a skinny dip with you?"

"Oh Jesus!" Pugsley exclaimed. "Never even thought of that."

"Get a woman naked whenever you can. It's never a bad idea."

"I suppose." Pugsley paused. This opening was too inviting to ignore. "Have you ever paid for it, Jack?"

"Paid for what?

"You know … sex."

"Well, a guy like me always pays for it, one way or another. A mink coat, a fancy restaurant meal, some flashy jewelry. Nothing's truly free in this world – especially not pussy."

"Yeah," Pugsley persisted, "but have you ever directly paid a woman to have sex with you?"

"You mean a whore?"

"They're called sex workers now, I believe."

"Well, that's a pretty personal question, Pugs. But since you're a buddy of sorts, I'll admit that yes, I have. What about you?"

"A few times. Only when drunk, though," Pugsley lied.

Clifford roared and slapped his knee. "Only when drunk! Love it!"

Now or never, Pugsley thought. "Speaking of which, Jack, I'm working with a reporter at the *Advocate* on a story about a young prostitute, Jenny Birchmount, who was murdered about 20 years ago. Do you remember her?"

"Sounds familiar," Clifford said breezily. "Should I?" If Jenny Birchmount's name meant something to Clifford, he was concealing it well. *Time to up the ante*, Pugsley thought.

"Well, I was told the police had you pegged as one of the leading suspects in her murder," he said.

Clifford's customary expression of barely suppressed amusement vanished in an instant, replaced by something that looked like utter consternation.

"Who the hell told you that?" he demanded.

"One of my police sources," Pugsley said quietly. Clifford's face, and the alarmed expressions washing over it, had his full attention.

"The cops did ask me where I was when the hooker was killed," Clifford slowly recalled, seeming to search his memory, all traces of badinage scrubbed from his voice. "They wouldn't have done that if they didn't think I was a suspect, I guess. But I never heard from them after that."

"Did you own a black luxury car at the time?" Pugsley asked.

"Shit, I don't know. When are we talking about?"

"November 1985."

"Jesus, I can barely remember what I did yesterday," Clifford grumbled. "Is it important?"

"It could be," Pugsley said. "Jenny's murderer was driving a car like that."

"Fuck. Fuck, fuck, fuck," Clifford sputtered. "Let me think. Let me think." He shut his eyes and furrowed his brow, the effort of struggling with his failing memory almost physical.

"Was that when I owned the Corvette?" he muttered to himself. "No, that was in the early 80s. I think … I think … yes, it was the Merc." He turned to Pugsley. "I owned a Mercedes at that time."

"Black?"

"Yes, black, dammit," Clifford confirmed. "But so what? Lots of people drive black cars. Most of them aren't murderers."

"What about you, Jack?" Pugsley asked softly. "Are you a murderer?"

Clifford gasped, then scowled. "That's why you wanted to see me. You think I murdered the whore!"

"Did you?"

"What the fuck?! I never murdered no one!" Clifford shouted, proper grammar deserting him in the stress of the moment. He rose to his feet, face flushed with anger. "We're done here," he announced, turning to walk away. Then he stopped and glared at Pugsley.

"If you put any of that crap in your rag of a newspaper," he snarled, "I'll sue the pants off you. Literally. You won't be able to afford pants when I'm done with you."

And with that, Clifford turned and strode from the bar.

●●●

"So," Fawzia Hassan asked Pugsley the following day, "how'd your little chat with Jack Clifford go? Did he confess?"

Pugsley snorted. "Hardly. He threatened to sue me for the very suggestion."

"Sounds like you hit a nerve."

"Maybe. But even if I did, I'm not sure it means much."

"OK," Hassan said. "Tell me why."

"Well, put yourself in his shoes. Someone you know, a friend of sorts, asks if you killed someone. Even if you didn't – *especially* if you didn't – you're not going to take that well."

"So, you don't think he's our guy?" Hassan asked.

"He might be guilty as hell. He did confess to seeing um, sex workers, after all."

"He did? That sounds important."

"Perhaps," Pugsley said. "But when I first brought up Jenny's name, he didn't seem alarmed. I was watching his face, and there wasn't a ripple of concern."

"Maybe he's just really good at hiding his emotions," Hassan mused. "A lot of psychopaths are masters of deception, or so I've heard."

"True," said Pugsley. "But … is Jack really a psychopath? I'm not so sure. He tends to let his personality hang out – no secrecy, no artifice. He's gone through three wives and couldn't be bothered to raise his own kids, so that's a sign of something, I guess. And he can be a real asshole when he wants to be. But he appears to love his grandkids, so there might be a decent human in there somewhere, though you might have to squint to see it."

"So … you don't think he's our guy," Hassan said again, a statement this time rather than a question.

"I'm not saying that. He may be. We certainly can't rule him out, but …" Pugsley said.

"…but there's no smoking gun," Hassan said, finishing his sentence, disappointment in her downcast eyes.

"A bit of smoke, but no gun," Pugsley said.

"Maybe we should go back to the cops and see if they'll tell us anything more about Jack Clifford," Hassan suggested.

"Sure. Don't think they'll say much, but I'll see if Lachance will tell me if we're on the right track or not," Pugsley said.

"And if that doesn't work …?"

"Well, there are other names on the suspect list."

Part Two
Exile and Romance

Fourteen

OTTAWA, FEBRUARY 1987

Norman Pugsley peered into the office refrigerator, searching for his packed dinner. The fridge was overstuffed with his colleagues' food, some of it well beyond its best-before date: limp salads, wizened apples, questionable curries, carcinogenic casseroles, souring milk and other unrecognizable organic matter. Though newsroom denizens reflexively lamented the appalling state of the fridge, efforts at clean-up had failed miserably. It was a textbook tragedy of the commons.

Pugsley had been toting his dinner to work for the past year, ever since his bosses at the *Advocate* had bounced him onto the night news desk as punishment for his role in the Senator James Brody debacle.

"It wasn't all your fault, Norm," editor-in-chief Gordon Davis told him at the time, "but some of it was. The publisher wanted to fire you. Hell, he seriously considered firing me. I was able to save your ass. You should be thanking me."

Davis had waved away Pugsley's objections that he was being made a scapegoat, that the person responsible was city editor Morgan J. Peck. Peck had been fired, he reminded Pugsley, and police reporter Jake Berger had been demoted to copy boy.

"You're a veteran reporter, Norm. You never should have raised Senator Brody's name unless you were certain he was a suspect. And writing a draft of the story before it was pinned down? What were you thinking?" Davis shook his head. "Like it or not, you lit the fuse. The publisher and I believe there have to be consequences for that."

For Pugsley, those consequences had included a five-day suspension and the abrupt loss of his star status as investigative reporter. He was exiled to the Siberia of the night news desk, where he was tasked with designing inside news pages and editing the assigned stories. In journalistic parlance, he was what was disparagingly referred to as a "rim pig," a faceless deskman who sat around a horseshoe-shaped table, handling other people's writing.

When he broke the news to Maryanne, she was indignant on his behalf. "After all you've done for that newspaper, this is how they treat you?" she fumed. "You should quit and go work for someone who appreciates you."

"Believe me, I'm tempted," Pugsley said. But he knew it wouldn't be that simple. He had a wife and child. He loved being a journalist and there weren't many alternatives to the *Advocate* in Ottawa. And who would have him? His sudden infamy had spread. A job as a government flack, while theoretically an option, was unappealing.

The demotion – there was no other way to describe it – crushed his spirit. He'd lived a charmed life, but now he felt it was over.

At first, Pugsley was defiant. They wanted to dump him on the news desk? Fine. He'd be the best damn desker ever. His headlines would sparkle. He'd edit like Ben Bradlee. He'd outwork, outsmart and outshine every other editor at the paper. He'd be so unmissably excellent his bosses would *have* to recognize their error.

Months later, when that hadn't worked – unless there was a cock-up, few senior editors paid much attention to the essential work of the night desk – he did a strategic 180, morphing into perhaps the worst editor in the paper's long history: heroically unmotivated, superbly uninspired and epically absent.

That attracted his bosses' attention, all right, but not in a good way. They threatened him with discipline and made it clear his job was at risk.

Pugsley eventually settled for mediocrity. He showed up for work, cut stories to fit the available space rather than trying to improve them, wrote competent if uninspired headlines, proofed a few dull pages for typos. Then he came in the next night and did it again.

As the weeks and months passed, Pugsley felt his morale crumble. His new responsibilities struck him as tedious and mechanical. The only real creative outlet was writing headlines. But the fleeting satisfaction he derived from writing an occasional artful heading did little to lessen his sense of betrayal.

The more he thought about how he'd been treated, the more embittered he became. Not only had the newspaper quickly dropped the Jenny Birchmount story after the Senator Brody fiasco, but the police also seemed to lose interest as well. In his lowest moments, he imagined he was destined to play out the string of his professional life as a barely tolerated cog in the *Advocate* machine.

To add to his misery, his new role had completely upended his family life. His shift now started at 5 p.m. and ended at midnight. Instead of enjoying dinners with Maryanne and Barbara, he had to pack a meal, reheat it in the office microwave and eat at his desk. When he finished work at midnight, no one was awake at home to help him unwind. By the time he rose in the morning, Barbara was at school and Maryanne had left for her job at the grocery store. He felt unmoored, disconnected for the first time in his adult life from the people he loved.

He sensed his unhappiness was affecting his relationship with his wife and daughter but felt helpless to act differently. On the rare occasions when they were able to spend time together, he was morose and withdrawn, seemingly unwilling or unable to engage, often simply staring aimlessly into space.

At first, Maryanne tried to be supportive. "The important thing is we have each other," she told him. "Our love will see us through this. It matters much more than any stupid job."

She was right, of course. Pugsley knew that. But that stupid job had defined much of who he was. So much of his self-worth had come from being a star reporter at the *Advocate*. In the blink of an eye, his feckless bosses had taken that away.

Now, six months later, Maryanne was losing patience. Uncharacteristically, the other day she'd snapped at him. "You're your own worst enemy, Norm," she fumed. "Stop with the pity party and take charge of your life. Jesus!"

Things couldn't continue like this. Their relationship was hanging by a thread. Something had to change.

But what?

•••

Those who toiled on the *Advocate*'s night news desk had rituals and diversions to help them cope with their unrewarding work and terrible hours. Smoking, once endemic in the newsroom, had been banned two years earlier. To compensate, those unable to shake nicotine's grip took frequent smoke breaks in an alley behind the building – breaks that could, and often did, consume upwards of 15 minutes of every working hour. Night desk veteran Henry Millchuck was in a league of his own. He routinely spent more of his shift smoking in the alley than working in the newsroom, an achievement noted by colleagues with a mixture of awe and resentment.

Any excuse, however tenuous – an election night, a breaking news story of consequence, bad weather – prompted night news editor Carl Dunning to order half a dozen pizzas from the nearby Impresario restaurant, smothered in cheese and sometimes studded with pineapple, to the horror of purists. He'd charge them to the company tab, lay them on a table near the news desk and bellow "Pizza time!" in a resonant baritone that carried easily to all corners of the newsroom. The response of employees was Pavlovian. Like scavengers on carrion, they scooped up multiple slices, swiftly inhaled them and returned for more.

Then there were the Friday night drink-ups. Any night qualified, in fact, but the Friday sessions were *de rigueur*. The killjoys in Human Resources had banned alcohol in the workplace after one too many newsroom Christmas parties dissolved into drunken disarray. But the HR office was long shuttered and empty at 11 p.m. Fridays. When deadline passed and the last page was sent to press, desk editors cracked open their beer, wine and Scotch, HR be damned. It was a satisfying moment of middle-finger defiance.

Pugsley had been slow to participate in these rituals. Though an occasional smoker, he largely abstained while in the office, slipping out perhaps once a night for a quick nicotine hit. He liked pizza, but his intestines responded poorly to the Impresario's lactose-heavy pies. And while he enjoyed beer as much as the next man, for a long time he was too dispirited to share drinks with his colleagues after work.

That began to change one Friday night. When deadline had passed, one of his co-workers, Jimmy Nolan, a grizzled news desk veteran, cracked open a 12-pack of Labatt's Blue and pulled one of the long-necked bottles out of the carton.

"Beer?" he said, offering one to Pugsley.

"What?" Pugsley said, startled. "Oh … no thanks, Jimmy. Not really in the mood."

Nolan gave him a searching look. "What's going on with you, Norm? You've been on the desk for months now, but you don't feel like you're really here. Sure, you show up for work, but you barely talk. And you never join us for a drink after deadline. You can't wait to skedaddle out of here."

"I have my reasons," Pugsley said.

"Well, what are they?" Nolan demanded. "Somewhere you've gotta be? A pussy party or something?"

"What? God no. I'm a married man."

"That means you don't like sex?"

"No. I mean, yes. I like sex, OK? But only with my wife."

"So that's what you do? Rush home and have sex with your wife?"

"Jesus, Jimmy. What kind of a question is that?"

"Just gathering the facts, Norm," Nolan said evenly. "You know, like journalists are supposed to do."

"Look," said Pugsley, exasperated. "This has nothing to do with sex or my wife. I'm just bummed. Sorry … I'm not good company right now."

"So, you're sulking because the bosses bounced you onto the desk? That's why you're shunning us?"

"I'm not shunning you, for chrissakes."

"Sure feels that way."

Pugsley glowered at Nolan for a moment. "Give me that damn beer," he said abruptly.

Nolan smiled and passed the beverage to Pugsley. "Now you're talking."

Pugsley took a lengthy pull, smacking his lips in appreciation.

"Looks like you needed that," Nolan observed.

"Maybe. You could be right." Pugsley raised the bottle to his lips again, nearly draining its malty contents. It had been a while since he'd allowed himself such an indulgence. Too long, really. He turned to Nolan. "Got any more of those?"

•••

The beer with Jimmy Nolan lubricated something inside Pugsley that had been seized up since his banishment to the night news desk. He began looking forward to the Friday night drink-ups, even contributing six-packs and the occasional bottle of Canadian Club rye whisky to the common stash. He discovered that a late-night tipple with his fellow news desk inmates helped him relax. There was no point in rushing home, after all. Maryanne would be hibernating in bed.

As alcohol loosened inhibitions and tongues, conversation often turned to the innumerable failings of their bosses. Pugsley was surprised and oddly gratified to learn that most of his colleagues shared his low opinion of the people who ran the newspaper. Several, in fact, held views more jaundiced than his own.

"Garrett Smythe is nothing more than Gord Davis's bumboy," fellow rim pig Steve Woolsley declared with a scowl that conveyed his contempt for the *Advocate*'s assistant managing editor. "He's a talentless arse who's in way over his head."

"And don't get me started on our illustrious night news editor," added Woolsley, who'd retained his broad Liverpudlian accent despite decades in Canada.

The reference to night news editor Carl Dunning prompted a round of knowing head shakes and grimaces from the assembled desk denizens. Once he selected the stories for Page One, Dunning customarily vanished for a few hours, ostensibly to eat dinner. When he returned an hour or so before deadline, glassy eyed and flushed with something more potent than steak frites, he routinely caused chaos by changing the Page One lineup.

"Oh yeah, our friend Dunning is a piece of work," Jimmy Nolan said. "Not sure where he goes every night, but if you've ever had the misfortune to smell his breath, you'll know it wasn't AA."

"My guess is he's off boozing with Rob Sutherland's gang," chimed in Jordan Jackson, who handled sports pages on the night desk. Sutherland, the *Advocate*'s managing editor, was a solid newsman when sober, a state he endeavoured to avoid whenever possible.

"Rob Sutherland's gang?" Pugsley said quizzically. He was aware of the managing editor's affinity for alcohol in any form, but this was the first he'd heard mention of a "gang."

"You haven't heard the story?" asked Woolsley.

"No."

"Good God, man. You've led a sheltered life," Woolsley said, summoning up a facsimile of incredulity. "Rob has copyboys deliver little brown envelopes to selected people in the newsroom. Inside, there's a drawing of a beer stein and the words, 'On tap tonight.' "

"That's weird. What's it mean?" Pugsley said.

"It means Rob wants his drinking buddies to join him at the Press Club after work," said Nolan, jumping back into the conversation. "Not just for a drink. For the whole friggin' evening. Until last call."

"And that actually works?"

"Damn right it does. He's the managing editor, after all," Woolsley said.

"Haven't you ever wondered how incompetent bastards like Smythe and Dunning got promoted into management jobs?" Nolan said. "Rob rewards his friends. And the surest way to be Rob's friend is to drink with him."

These stories left Pugsley's head spinning. He'd always believed the paper rewarded talent and hard work. Of course, that was before his own disillusioning fall from grace. That seemed hopelessly naïve now.

"That's disgusting!" Pugsley said, to grunts of agreement from his colleagues. His brain had a different take, though, which he chose not to articulate. It saw a path to a different future.

Fifteen

ALGONQUIN PARK, AUGUST 2006

"You packed a *suitcase*?" Pugsley said, unable to scrub the note of incredulity from his voice.

"Well, yes. I need *something* to put my clothes in, don't I?" said Renata Richter, gripping the handle of her hard-sided Bugatti travel bag.

"Yes, but Renata, we're going canoe camping. Nobody brings a suitcase canoe camping."

"No? What *do* they bring?"

Pugsley was already regretting his rash offer to take Richter camping. "A backpack. A duffel bag maybe. Something soft that will fit inside a canoe."

"Well, I don't own any of … those things," said Richter. "Let me think." She frowned, then brightened. "I do have an old suitcase with soft sides. Would that work?"

"I dunno. Lemme see it," Pugsley said, more brusquely than he'd intended. Richter led him into a bedroom in her 12th-floor condo, rooted around in a closet and emerged holding a battered Swiss Gear suitcase, fetchingly finished in red polyester. "I took this one with me on safari in Botswana a few years ago. It got bashed around a bit, even though we had porters, of course, so I don't use it much anymore."

"The moose will certainly see us coming," Pugsley said, eyeing the brightly coloured luggage with resignation, "but I guess it's better than nothing."

Richter popped open the Bugatti bag and began shifting its contents into the Swiss Gear case. Out came a couple of pairs of capris, two bathing suits, a pair of pyjamas, some shorts, four short-sleeved tops, three pullovers with long sleeves, a white hoodie, silk socks and frilly undergarments, two pairs of running shoes, a scoop-necked evening dress, jewelry …

"Whoa," Pugsley cried, pointing at the dress and jewelry. "Why are you bringing those?"

"I just thought we might like to dress for dinner," Richter said.

Lord preserve me, Pugsley thought. "We'll probably eat dinner sitting on a log in front of a campfire."

"So … I should leave the dress and jewelry at home?"

"Yes. And while you're at it, why don't you take out a few of these other clothes? We're only going away for a couple of nights."

When the repacking was complete, Pugsley loaded Richter's suitcase into his Ford Explorer. "Oh, look at that!" Richter exclaimed when she saw the green Swift canoe strapped to the SUV's roof. "Is that safe?"

"Solid as a rock," Pugsley replied as he helped her settle into the passenger seat. He assumed his position behind the wheel and they were off. "Algonquin Park here we come!" he intoned, casting a sideways glance at Richter.

"Goodness," she said, with what sounded like forced gaiety. "What fun!"

Before long, the flat farmland of the Ottawa Valley gave way to hillier terrain. They rumbled through the village of Eganville in the Bonnechere Valley, skirted the broad expanse of Golden Lake, ascended steep hills to Canada's first Polish settlement in Wilno. About three hours after leaving Ottawa, they reached the east gate of Canada's oldest provincial park, encompassing 2,400 lakes in an area twice the size of Rhode Island.

"What a lovely place," Richter marvelled at the rugged Canadian Shield landscape. "I can't believe it's taken me 54 years to get here."

"Whaddya mean, 54 years?" Pugsley asked.

"I'm 54, Norman, and this is my first time in Algonquin Park."

"Oh … really? You're 54?"

"Is that a problem?"

"Not at all. It's just that you look a lot younger."

"Flatterer."

"No really. I thought you were late 40s, max."

Richter gazed at him, bemused. "Your eyesight must be failing."

Pugsley shook his head. "Just had it tested. 20/20."

"Not sure I believe you," Richter blushed. "But I'll suspend my disbelief for now."

•••

After about half an hour, Pugsley pulled off the highway onto a road leading to the Portage Store at the south end of Canoe Lake.

"We'll start our trip here," he told Richter. "But first, I need to pick up the equipment I rented for you."

"You rented equipment?"

"A tent, sleeping bag and a sleeping pad. Figured you'd need them – unless you'd rather sleep with me." That was meant as a joke, but he knew it had come out awkwardly. Richter caught her breath. "No, Norman, thanks anyway. I should probably sleep in my own tent."

"Suit yourself," Pugsley laughed, doubling down on his lame attempt at humour. "Why don't you wait at the car while I get the stuff?"

A few minutes later, Pugsley returned bearing the camping gear. "Now," he said, "let's get that canoe off the roof." He released a few straps, then turned to Richter. "Could you give me a hand here, Renata? It's a lot easier when two people do this."

"I suppose," she said dubiously, "if you show me how."

"It's dead easy. You grab the front of the canoe, I'll grab the back and on the count of three we'll lift it, flip it and set it down on the ground."

Richter nodded, but her wide-eyed expression betrayed her unease.

"Ready?" Pugsley said. "One. Two. Three. Lift!" Richter hoisted the canoe shakily above her head and held it there for a moment. Then, without warning, it slipped from her hands. The bow hit the ground with a mighty thwack, narrowly missing her feet.

"Christ in a kayak!" Pugsley cried.

"Oh, Norman!" a shaken Richter said. "Did I wreck your lovely canoe?"

Pugsley set his end down and checked for damage. There appeared to be none. "These Swift canoes," he exclaimed, "they're built like tanks.

Amazing!"

"*Fucking* amazing," blurted Richter, in a rare recourse to obscenity.

The hint of a smile on his face, Pugsley carried the canoe to the water's edge and proceeded to pack it. It took several attempts to wedge Richter's red suitcase in securely, but the vessel swallowed everything else with ease.

Richter clambered in and settled into the bow seat, clutching her paddle. Pugsley pushed the boat into the shallow water and stepped in. Using his oar as a lever, he propelled the canoe into deeper water and began to paddle.

The winds that customarily whistle down the narrow end of Canoe Lake buffeted the canoe, making it difficult to stay on course. Richter tried to compensate by shifting her paddle from one side to the other every half-dozen strokes.

"You don't need to do that," Pugsley told her. "Just paddle on one side. I can steer. That's why God invented the J-stroke."

"What's a J-stroke?" Richter asked.

"Basically, as I'm finishing my stroke, I pry the paddle away from the side of the canoe. It makes a kind of a J in the water. That's a J-stroke."

"A stroke named for its shape in the water," Richter mused, turning her head and smiling at Pugsley. "I like it. Sort of the paddling equivalent of onomatopoeia."

He gave her a puzzled look.

"You know, words like buzz or splash or hiss that echo the sounds they describe when spoken aloud."

"Oh, sure. I learned that in school," Pugsley replied.

They fell silent after that, lulled into a Zen-like state by the rhythm of their paddles and the tranquility of their surroundings. As they passed Camp Wapomeo, a summer camp for girls on two islands in the middle of Canoe Lake, Pugsley suddenly remembered something he thought might interest Richter.

"You know, Renata, a famous painter drowned in this lake a century or so ago," he said.

Richter straightened up in her seat. "Of course! It was Tom Thomson, wasn't it?"

"Yeah, that's him. He was a big deal in the art world, I understand."

"Only one of the most influential Canadian painters ever," Richter said fervently. "He was a contemporary of the Group of Seven, considered by many to be an unofficial member."

"Is that so?" Pugsley knew little about the Group of Seven beyond the fact they were famous. Many of their paintings were on display in Ottawa at the National Gallery of Canada, but he'd ventured inside only once, when his daughter was in her teens.

"There's some sort of memorial to the guy on this lake," he said, trying to disguise his ignorance.

"Oh, I'd *love* to see that," Richter said. "Can we stop?"

Despite paddling on Canoe Lake many times, Pugsley had never sought out the Thomson memorial. He didn't exactly know where it was but was loathe to admit that.

"Um, sure. Lemme double-check my map to confirm it's where I think it is." He studied the map for a moment. "Yes, just as I thought. It's straight ahead, on that point."

Minutes later, they landed and approached the weathered memorial cairn, erected in September 1917, barely two months after Thomson's death. Richter reverently read aloud the inscription, written by Group of Seven artist J.E.H. MacDonald.

"To the memory of Tom Thomson, artist, woodsman and guide, who was drowned in Canoe Lake July 8th, 1917," she began. "He lived humbly but passionately with the wild. It made him brother to all untamed things of nature. It drew him apart and revealed itself wonderfully to him. It sent him out from the woods only to show these revelations through his art and it took him to itself at last."

Richter looked at Pugsley, eyes glistening with emotion. "Oh Norman. It gives me goose bumps."

"Yeah. Me too," he said. To his surprise, he meant it.

•••

A few minutes paddling brought them to the north end of Canoe Lake. "There's a short portage here," Pugsley announced.

"You're not expecting me to carry the canoe, are you Norman?" Richter asked with alarm as she made a wobbly exit from the canoe.

"I've seen what you do to canoes," he smiled. "Just carry your suitcase and some of the other gear."

Pugsley unloaded the canoe and flipped it easily onto his shoulders. The fluidity of his move impressed Richter, who grabbed the suitcase, her sleeping bag and purse. "We'll come back for the rest," Pugsley told her.

They followed a path for about 300 metres, arriving at a narrow section of Joe Lake. Pugsley set the canoe down and Richter, puffing noticeably, gratefully unburdened herself beside him.

"Are you OK?" Pugsley asked.

Richter wiped a sheen of sweat from her brow. "Between the paddling and portaging, I'm looking forward to reaching our campsite."

Pugsley checked his watch. Nearly 4 p.m. "Good news, then. We'll be camping tonight on this lake. Should be there in less than an hour."

"I think I can manage that," Richter said, fanning her face with a hand.

"Tell you what," Pugsley said. "Why don't you stay here, and I'll get the rest of the gear?"

Pugsley reappeared 15 minutes later, staggering under a load that included his backpack, two tents, his sleeping bag and fishing gear. He dumped the items beside the canoe. "Jesus," he wheezed, "that was heavier than I expected. But at least my heart didn't give out."

"You're amazing," Richter said. "I had no idea you were so strong."

"I bet you say that to all the men who take you camping," he smiled.

"Every single one," Richter said gravely. "What's next?"

"Still gotta get the cooler. Even I couldn't carry everything in one load."

When he returned, they loaded the canoe and set off again until, not far from Joe Lake's northeast end, Pugsley spotted an empty campsite.

"This looks good," he said, steering the canoe towards shore.

"Anything looks good to me right now," said Richter, whose shoulders were begging for mercy. There was another issue, as well.

"Norman," she said, "will there be an outhouse at the campsite?"

"An outhouse? No. There'll be a thunderbox."

"What's that?"

"An outdoor privy," Pugsley said. "No walls, but you can sit down and do your business. Good news is you don't have to flush."

Richter frowned. "There's no privacy?'

"Don't need it. You'll be out in the forest, some distance from the campsite. No one will be watching – except maybe a moose."

After landing the canoe, Pugsley unloaded the gear and secured the boat. "Now," he said, "let me show you that thunderbox."

"Yes, please," Richter said, through gritted teeth.

He led her along a trail. A minute or so later, a squat wooden box with a hinged lid came into view. Pugsley raised the lid, exposing an egg-shaped hole on the box's top.

"There you go," he said. "Have at 'er."

Pugsley returned to the campsite and had begun unpacking the tents when Richter reappeared, a beatific smile on her face.

"That was sublime!" she exclaimed. "I felt at one with nature sitting there in the middle of the forest."

"You must be quite relieved," Pugsley chuckled. "Let's finish setting up the tents."

While Richter watched, Pugsley snapped the tent poles together and slipped one into a corner grommet. After clipping it to the tent body, he secured the other end in a grommet on the opposite side, then repeated the process with the second pole. As if by magic, the tent rose and assumed its shape.

Pugsley glanced at his tenderfoot companion. "Can you pass me some stakes?"

Richter looked momentarily confused. "Oh, tent stakes," she said, the light dawning. "Not the kind you cook. I see." She handed a few to Pugsley, who used them to batten down the corners of the tent.

"And now, the fly," he said briskly.

"Oh," she said. "Should I avert my eyes?"

Pugsley stared at Richter for a moment then burst into laughter.

"Not *that* kind of fly," he said. "The *tent* fly. It keeps the rain out."

"Oh, my lord," Richter said, her face colouring. "I certainly have a lot to learn about camping, don't I?"

Pugsley picked up the fly fabric, positioned it over the tent and pegged down the corners. "Your turn," he told Richter.

She unrolled her tent and spread it out on the ground. Within minutes, it was up, secured with stakes in each corner. "That wasn't so hard," she said, pleased with herself.

"Aren't you forgetting something?"

"What?"

"The groundsheet. It goes under the tent."

"Oh fiddle-faddle," she said. "Do I have to start over?"

Pugsley shook his head. "Just pull out the stakes. I'll lift the tent and you can position the groundsheet underneath."

Once that was done, they wrangled the fly into place. "There you go," Pugsley said. "Why don't you move in while I get dinner going?"

While Richter nested, Pugsley lit a campfire, ignited his camp stove, and began preparing their meal.

After 20 minutes or so, Richter emerged, wearing pink capris and her white hoodie, and ambled over to where Pugsley was working. "I'm ravenous," she said, eyes alight with anticipation. "What delicacies are you preparing for us tonight?"

"Dogs and burgs," he grunted, "with a salad on the side."

Her face fell. "Hotdogs? And hamburgers?"

"Yup."

"I'm supposed to eat one of each?"

"Oh no. You can have as many as you like."

Richter couldn't recall the last time she'd eaten a hotdog. "I'm really sorry, Norman," she said, thinking fast, "but I'm allergic to hot dogs. It's the nitrates, I think."

"Huh. Never met anyone allergic to hotdogs before. But no problem. You have the burgs and I'll have the dogs."

Richter suppressed a sigh. "You said there's a salad?"

"Absolutely," Pugsley said. "I know ladies are into things like that, so I made sure to bring some."

"That's so thoughtful. I do love a good salad. I could make a meal of salad alone."

"Terrific." Pugsley reached into the cooler and pulled out a bagged Caesar salad. "This is one of my favourites. Got it on sale at Walmart."

Resigned to a dismal meal, Richter was surprised to find she enjoyed her hamburger. Even the bagged salad and the boxed Merlot Pugsley offered were somehow tolerable.

"There must be something about sitting on a log around a campfire that makes food taste better," she mused. "I'm not normally a big hamburger fan, but this one is quite tasty."

"Should be," said Pugsley, between bites of his third hot dog. "It's prime rib. Premium stuff."

As the sun dropped and the shadows deepened, they sat around the campfire, mesmerized by the dancing light, fending off mosquitoes, chatting about inconsequential things. Richter listened as he told her tales of canoeing northern rivers with Pierre Trudeau and other camping adventures, perplexed but charmed by his mysterious love of a thing so foreign to her, yet captivated by the dazzling dome of stars overhead. Even the bugs seemed only a minor inconvenience.

With the fire burning down to embers, Pugsley suggested it was time to turn in. "We'll want to get an early start tomorrow to make sure we get the best possible campsite."

"We're not staying here? I was just starting to like it."

"I've got my eye on a spot on Burnt Island Lake. It's not far from here. You'll like it even more there."

"If you say so," Richter said. Turning on a flashlight, she navigated the pitch-dark to her tent. "Good night, Norman. And thanks for the, um … *interesting* day," she said, silently recalling the ancient Chinese curse.

"Sleep tight, Renata," he said, turning towards his own tent. All in all, Pugsley was pleased with the day – and with himself. His companion, though ignorant of the outdoor life, had been charming and was learning quickly. He fell asleep smiling.

Hours later, he was enjoying a dreamless sleep when the sound of someone unzipping his tent startled him into wakefulness. Richter, clad in flannel pajamas with a floral motif, poked her head inside and caught him in the beam of her flashlight. She had a sleeping bag tucked under one arm.

"Wha … What's the matter, Renata?" he asked groggily, shielding his eyes.

"I heard a noise," she said, voice quavering.

"What kind of noise?"

"I don't know. An animal. Something close by. Can I sleep in your tent tonight?"

"Jesus. What time is it?"

"Around 2 a.m. I think."

Pugsley wanted to say she'd be fine, that animals rarely attack people in their tents. But he doubted she could be reassured.

"Yeah, all right," he said, shifting to the left. "Put your sleeping bag here."

"Thank you, thank you." She laid her bedding next to his and slipped inside. "You're a prince, Norman Pugsley," she said, gently taking his beefy hand in hers. Within minutes, she was snoring lightly. Pugsley, now wide awake, listened to her even breathing and wondered what he was getting into.

•••

The sun wasn't yet above the horizon when Pugsley arose. It would be wrong to say he woke early. He hadn't truly slept since Richter joined him. Gingerly freeing his hand from her failing grip, he slipped on a pair of Crocs, quietly unzipped the tent and stepped outside.

He could already see it was going to be a classic late-summer day. The lake was preternaturally calm, the sky cloudless and ripe with cerulean promise.

After a productive visit to the thunderbox, he began preparing breakfast. Rashers of bacon, fried eggs, navel orange quarters, Texas toast grilled over a fresh campfire. He was about to rouse Richter when she emerged, sleep-tousled, from his tent.

"I like your pajamas," was the first thing she said, assessing his black-and-red plaid sleepwear with an approving eye.

"Yours aren't bad, either," Pugsley said, diplomacy trumping frank assessment.

"Look at us, both in our pajamas," she laughed. "Just like an old married couple."

"Ahem, yes. Breakfast is served," he announced, quickly changing the subject.

"Is there any granola?" she asked, with comical optimism.

"Eggs and bacon."

"Poached?"

"Over easy."

After breakfast they packed up and set off for their next destination, entering Little Joe Lake through a narrow channel. A group of buildings was visible on the lake's southern shore.

"What's that?" Richter asked, pausing her paddling and pointing.

"A resort. Arrowhead Pines or something."

Richter perked up. "Really. What's it like?"

"Dunno," Pugsley said, continuing to paddle. "Never been there."

"Why not? It looks lovely."

"Yeah, maybe. But it's the sort of place that serves smoked salmon and eggs Benedict for breakfast. Not really my style."

"It sounds *fabulous* to me," Richter said. "Can we paddle over for a closer look?"

Pugsley checked his watch. It was only a little after 9 a.m. "Guess we have time for a quick peek."

Soon they were gliding past manicured grounds dotted with log structures. They caught a glimpse of a tennis court and a stash of canoes and kayaks. What most attracted Richter's attention, though, was the red-roofed, hexagonal waterfront dining room and its massive wrap-around veranda. She shouted to a guest lolling on the dock, "Is this Arrowhead?" The amused patron responded, "Arowhon. It's called Arowhon."

"My God. That looks *amazing*." Richter turned her head in Pugsley's direction. "You could get me here in a heartbeat."

"I'll keep that in mind," he said, pivoting the canoe and propelling it northward with increased urgency. After a few minutes, they arrived at a swampy section of the lake that narrowed until they reached a shallow meandering stream.

"You have to be alert in here, Renata," he called from the stern. "There are lots of twists and turns and underwater logs and whatnot."

They did well enough at first, easily navigating corners and narrow openings. But Richter, distracted by the sylvan beauty of their surroundings, kept losing focus. More than once, the canoe ploughed into a half-built beaver dam or other obstruction.

"Pay attention, Renata!" Pugsley admonished.

"I'm sorry," she said. "The scenery is just so breathtaking."

At last, they reached a portage. It took two trips to carry the canoe and their gear to the next lake. Richter returned with Pugsley for the second load this time to share the burden.

After a brief paddle and one final short portage, they arrived at Burnt Island Lake. They passed a small island and followed the lake's south shore to the first campsite. To Pugsley's delight, it was unoccupied.

"We're here," he announced. "This is our campsite."

They unloaded their gear, located the thunderbox and began setting up their tents. Richter remembered to deploy the groundsheet and managed most of the set-up herself, including what she called "the GD fly."

By the time the set-up was complete, it was nearly noon. "Don't know about you, Renata, but my stomach's rumbling," Pugsley said, rubbing his petulant paunch. "Feel like a bite of lunch?"

"What did you have in mind?" she asked, fearing his answer.

"Let me surprise you. Why don't you check out the lake while I prepare something?"

It didn't take long before he called her back. "Peanut butter and banana sandwiches!" he said, chuffed at his culinary creation. "Bet you haven't had one of those in a while, eh?"

"Never."

"Normally I'd toast the bread, but I'm a little short of toasters. It still should be good."

"I'm sure it will be … what's the right word … unforgettable?" Richter replied. She took a tentative bite, chewing cautiously as if fearful of choking on bones. It wasn't good, exactly, but it wasn't horrible either.

"Well, what do you think?" Pugsley said. "You like it?"

"It's … better than I expected."

"You know, Renata," Pugsley said, ignoring her tepid endorsement, "this is a special campsite. The Grand Trunk Railway set up a summer resort on this very spot nearly a century ago. They called it Minnesing Camp. There was a main lodge and a bunch of cabins. Everything's long gone, of course, but you can still see some of the ruins."

"That's fascinating," Richter said. "What happened to the resort?"

"Some guy from California turned it into a religious retreat. For a time, Bible-thumpers from around the world came here to study the life of Jesus." A slow smile spread across his face. "Can you imagine? Christ on a bicycle!"

"I doubt they used that expression."

"Probably not."

When they'd finished lunch (Richter discreetly tossing part of her sandwich into the bush), Pugsley showed her the remains of the resort. There were several tall stone chimneys, a staircase and the remnants of a foundation.

"I love this!" she declared. "It's like a time machine. It transports me to a vanished age, and I can imagine the people who were here long before us. What were their lives like?"

"Never thought about it like that," Pugsley admitted. "It certainly is … nifty. Very nifty."

Later, Pugsley suggested they try some fishing. "It's the middle of the day, not the best time to catch fish, but who knows? We might get lucky."

Richter had never fished. Indeed, the idea of trying to impale a living creature on a hook repulsed her. "I'll just watch, if you don't mind."

Pugsley gathered his fishing gear and they launched the canoe, paddling along the shore. "There's some monster lake trout down there," he told Richter, "but they like it deep. We're more likely to hook a bass if anything." He tied on a spinnerbait, drew back his arm and cast the lure about 80 feet from the boat.

"My goodness!" Richter exclaimed. "You can really make it fly."

Pugsley wasn't the sort of man who blushed easily, but Richter's appreciation triggered a strange glow in the vicinity of his neck.

"Thanks Renata. I've been doing this for more than 50 years. If I'm not good at it by now, I never will be."

For the next hour or so, Pugsley cast his line repeatedly into the lake waters, pausing occasionally to paddle to different locations. His form was nearly perfect, but the results were always the same. The fish just weren't interested.

"Just as I thought, it's the wrong time of day," he said, irritated and mildly embarrassed by his piscine washout. “We might as well pack it in.”

“Could you show me how to cast?” asked Richter. With the probability of catching a fish effectively nil, animal cruelty was no longer top of mind.

Pugsley was pleased by her interest. “First, take your right hand and hold the rod just above the reel. There should only be a foot or so of line at the end of the rod when you cast.”

“Like this?” Richter said.

“That’s good. Now open the bail away from you.”

“The bail?”

“That’s the lever on the reel that holds the line in place. Opening it releases the line and allows you to cast.”

“Done.”

“Excellent. Now take your index finger and lightly pick up the line. Then take your other hand and hold the rod near the base. Lift the rod over your right shoulder and cast up and out.”

Richter followed his instructions, nearly hooking Pugsley’s shoulder with the lure.

“Oh! I’m so sorry,” she said, mortified. “Are you OK?”

“No harm done. Give it another try.”

This time, the line unspooled and the lure travelled about 50 feet before plunking into the water. Richter beamed. “That’s unbelievable. I can understand why you …”

Before she could finish the thought, there was a sudden sharp tug on the line, so intense it nearly ripped the rod from her hands.

“What’s happening?” she cried.

“I don’t believe it,” Pugsley said. “You’re catching a fish!”

Richter stared at him. “Oh no! I don’t … I can’t … Can you take over?”

“You can do it, Renata. Just keep the rod at a 45-degree angle to the water, pointed at the fish. When it stops taking line off your reel, lift the tip of the rod and start reeling the line in as you lower it. Then repeat.”

After 10 minutes or so, a rather large fish, frenzied and thrashing, surfaced a few feet from the canoe.

“It’s a lake trout. A big mother,” Pugsley exclaimed, wide-eyed. “See if you can bring it closer to the boat and I’ll try to net it.”

Richter felt like she was having an out-of-body experience, watching someone she barely recognized struggling to land the giant fish. But somehow, she managed to draw it close enough for Pugsley to scoop it up in his net.

"My God," he exclaimed, "that's gotta be a five-pounder at least." He looked at Richter with something approaching awe. "Woo-hoo! We're gonna eat like royalty tonight, Renata!"

Back at their campsite, Pugsley gutted and cleaned the fish while Richter took refuge in her tent. "It's safe to come out now," he said when the job was done.

"I was going to whip up some pasta tonight," he told her, "but this will be so much better." And it was. So good, in fact, that Richter asked for seconds. "If we only had some chilled Chablis, this would be perfect," she sighed, eyeing him with fresh appreciation.

When it came time to turn in, they unrolled their sleeping bags, retreated to separate quarters to change into their pajamas, and settled in side-by-side in Pugsley's tent.

Richter propped herself up on an elbow and gazed at Pugsley. "That was an amazing day, Norman. Thank you." She leaned over and gave him the briefest of kisses, his moustache tickling her lips.

"Good night, sweet one," she murmured, then turned away.

Sixteen

OTTAWA, 1987-88

It was a few minutes past midnight and the Press Club was hopping. Boisterous groups of men – almost everyone there was male – filled the premises. Some, jackets and ties askew, leaned unsteadily on the club's long oak bar. Others played snooker or hurled sharp projectiles in the general direction of a dart board. Still others sat with colleagues in darkened corners, their raucous conversations punctuated by braying laughter and the occasional curse. Some were journalists. Some were political aides. Some were employed by companies seeking government favour. But to a man, they were drunk. Potted. Stewed. Feeling little, if any, pain.

This bacchanal of booze greeted Norman Pugsley when he arrived at the club minutes after finishing a Thursday night shift on the *Advocate*'s news desk. He knew managing editor Rob Sutherland and his gang would be there. Though he hadn't received one of Sutherland's invitations, he'd wagered that wasn't strictly necessary.

It didn't take long to spot Sutherland, surrounded by a small posse of *Advocate* colleagues at a corner table. Night news editor Carl Dunning was present, eyes glazed, hair dishevelled. So were sports editor Casey Turnbull and assistant managing editor Garrett Smythe.

Pugsley started to approach them, then hesitated. Ever since he'd heard about Sutherland's gang, he'd been debating whether he should try to join them. It didn't feel honourable. Cozying up to Sutherland, a man he'd never admired, was the worst sort of cynical ploy. But perhaps it was the only way to start rebuilding a career that had been so callously derailed by his bosses.

While Pugsley dithered, Dunning spotted him from a distance.

"Why, if it isn't Norm Pugsley," he said to the room at large. Sutherland and his acolytes swivelled in their chairs to peer at the unexpected interloper. From their flushed expressions, it was impossible to tell whether they were happy to see him or not.

"Pugsley!" Sutherland barked. "What the fuck brings *you* here?"

Pugsley had rehearsed what he would say should that question be posed. "Just got off work and had a hankering for a drink," he began. "I'd heard about you lads gathering here. Sounded like a good time, so I thought I'd pop by."

Sutherland scrutinized him woozily. "Don't think you were on my invitation list," he mumbled.

"You're right. But I thought maybe if I bought a round, you wouldn't mind too much if I joined you."

Sutherland beamed and leaned back in his chair, nearly toppling backwards before steadying himself. "That sounds like a good idea. What do you think, boys? Should we let Pugsley buy us a round?"

There were murmurs of assent. They were journalists, after all. Turning down free drinks was almost unthinkable.

"It's nunanimous," Sutherland said, mangling the four-syllable word. "Pull up a chair."

"Thanks Rob." Pugsley collected the orders – a gin martini for Sutherland (stirred, not shaken), Scotches for Dunning and Smythe, and draft beers for Turnbull and himself – and headed for the bar. He returned minutes later bearing the drinks on a tray.

"Careful, Pugsley," Smythe said, "that's precious cargo ya got there." Pugsley acknowledged the comment with a smile, passed out the drinks and settled into a chair.

"To Norman Pugsley!" Sutherland said, shakily raising his glass. "Cheers!"

"To Pugsley!" the others echoed.

"To Rob and his gang," Pugsley replied. "Thanks for letting me join you tonight."

"Just keep buying the drinks," Casey Turnbull said with a snort.

"So, Norm," Sutherland said amiably, "how's life on the night freaking desk?"

Pugsley wanted to say it was awful, that he was bored silly, that it was an injustice of the first order for him to be there at all. Instead, he conjured up a small smile and said, “Oh, you know, Rob. It’s not so bad. The hours suck” – that elicited a chorus of snickers – “but I’m learning a lot.”

Sutherland peered at him, struggling to keep his eyes in focus. “Good to hear. If that had happened to me, I’m not sure I would be so … so …” Sutherland paused, wracking his booze-addled brain for the right word.

“Chipper?” Dunning suggested.

“Craven?” Smythe offered unhelpfully.

“Sanguine?” Pugsley said.

“That’s it, sangreen,” Sutherland affirmed, even two syllables problematic now. “You know, Norm, don’t repeat this, but I never thought what happened to you was right. Old man Sherman was in a rage and Gord Davis didn’t have the balls to stand up for you.”

After that, Sutherland added Pugsley to his invitation list. Two or three times a week, a small brown envelope would appear in his mail slot, signalling another Press Club conclave. Pugsley invariably appeared and bought a round or two, solidly ingratiating himself with Sutherland and his companions.

When Sutherland organized a booze-soaked bus expedition to Montreal to watch the Expos play the New York Mets, Pugsley made sure he was free to go. He was also reliably available for Sutherland’s semi-regular outings to the Bare Bodkin, a popular strip club in the ByWard Market district.

His ploy appeared to be working. He’d become what Sutherland prized most: a reliable drinking companion. If the other members of the gang had reservations about him, they didn’t voice them.

Maryanne, however, wasn’t thrilled when Pugsley rolled into bed at 3 a.m., stinking of alcohol. Nor was she impressed by his frequent hangovers, which left him twitchy and even more remote.

“I’m worried about you, Norm,” she said one night after her husband staggered up the stairs to their bedroom. “You’re drinking too much and you’re not around enough – always heading off somewhere with your buddies. Are you going through male menopause or something? A midlife crisis?”

Pugsley protested it had just become part of the job. He was too embarrassed to tell her the ignoble motive he actually had: to restart his career by sucking up to the boss.

Maryanne looked at him narrowly. "You're not having an affair, are you?"

"Jesus, Maryanne. Why would you even ask that?"

"Well, are you?"

"No. Of course not."

"Don't suppose you'd admit it if you were," she huffed, turning away.

"For chrissakes, Maryanne. Everything I'm doing I'm doing for us. For the family."

She whirled to face him. "It sure doesn't feel that way. Barbara's at a very vulnerable age. She needs your support. I used to love our conversations, but we almost never talk anymore. And I can't remember the last time we made love."

Pugsley had to admit she had a point. The physical side of their marriage had withered since his fall from grace. Working nights was partly to blame. So was his boozing with Sutherland's gang. It hardly made him an attractive lover. But if he were being honest, he was rarely in the mood. His melancholy over his seemingly lost career was crowding out the joyful things in life.

"Look, Maryanne," he said, "we're going through a rough patch. But I'm trying to fix it. I have a plan. If everything works out, I'll get my career back on track and we'll get our lives back."

Maryanne shot him a baleful look. "Bugger your career," she said.

•••

"Got a moment, Pugsley?" Sutherland said as another night of heavy drinking wound down at the Press Club. "I have some news for you."

Sutherland leaned over, his martini breath in Pugsley's face. "Keep this under your hat," he slurred, "but our publisher's gonna retire in January. Know what that means?"

Pugsley shook his head. He had no idea why Sutherland was sharing the information with him.

"It means opportunity!" Sutherland said with a sly smile. "Opportunity for you!"

"What do you mean?"

"C'mon, Pugs, don't be cute. You know damn well you were bounced to the night desk because Clark Sherman wanted to punish your ass. You also know a lot of people, me included, think you got a raw deal. You do the math."

The wheels were turning, albeit sluggishly, in Pugsley's befogged brain as he tried to process what Sutherland was telling him. Did he dare to hope that his fortunes might change? Yes, he did.

"Are you saying that once the publisher goes, I'll be able to get off the night desk?" he ventured.

"No. I'm not saying that," Sutherland replied, poker-faced as a person can be after seven martinis.

Pugsley's face fell.

"What I *am* saying, though, is things are going to change for you. For the better." Sutherland grinned and flung a comradely arm around Pugsley's shoulders. "How'd you like to be night news editor?"

The question, which came out of the blue, caught Pugsley off guard. He stalled for time. "What's happening with Carl? Is he leaving the paper?"

"No, nothing like that. He's far too valuable to me. And the paper, of course." Sutherland emitted three percussive hiccups. "Christ. Sorry about that," he said, wiping his mouth with a sleeve.

"Carl has been night news editor for three years now. He needs a break, and I could use another assistant managing editor. I've been pushing for one for a while, but fucking Sherman always turned me down. Once he's gone, Gord Davis has promised to sign off. So you see, my good fellow, our esteemed publisher's retirement works for both of us."

Night news editor was far from Pugsley's dream job, but at least it was a promotion. A small step, perhaps, but in the right direction.

"I wasn't expecting anything like this," he lied. "I don't know what to say."

"It's easy," Sutherland said. "Say yes."

"All right, then. Yes. And thanks, Rob."

"Hey, you're welcome. You've earned it, Pugsley." Sutherland lowered his voice. "Just so we're clear. Carl figured out how to do the job and still slip away for the odd drink with me and the boys. I hope you can manage that too."

More than the odd drink, Pugsley thought. Carl Dunning was the absentee landlord of the night news desk. But if that was OK with Sutherland, who was he to argue?

•••

Maryanne didn't seem very enthused when he broke the news of his impending promotion.

"So, you'll still be working nights?" she asked dully.

"Well, yes, for now. But it's just a first step. I'm sure I'll be back on days before long."

"Really? Did they tell you that?"

Pugsley knew he'd likely be night news editor for at least a couple of years. The position, with its terrible hours, was difficult to fill. But that wasn't what Maryanne wanted to hear.

"Not in so many words," he parried. "But Rob and I are buddies. If I ask, I'm sure he'll get me off nights as soon as he can."

Maryanne wasn't placated. "What about your drinking, Norm? Will that change at least?"

Probably not, Pugsley thought. Sutherland had made it clear he expected him to remain a booze buddy. But once again, that wasn't what his wife wanted to hear.

"Some drinking goes with the job, Maryanne," he argued. "It's about building relationships. But look, I'll be more or less putting out the newspaper. So I'll have to take that into account."

"What does that even mean?" Maryanne said wearily. "Just give me a straight answer for once. Will you still go to the Press Club until all hours and come home drunk?"

"Maybe. Sometimes."

"So nothing's really changing, is it?

"Of course it is. I'll be a manager. My career is back on track."

"But you'll still be a stranger to me and Barbara. A drunken stranger."

•••

Just as Sutherland had promised, *Advocate* publisher Clark Sherman announced his retirement in January. Two weeks later, Carl Dunning was promoted to assistant managing editor and Pugsley was named night news editor.

"Congratulations Norm," Dunning told him. "Well played."

"You too, Carl. You gotta do what you gotta do, right?"

"Right."

In deference to his wife's complaints, Pugsley tried to scale back his drinking at first. But Sutherland was having none of it. If anything, his invitations showed up more often in his mail slot. If Pugsley tried to beg off, Sutherland would purse his lips. "That's very disappointing, Norm," he'd say, a bit ominously. "You know how much I count on you."

Pugsley tried to explain. "My wife's really on my case," he said, hoping for some sympathy and understanding.

Empathy wasn't one of Rob Sutherland's traits, though. "Are you a man, Pugsley? Or are you a mouse? If you're a man, you won't let your wife henpeck you. You're supposed to be the king in your castle. Act like one."

Sutherland also ramped up the frequency of his command-performance visits to the Bare Bodkin. Short of a death in the family – and it was unclear whether even that would suffice – Pugsley was expected to be there.

One night, a stripper named Maria Callous was on stage. Sutherland nudged Pugsley and smirked. "Watch this girl," he told him. "You won't believe what she can do with ping-pong balls …"

The stripper indeed had a freakish talent. For his part, Pugsley was more appalled than impressed. Sutherland, though, hooted his febrile appreciation.

"What did I tell you?" he crowed to Pugsley, who forced a smile and nodded. He was trapped and he knew it. It's not that he didn't enjoy a drink or even an occasional pole dance. But those were no longer his choices. Rob Sutherland was calling the shots.

Maryanne knew nothing of his deal with the devil. If he told her, she wouldn't understand. She'd tell him to quit his job. And that was unthinkable. He'd spent nearly two decades of his life at the *Advocate*. He couldn't throw that away.

One Saturday, a few months after his "promotion," his 19-year-old daughter, Barbara, accosted him.

"You're not going out *again*, are you?" she asked.

"I'm afraid I have to," he said. "It's business."

"You have a business meeting on a Saturday night?"

"That's the newspaper racket, honey. It's not a 9 to 5 job."

Barbara couldn't hide her disappointment. "I was hoping you'd come with me to see Iron Man at the Cineplex tonight," she grumbled. "It's supposed to be really, really good."

Pugsley felt a stab of guilt. "I'm sorry, Barbara. Maybe we can see the movie next weekend."

"Sure. Maybe," his daughter said, without conviction.

When Pugsley lurched though the door after midnight, Maryanne was waiting for him in the living room.

"You're still up?" he asked, trying and failing to conceal his fermented state.

"I was waiting for you," she said. She wasn't smiling.

"You didn't have to do that," Pugsley said. He could sense he was in trouble but wasn't sure why.

"Yes, I did," she said. "Norman, we need to talk."

"OK. Why?"

"One of my friends was having dinner in the ByWard Market tonight. She saw you and your buddies go into a strip club there."

Pugsley's sodden brain was suddenly on high alert, flashing an urgent warning: *Not good. Not good. Not good.*

His first instinct was to deny it was him. But Maryanne was his wife, the mother of his only child. Sutherland's dissolute company had coarsened him, but some shred of decency still survived. He couldn't bring himself to lie to her.

"It's true," he said, gambling he'd get credit for honesty if nothing else. "Rob and his gang wanted to go there."

Maryanne looked at him levelly. "What about you? Did you want to go too?"

"Not especially."

"So why did you? Why didn't you just come home?"

Pugsley could feel the vice tightening. "I couldn't. Rob wanted me there."

"So what?" Maryanne said. "Rob isn't God. You could have said no."

There was no alternative now. It was confession time.

"You don't understand, Maryanne. I have to stay in Rob's good books. My career depends on it."

"You expect me to believe your career depends on going to a strip club with Rob Sutherland?" she asked, incredulous.

Pugsley couldn't meet her gaze. "Rob rewards his friends, but not if they let him down."

"Let me get this straight," Maryanne said. "You're telling me you have to do whatever Rob wants for the sake of your bloody job?"

"Pretty much."

"Even if it hurts the people you're supposed to love?"

"I never meant to hurt you or Barbara," Pugsley protested.

"But you have, Norm. You have." Maryanne wiped away a tear. "You're barely here, and when you are, you're usually drunk or hung over. We feel … abandoned."

"What do you expect me to do?" he asked sullenly.

"Put your family first. Tell Rob Sutherland to fuck off."

"Jesus, Maryanne. I can't do that. It would ruin me."

Maryanne bowed her head as if in silent prayer. When she finally spoke, her words were tinged with sorrow. "I guess you've made your choice," she said. "I'm going to bed. Please don't join me."

Seventeen

OTTAWA, EARLY SEPTEMBER 2006

"No luck?" Fawzia Hassan asked, though the look on Pugsley's face had already conveyed the answer.

"No luck," he confirmed. "When I raised Jack Clifford's name with my cop contact, Bernie Lachance, he buttoned his lip. Complete poker-face. I couldn't get a read one way or the other."

Pugsley scowled. It hadn't helped that Lachance had taken a month-long vacation to France. During that period, they hadn't been able to speak to him. "What a waste of time," Pugsley groused.

"He didn't warn you off, though," said Hassan. "I guess that means Clifford's still a suspect, right?"

"Well, we know he sees prostitutes. We know he was driving a black Mercedes at the time Jenny was killed. And we know he was one of four names on the police list of suspects. All of that points to him as the possible killer. What we don't have is proof."

Pugsley glanced at Hassan. "What about the other names Lachance gave us? It appears none of them had solid alibis when the cops checked them out."

"Funny you should mention that," Hassan said. "I did a little poking around while you were off on your camping trip with my boss."

The reference to Renata Richter made Pugsley squirm. He wasn't quite ready to go public with their relationship, whatever it was exactly. He was still trying to figure that out himself.

"And what have you found out?" he asked, eager to move the conversation along.

"Believe it or not, two of the other three suspects are dead," Hassan said. "One of them, Bradley Gibson, was a divorce lawyer who was shot and killed by the husband of one of his clients."

"I remember that case!" Pugsley exclaimed. "The husband thought Gibson was boning his wife, as I recall."

Hassan's eyebrows shot up.

"Sorry, Fawzia," Pugsley said, regretting the crude expression. "I meant he thought the lawyer was having, um, sexual relations with his wife."

"Ah."

"What about the other dead guy?" Pugsley asked.

"Laurent Dupont. A dentist," Hassan said. "Died five years ago while on vacation in Africa. Apparently killed by a hippo while canoeing in Zimbabwe."

"Jesus," murmured Pugsley. "So, who's left?"

"Guy named Günter Grunwald," Hassan said. "I haven't been able to track him down. He used to work for the federal government as an auditor, I think, but he retired four years ago. I can't find him in Ottawa. Maybe he moved somewhere warm."

"Good work, Fawzia. I'm impressed."

"So where do we go from here?" Hassan asked.

"Well, the dead guys are dead," Pugsley said. "That's a problem, obviously. Since either of them could have done this while alive, we may never know. Still, the lawyer, Gibson, sounds like he might have been a stickman … a guy who had lots of sex," he quickly added, noting Hassan's expression. "Especially if he was doing it with a client. He might be our guy."

"But if he is, how can we prove it?"

"Not easily," Pugsley conceded. "Today, the police might be able to finger him using DNA testing. Unfortunately, that wasn't in use when Jenny was murdered. I guess the cops could exhume Gibson's body to get a DNA sample, but they'd probably need more evidence of his guilt before they could do that. If Gibson was married, we could talk to his widow. Maybe she knows something. Or we could talk to the woman he was … you know … having sexual relations with."

"Sounds like a longshot," Hassan said gloomily.

"It is. But we need to check it out. We should also try to track down dentist Dupont's family and see what they can tell us."

"What about the auditor?"

"I don't know, I always think of auditors as by-the-book types," Pugsley said. "Not really the sort who murder people, my gut tells me. But we definitely should try to find him. My gut's been known to be wrong now and then."

"OK," Hassan said. "I'll see what I can unearth about the two dead guys. Can you try to locate Grunwald? I struck out, so maybe a fresh set of eyes …"

"Sure. Leave it to me."

•••

Beauregard Fisher peered over the top of his glasses. "Well Norm, how's the old ticker? Any issues?" It had been a year since Pugsley's near-fatal heart attack in Athens and whether he liked it or not, it was time for another checkup.

"Everything's good, Beau. No chest pain and I've got plenty of energy. I even went canoe camping a couple of weeks ago."

"Not by yourself, I hope."

"No, I had a … friend with me."

"You almost died, Norm," Fisher reminded him. "I'm glad you're doing well, but you have to realize you're still at risk. Don't push yourself too hard."

"Don't worry. I'm taking it easy. And look, Beau," Pugsley said, sucking in his gut and rubbing his belly. "I'm practically skinny."

Fisher smiled. "Let's not get carried away, Norm. You've lost weight but only a blind man would call you skinny. What do you weigh now?"

Pugsley was in the habit of weighing himself on the bathroom scale before breakfast – naked, after emptying his bladder. This strategy usually produced the most satisfying result. That morning, he'd weighed in at 197 pounds, up a bit from the previous week.

"Around 195, typically," he told Fisher. *Close enough*, he thought.

"Hmmm," Fisher said, assessing the curve of his abdomen. He gestured in the direction of his medical scale. "Step on that and we'll get an official reading."

Pugsley suppressed a groan. "I always weigh more at the doctor's office," he grumbled, stepping onto the scale gingerly, as if that might somehow produce a better result. Fisher adjusted the sliding weights until they were in balance. "Two hundred and two pounds," he reported, without comment.

"Impossible," Pugsley sputtered.

"The numbers don't lie, Norm. But look, you're still down nearly 20 pounds. You must be doing something right. Congratulations."

"Yeah, thanks," Pugsley said. "I try to have a couple of walks a day if the weather isn't too crappy. I'm cooking more of my own food, even healthy stuff like broccoli every now and then. And I'm barely drinking at all, I'm sorry to say."

Fisher nodded approvingly. "Sounds like you're on the right track. Let's have a listen to your heart and I'll let you go."

The stethoscope revealed nothing alarming. Pugsley began to button up his shirt.

"Oh Norm, I nearly forgot," Fisher said. "Deirdre is on the board of the Rape Crisis Centre. They're having a fundraising dinner next week and ticket sales have been sluggish. I know she'd love it if you could come."

Fundraising dinners for rape crisis centres weren't high on Pugsley's wish list, but Fisher was a friend as well as his doctor. "Sure Beau. How much are the tickets?"

"$500."

Pugsley blanched but said nothing.

"If that's too much," Fisher offered, "I can pay part of the price."

Yes! Pugsley thought but did not say. "I wouldn't dream of it," he replied instead, forcing a smile. "It's such a good cause. I'd be delighted to support Deirdre's group."

"Terrific! I'll let her know." Fisher lowered his voice and leaned towards Pugsley. "Between you and me, I find these events tedious. It will be great to have you there."

"Looking forward to it," Pugsley said miserably.

•••

For the first time since his retirement from the *Advocate*, Pugsley dusted off his only suit, polished his black dress shoes and picked out his favourite tie – unfashionably wide and dotted with tiny Toronto Blue Jays logos.

If he had to go to a fundraising dinner for the Rape Crisis Centre, he was bloody well going to look his best, he'd decided. He studied himself in the mirror, mostly with approval. His hair and moustache were trimmed. Thanks to his weight loss, the suit fit well, with none of the lamentable bulges he'd noticed the last time he wore it. The Blue Jays cravat added a jaunty finishing touch, he believed.

The crowd was already gathering in the Château Laurier's sumptuous ballroom when he arrived just before 6 p.m. He spotted Fisher across the room, chatting with an attractive blonde woman who looked to be in her late 20s. Unsure whether to interrupt them, Pugsley hung back until Fisher waved him over.

"Hey there, Norm," he said. "Glad you're here." He gestured at the woman. "Let me introduce you to Marilyn O'Malley. She's a volunteer at the Rape Crisis Centre. Norm ran the *Advocate* for donkey's years, Marilyn."

"You don't say," O'Malley said, barely disguising her boredom. "Sounds important. Forgive me but … what's the *Advocate*?"

"Only the newspaper in town," Pugsley said, mildly irritated by her ignorance.

"Of course. Sorry. I get all my news on the Internet."

Fisher rolled his eyes and offered a sympathetic smile. "Young people these days, eh Norm?"

Pugsley grunted and O'Malley seized the opportunity to make her escape, mumbling something about fixing her already impeccable hair.

"Lovely young woman," Fisher said, watching her recede. "It's all downhill from here, I'm afraid. Prepare to be …"

But Pugsley had stopped listening. He was transfixed by another woman, spectacularly turned out in a slinky silver dress. With a start, he realized it was Renata Richter. With her – indeed, acting as her escort – was none other than Bliss Browning.

"Excuse me, Beau," he said, eyes never leaving Richter and Browning. "A couple of my former colleagues just walked in. Gotta say hello."

Richter's face lit up as he approached. "Norman! I didn't expect to see you here."

"And I had no idea you were coming. And Browning," he said, eyeballing the former travel editor. "What the hell? I thought you were in Greece. Why are you here?"

"Hope you're not too shocked," Browning smiled. "I'd hate to be responsible for another heart attack like the one you had in Athens."

"No danger of that," Pugsley laughed. "I've turned over a new leaf. And my doctor is here, just in case. Seriously, though. How is it that you're here?"

"Renata invited me," Browning said. "I happened to be in town for a few days and she had a spare ticket. So, I'm her date."

"Bliss is too modest to mention this," Richter said, jumping into the conversation, "but he just took second place in National Geographic's travel writers' competition for his series on Botswana. He had to fly to New York City from Athens to pick up his prize, so he decided to tack on a quick trip to Ottawa."

"Well, well," Pugsley said. "Congratulations are in order." Pugsley hadn't read much of the travel series, but this wasn't the moment to confess that. He was struck anew by the change in Browning. At the paper, Browning had been the poster boy for forgettable, timid and cowering. Now, he seemed at ease, comfortable in his skin, even – dare one think it? – modestly impressive.

"Thanks Norman. I'm still having trouble believing it myself."

"As for you, Renata," Pugsley said, turning his attention to the editor, "you look … ravishing. Dazzling. Gorgeous. Where'd you get that dress?"

Richter, delighted by his flattery, responded: "It's been hanging in my closet, waiting for just the right occasion."

"Well, thank God you broke it out tonight. You're a vision of loveliness," he gushed.

"Stop it," Richter protested, though Pugsley thought he detected a faint blush on her face. She squinted, her gaze focused on his chest. "That's quite a tie," she said.

"Thanks, Renata. It's my special Blue Jays tie. Do you like it?"

"Well, it certainly is … special."

"I'm here with my doctor, Beau Fisher, and his wife, Deirdre," Pugsley said. "Why don't the two of you join us?"

"That would be lovely," Richter said. "I only know Dr. Fisher by reputation, but I have met Deirdre. She was in to talk to the editorial board about the Rape Crisis Centre a few months ago."

Fisher and his wife were already seated when Pugsley's party ambled over. He made the introductions, adding: "I've invited them to sit with us. I hope you don't mind."

"By all means," said Fisher, glancing at Deirdre for affirmation. Oddly, she made no response. Didn't acknowledge him at all, Pugsley noticed, though she did manage a wan smile.

"Well, here we are," Pugsley said, once everybody was seated. "Does everyone have wine?" Hearing no dissenters, he raised his glass. "Then let's have a toast!"

"To the Rape Crisis Centre!" he exclaimed. Even as he said it, he knew it was a peculiar toast, but the others followed suit. "The Rape Crisis Centre, the Rape Crisis Centre," they chanted, clinking glasses.

A server soon arrived and placed steaming bowls of soup at every place.

"What's the soup?" Pugsley asked.

"Wild mushroom bisque," said the server.

"Marvellous," Richter enthused. "Love, love, *love* wild mushrooms."

Pugsley liked domesticated mushrooms well enough but had limited experience with the untamed variety. Cautiously, he sipped a spoonful. To his relief, he liked it.

"Yeah, wild mushrooms, hooray," he proclaimed. "Great stuff. Also, the bisk."

"Bisque," said Richter, correcting his pronunciation.

"Yeah, that's what I said."

Fisher noted their byplay with amusement. "You two are just like an old married couple," he joked. "They remind me of us," he said, nudging his wife. "Uh-huh," Deirdre grunted.

Richter chimed in. "You might like to know that you're in the presence of an award-winning journalist," she told the Fishers. "Bliss just won second prize in a competition among travel writers from around the world."

"Well done!" exclaimed Fisher, turning to Browning. "What was your story about?"

"It was a massive series about my safari trip to Botswana," he replied.

"Don't worry if you didn't read it. I doubt many people did."

"Nonsense," scoffed Fisher, who was indeed unaware of Browning's series. "I devoured every word. It was terrific. Made me want to go to … where was it again?"

"Botswana."

"Right. Botswana. It's on my bucket list now, thanks to you."

The server whisked away the empty soup bowls and replaced them with plates of salad.

"Oooh, baby spinach, feta and … are those caramelized pears?" Richter asked, taking a nibble. "Yes, they are!"

Pugsley normally disliked the gritty texture of pears. But the caramelized versions were succulent, and he devoured every slice.

After his forays into exotic cuisine, he was relieved to be able to order prime rib as his main course. "Well done, please, my good man," he told the server. Everyone else chose the miso maple marinated salmon.

"Say, Norm," Browning said at one point, between mouthfuls of salmon, "are you and Fawzia making any progress on that Jenny Birchmount story?"

Pugsley nearly choked on his well-done beef. Fisher had advised him against taking on the assignment for health reasons. As far as his doctor knew, he'd followed his advice. Now Browning had unwittingly spilled the beans.

Hoping Fisher hadn't heard the question, Pugsley responded *sotto voce*, barely above a whisper. "We're working on it but no breakthroughs yet," he mouthed.

"Sorry, Norm. Can't hear you," Browning said loudly.

"Yes, Norm," said Fisher, who'd heard Browning's question. "I'd like to hear about this, too."

"Um, we're … we're making some headway. We've narrowed it down to a few suspects. But, well, two of them are dead and … we just don't know about the others."

Fisher frowned slightly. "We talked about this, Norm. I thought it was a bad idea to take on unnecessary stress after your heart attack."

"I'm sorry I didn't tell you, Beau," Pugsley said, turning to Fisher. "Renata really needed my help. Fawzia's a junior reporter and she wasn't getting anywhere. Besides, it really hasn't been very stressful. It's almost fun to return to the fray."

Pugsley kept talking, though he knew he was babbling. "We even managed to discover that there's one very interesting name on the suspects list."

"Anyone we know?" Fisher asked, a slight smile signalling he was joking.

"It's too soon to talk publicly about it," Pugsley told him.

Fisher nodded. "Well, I hope you nail the bastard – just don't go at it too hard."

The table chatter moved on as the ever-efficient server cleared their plates and brought dessert – a choice between chocolate ganache and crème brûlée. Pugsley was more of an apple pie man but chose the ganache because at least he knew what chocolate was.

"They'll be doing speeches soon," announced Deirdre, who'd been quaffing white wine steadily during dinner but saying little. "I'm going to make a dash for the ladies' room."

"I'll go with you," Richter said, rising from her chair.

The three men watched as they walked toward the restroom.

"Have you ever noticed that women go to the washroom in packs?" Fisher said. "What's that about? I mean, *guys* don't do that." Browning and Pugsley laughed in agreement.

Minutes later, the master of ceremonies was at the mic, preparing to introduce the featured speaker, Lee-Anne Harris, executive director of the Rape Crisis Centre.

"Deirdre and Renata are going to miss the speeches if they don't hurry up," Fisher said, checking his watch.

"Probably powdering their noses, or whatever women do in washrooms," ventured Pugsley.

Harris began her speech. "As most of you know, the Rape Crisis Centre has been serving victims of sexual assault in our community for more than three decades," she began. "We're proud to provide feminist services from an anti-racist/anti-oppressive perspective."

Fisher rolled his eyes. "Riveting stuff, isn't it?" he muttered. Pugsley responded with a weak smile, but Browning grimaced. "They do important work," he pointed out. "Sexual abuse and harassment are real problems for women. We men need to be more supportive if we want that to change."

"You're right," Fisher quickly acknowledged, abashed. "I didn't mean to suggest otherwise."

Harris ran through the centre's counselling services and therapeutic groups and its plans for the future. She was wrapping up when Richter and Deirdre returned and took their seats.

"Jesus, Deirdre, what were you two doing?" Fisher whispered. "We were starting to worry."

"It's my fault," Richter said apologetically. "We got talking and I just lost track of time." She glanced at Pugsley. "Norman knows what I'm like."

Fisher's wife said nothing. Pugsley couldn't help noticing her silence. And wondering what had really been discussed in the ladies' room.

Eighteen

MONT-TREMBLANT, QUEBEC, LATE SEPTEMBER 2006

The resort town of Mont-Tremblant was a feast for the eyes. It was the final week of September and the fall colours in the Laurentians were nearing their peak: the hallucinogenic reds of the sugar maples, the mellow yellows of the birch, the defiant greens of the immutable balsam firs.

"I know it's considered the off-season," Renata was saying as she steered her Mini Cooper through the mountainside town's streets, "but it's my favourite time of year here. The colours are utterly magnificent."

Pugsley couldn't disagree. But he had mixed emotions about the trip. The idea of spending time with Renata was appealing, as unlikely as that would have seemed until recently. Yet he was genuinely apprehensive about the luxe weekend she had planned.

They'd be staying at the Hotel Apotheosis, Mont-Tremblant's most luxurious boutique hotel. Nothing wrong with luxury, but Pugsley suspected it came with uncomfortable baggage. Gourmet meals of unknown provenance. French wines. The spa and its inventory of terrifying treatments. All well outside his comfort zone, but since she had earlier accepted his challenge to go camping, there was no escape.

Though Pugsley had offered to drive Renata's Mini Cooper to Mont-Tremblant – he was, after all, the man – she would have none of it. She turned out to be an aggressive driver, accelerating rapidly and routinely exceeding the speed limit. On the twisty highway leading to Mont-Tremblant, her driving struck him as borderline reckless, forcing Pugsley to brace himself on curves.

"Do you think maybe you should slow down a bit?" he asked at one point.

She gave him a sideways glance. "Please, Norman. Just relax and enjoy the ride."

At last – or so it seemed to him – they arrived at a four-storey château of stone and wood perched near the shores of Lac Tremblant, a long, narrow body of water hemmed in by dense forest and mountainous ridges. She pulled up to the entrance and handed her car keys to an attendant.

"Valet parking. I'm impressed," Pugsley said.

"Oh, we're just getting started," she replied, smiling.

The lobby of the Apotheosis was soaring and expansive, richly appointed with dark wood and Italian white marble, and furnished with a tasteful collection of leather wingback chairs. A graceful spiral staircase connected the lobby to the restaurant level below.

Its beauty and grace left Pugsley almost speechless. "Wow," was all he could muster. "Just wow."

A bellman led them to adjoining rooms on the second floor. Each featured a king-sized bed, a wood-burning fireplace and a picture window and balcony overlooking the lake.

"Why don't we both settle in?" Renata suggested. "I'll rap on your door when I'm ready to show you around."

Pugsley retreated to his room and unpacked his small suitcase. His nerves were still a-jangle from the harrowing drive, but he could feel himself calming down. He was in a beautiful place with an intriguing woman.

A few minutes later, he heard a knock on the door that separated their two rooms. Renata was there, looking smashing in yoga pants – a fetching shade called wild indigo – and a grey half-zip top.

"Ready to explore?" she asked.

"Hell, yes."

She showed him the hotel's outdoor infinity pool. "It's unheated, so at this time of year it becomes part of a Nordic bath experience," she said, clapping her hands excitedly.

"What, exactly, is a Nordic bath, Renata?" Pugsley asked, though he had a premonition it wouldn't be good.

"Oh, you'll love it. First, we warm up in the steam room or the sauna. When we've worked up a good sweat, we jump into the cold pool. Don't worry," she said, noting his alarmed expression. "It's just for a minute or so. After we relax for a bit, we finish up in the outdoor Jacuzzi. Your whole body will tingle with pleasure."

It sounded like madness, but Renata was so enthused Pugsley couldn't bring himself to say so. Silently, though, he added Nordic baths to his long list of experiences best avoided.

Next, Renata showed him the hotel's spa, offering treatments ranging from Swedish massage to lymphatic drainage.

"I've signed us up for some treatments tomorrow," she said. "An anti-aging skin program for me and a mud bath for you."

This was unwelcome news indeed. Bathing in mud?

"Thanks Renata," he said, "but spas aren't really my thing."

"Have you ever tried one?"

"No. They don't interest me."

Renata looked exasperated for a moment. "Norman, the whole idea of this weekend is to embrace new experiences. I did that when you took me camping and I'm glad I did. Now it's your turn. For me."

Pugsley knew when he was beaten. "All right," he grumbled, "I'll have the mud bath. But I'll take a pass on the Nordic thingy."

Renata smiled enigmatically. "We'll see."

●●●

The dining room of the Apotheosis was the very definition of swanky: acres of teakwood, cushioned wingback chairs, white linen tablecloths, sculpted ceramic pillars and recessed lighting.

Pugsley was wearing his best suit – the one he'd worn to the Rape Crisis Centre fundraiser two weeks earlier, but without the Blue Jays tie this time. Renata, though, had opted for exotic. Her body was swaddled from neck to ankles in an ornately patterned caftan. On her head was a vintage white ostrich feather hat, though such headgear had been out of fashion for decades.

Pugsley was taken aback when she emerged from her room in that outfit. To him, she looked like a creature from another world. Not necessarily in a bad way, but decidedly unconventional. And Pugsley was, if nothing else, a conventional man.

But sitting there in the dining room, surrounded by low lighting and luxury, he had to admit she looked spectacular. They'd created a stir when they entered the dining room, drawing appreciative, perhaps even envious, looks from other patrons. He felt a swell of pride to be with such a remarkable woman.

Even so, he shuddered when Renata ordered a dozen oysters to share as an appetizer. "Aren't they raw?" he asked.

"Of course," she said. "But dress them with a bit of horseradish and mignonette sauce and you'll love them, I promise."

Fortunately, she was right. The oysters slid effortlessly down his gullet, trailing piquant flavours in their wake. A flute of champagne eased their passage.

The main courses were also a success: Arctic char with carrot and ginger purée and beet beurre blanc for her, and for him, venison rib, Duchess potatoes and spiced red wine pears. Even his wine – a 1999 Merlot from Château Pétrus – was agreeable.

"You know, Renata," he told her, wiping his mouth with his napkin, "I could get used to this."

She flashed a warm smile. "Me too."

Just before dessert, Renata pushed back her chair and rose to her feet. "You'll have to excuse me, Norman," she said. "I need to visit the ladies' room."

"OK. But try not to take as long as you did at the fundraising dinner."

She paused. "Remind me to tell you about that when I get back," she said.

The waiter had just delivered their chocolate soufflés when Renata reappeared. "My goodness," she exclaimed as she slid into her seat, "even the washrooms here are lovely. All marble and rosewood with Aveda toiletries. If I weren't having such a good time with you, I'd happily spend the evening there."

"Our soufull has arrived," Pugsley said, pointing to the dessert.

"It's soufflé, my silly darling," she said, so softly he wasn't sure he'd heard her properly. *Darling? Did she call me darling?*

"Weren't you going to tell me something?" he deflected awkwardly as they savoured the first mouthfuls of their dessert.

"Oh yes. Dr. Fisher's wife." Her serious face made a reappearance. "We were in the ladies' room so long that night, Norman, because she was upset."

"She did seem out of sorts," he said. "What was bothering her?"

"Her husband Beau is your doctor, right? And a bit of a friend?" She hesitated. "From what she told me, he often gets home late. He blames his job." She leaned forward, as one would when sharing a confidence. "But she thinks he might be having an affair."

"Beau? Having an affair? That's hard to believe." Pugsley remembered his own late nights away from his wife before their divorce, but of course, he'd been much younger then.

"Why? Men do, you know."

"Look, Renata, I've known Beau for decades. Even if his marriage to Deirdre were on the rocks, he'd never cheat on her. He's not the sort."

"I'm sure you're right," she said. She paused as if weighing whether to say more. "She told me one other thing. It's rather intimate. She said they don't have sex often anymore, but when they do, he likes it," she stumbled, groping for the right word, "a bit … kinky."

"Sounds like you think that's unusual," Pugsley said, with a faint smile.

"Well, isn't it? I mean, at their age?"

"Lots of couples like to play little games during sex, Renata. If it works for them, it's not a big deal."

"You're right," Richter conceded, "but Deirdre was worried that he might be picking up those … behaviours from somebody else."

"Jesus," Pugsley said, shaking his head. "You only just met the woman, and she told you all this stuff about her sex life? In the ladies' room?"

"Well," Richter said, "I think we may have bonded a little when she was at the *Advocate*'s editorial board that one time. And she'd had quite a lot to drink. I'm not sure she was thinking straight."

In the silence that followed, Pugsley thought about his own failed marriage and wondered if he could have done more to protect or strengthen his intimacy with Maryanne. "Tell you what," he said. "When we're back in town, I'll find a delicate way to have a word with Beau. For his marriage."

•••

The next morning dawned sunny and unseasonably warm. Pugsley was still cosseted in the luxury linens of his oversized bed when Renata rapped on his door.

"Norman," she called from her side of the door. "Are you awake?" *If I wasn't before, I certainly am now, he thought.*

"Just a moment, Renata." He rolled out of bed – it was a long way to the edge of the mattress – and slipped on the white silk housecoat provided by the hotel.

When he opened the door, he discovered that Renata was already dressed, wearing sonic pink yoga pants, a form-fitting black long-sleeve top and multicoloured Asics trainers.

"You're not dressed yet?" she said, glancing at her watch. "It's nearly 8:30. We need to have breakfast. I have a full day planned for you." There was nothing menacing in her words, but Pugsley felt alarmed. *Plans? What plans?*

"Give me five minutes," he said. He slipped on some jeans – freshly purchased for the occasion – and his favourite sweatshirt. Minutes later they were in the hotel restaurant, perusing the breakfast menu.

"I think I'll have the granola bowl," Renata said. "It's homemade and comes with berries and Greek yogurt. Magnifique!" She beamed. "What would *you* like?"

Pugsley would have enjoyed a couple of eggs over easy, some bacon and toast, but nothing that basic was on offer. Besides, Renata wanted him to be adventurous.

"Maybe I'll try the, uh …breakfast poutine?" He liked poutine but had never had it for breakfast and the hotel's version came with hollandaise sauce. That was adventurous, wasn't it?

Renata's smile dimmed slightly. "That's not a very healthy choice, Norman," she admonished. "But if that's what you want …"

After breakfast, Renata led him to the spa, a bounce in her step. "Time for our treatments," she said, eyes flashing with anticipation.

An athletic young woman named Noémie, with an accent that might have been charming under different circumstances, directed him to a change room. "Please take off your clothes and put on the robe," she said, pointing to a plush white bathrobe.

"All my clothes?"

"Your whole body will be in the mud, monsieur," she said with a sternness that brooked no dissent.

He did as he was told, then followed Noémie into another room where a large stone tub filled with a viscous brown substance occupied a position of prominence. It was steaming slightly.

"Now monsieur, please take off the robe and lower your derrière into the boue."

"What's … boue?" he asked.

"Ah, désolé monsieur. I mean the mud."

Pugsley wasn't a shy man, but standing starkers before an attractive woman decades his junior wasn't his usual practice. There appeared to be no alternative, however, so he slipped off the robe, modestly shielding his privates with a hand.

He eyed the steaming tub, which was filled with a mix of warmed mineral water, volcanic ash, organic peat and lake mud. "How do I get into that thing?" he asked.

"Ce n'est pas difficile," she insisted. "Just straddle the tub and gently lower yourself into the mud."

Standing astride the tub and bracing himself with his hands on both sides, he lowered his naked body backwards into the ooze until he hit bottom – literally.

Once fully immersed, he found the mud bath surprisingly agreeable. The Goldilocks temperature – neither too hot nor too cold – was pleasant and he felt a lifetime of accumulated stress seeping from his body. When his 15 minutes were up, he was reluctant to leave its soothing embrace.

The post-bath cleanup required him to lie face-down on a gurney while overhead jets of water hosed off the sludge. It was undignified but Pugsley, body glowing contentedly, no longer cared. Mud baths were his new favourite thing.

He slowly dried himself, dressed and ambled blissfully in the direction of the spa's reception area. Renata was waiting for him, her skin glowing.

She raised an eyebrow. "So? How was it?"

"Christ, Renata! That might be the best thing I've done in decades."

She smiled. "That's wonderful. Feel like a little yoga?"

Normally, Pugsley would have scoffed at the idea. In his view, yoga was the preserve of excessively limber young women. But after the mud bath, his joints had lost their usual creak. Indeed, they felt almost elastic. He threw caution to the wind.

"Why not?"

In the resort's gym, Renata unrolled two yoga mats. "We need to warm up. First, the legs. Lift each one, as if you're taking giant steps. Like this."

Pugsley followed her example, lifting his knees to hip height. It was easy at first, but after a minute or so he was puffing.

"Now, add the arms," she said, extending hers forward, to the side and over her head.

"Arms and legs at the same time?" he asked.

"Of course. Come on, old boy. It's easy!"

Easy for her perhaps, but for Pugsley the choreography was too complex. Rather than moving in a synchronized way, his arms and legs competed with one another. Renata didn't seem to notice, adding swinging leg circles, lunges and shoulder stretches to the regimen.

By the time she called a halt, the benefits of the mud bath were fading fast.

"Are we done?" he wheezed.

"The warmups," she said briskly. "Now, on to the yoga."

Sweet Jesus, Pugsley thought. *Will I survive this?*

"We'll start with an easy one," said Renata. "It's called the Mountain Pose."

"OK," he said dully. "What do I do?"

"Stand with your feet together and your arms at your side. Then straighten your legs, tuck in your tailbone and extend your arms up and then out as you inhale. After that, exhale, release your arms back to your side and repeat."

"That's it?" he said. *Maybe I can do this after all.*

She led him through several other moves, including the Cat Pose, the Downward-Facing Dog and the Warrior, all of which she executed with ease. He struggled, losing his balance repeatedly while attempting the challenging poses. They ended with the Corpse Pose, which as the name implies, requires participants to lie flat on their backs and emulate a dead person. It was by far Pugsley's favourite, and he was content to hold it indefinitely.

"All right, Norman. That's enough for now. You did well," she said, an appraisal even he recognized as absurdly generous.

Revived by the Corpse Pose, Pugsley was beginning to feel himself again – not to mention a bit peckish.

"Is it lunchtime?" he asked.

Renata glanced at her watch. "I believe it is. Let's have a bite, shall we?"

"Brilliant idea," he agreed.

He was pleased to discover the hotel bar offered club sandwiches, though the menu warned they came "*avec salade de tomates ancestrales et purée d'aubergine brûlée.*" Pugsley was reluctant to ask what that was in front of Richter, so he asked, "Can I get fries with that instead?"

"If that's what you prefer," the waiter sniffed.

Since this was the Apotheosis, the club sandwich was a gourmet version, with sun-dried tomato pesto and slices of avocado commingling with premium cold meats, slices of cheese and bacon. The fries, at least, were normal.

"So," he said, revived in body and spirit, "what's the plan this afternoon?"

"Well," Renata began, "we have a few options. We could take the gondola to the top of the mountain. The view from there is spectacular at this time of year."

That sounded innocuous enough. "Sure, let's do that."

Renata nodded. "When we're finished up there," she said, "if you really want to, we could come down on a zipline that goes over the forest …" Her voice trailed off uncertainly.

Pugsley stifled a cry of alarm. A zipline over the forest? What fresh insanity was this?

"Jeez, Renata," he sputtered, "I don't know about that." He lowered his voice to a near whisper. "I'm … afraid of heights." It wasn't true, but any port in a storm would do.

"Really? Me too," she said, relief plain on her face. "But no worries. We can hike down on some lovely forest paths."

"Great!" he said, disaster averted.

Renata gave him a long look. "I know you said you weren't keen on the Nordic bath idea, but after all that exercise I think it would be just the thing."

His instinct was to say no, but after dodging the zipline, he didn't want to shoot down another of Renata's ideas so quickly. And the mud bath *had* far exceeded expectations.

"All right," he said, adding with apparent, though bogus, enthusiasm, "let's do it!"

•••

As promised, the view from the top of Mont-Tremblant was dazzling, the countryside resplendent in its autumnal robes. The hike back down to the hotel was lovely as well, not least because it was downhill on well-marked paths.

Now it was time for the dreaded Nordic bath experience. Pugsley had briefly considered feigning illness – perhaps something heart-related, given his history – but didn't want to spoil what had been, for the most part, an enjoyable day.

They changed into their bathing suits at the hotel's spa. She was breathtaking in a form-fitting black-and-gold one-piece, Pugsley less so in baggy blue-and-white trunks he'd picked up on sale at Sport Chek for $4.88.

He couldn't help noticing how trim she looked, all too aware that his own body, still pudgy despite his recent weight loss, left something to be desired. *I don't remember ever thinking she was that sexy when we worked together,* he thought.

"Let's start with a Finnish sauna," Renata suggested. Pugsley had reached his mid-60s without experiencing a sauna of any nationality and wasn't prepared for the intense dry heat when they entered the wood-panelled room.

"Holy hell, Renata," he muttered, legs buckling slightly. "How hot *is* this thing?"

She peered at a thermometer on the sauna wall. "It's 85 Celsius." She beamed, as if that were something to celebrate. "That should really loosen us up." *Or kill us,* Pugsley thought.

Renata reclined on one of the sauna's benches, by all appearances deliriously happy. Pugsley huddled near her feet, futilely attempting to retract his steaming head, turtle-like, into his torso. After two minutes, he could take no more.

"I'm done," he declared and stood up. "I'll wait for you outside."

When she emerged 10 minutes later, none the worse for wear, Pugsley was chagrined. "Sorry, Renata, but I just couldn't handle the heat. So, I got out of the kitchen," he said, pleased with his feeble joke.

"No matter. I think we've heated up sufficiently. On to the cold pool!" she said. The thermometer showed a water temperature of 17 Celsius. *Not so bad*, Pugsley thought.

"Now Norman," Renata lectured, "the point of this is to close your pores and eliminate toxins. It's an essential step, but you should only stay in the water for a few seconds – a minute at most."

"No worries, Renata," Pugsley said. "I doubt I'll want to linger."

Without another word, she leapt into the frigid pool, completely immersing her body before popping back to the surface. "Oh, that's cold," she shivered. "But it feels *sooooo* good."

Pugsley could hardly back out now. He eased into the chill waters, which shocked his overheated body and snatched his breath away. "Christ on a …" he managed, the last word dying an unlamented death in his tightening larynx.

He was out of the pool as soon as he could manage it, shivering in a towel a full minute ahead of Renata. When she emerged, her expression could best be described as beatific. "My body is singing," she exulted. *Cold, Cold Heart by Hank Williams*, Pugsley thought.

"Are we done?" he asked, teeth chattering.

"There's one last thing." He braced for the worst. "The relaxation area."

"I like the sound of that," he said, perking up. He followed her to a solarium outfitted with lounge chairs and hammocks.

Perhaps not surprisingly, the relaxation area turned out to be Pugsley's favourite. He settled into a hammock as feelings of well-being spread from his shoulders to his toes. He'd nearly dozed off when Renata tapped him on the arm.

"Ready to do it again?" she asked, a mischievous smile on her face.

His eyes widened. "You're kidding, right?"

She shook her head. "For maximum health benefits, you should repeat it two or three times." Noticing his stricken look, she softened. "But since you're new at this, maybe not this time. Let's spend a few minutes in the outdoor hot tub instead."

Pugsley just wanted to have a nap, but immersion in a hot tub wasn't a bad alternative. "You're on," he said.

That night at dinner, he felt more relaxed than he had in years. "My God, Renata," he said, dissecting his roasted cod main course, "that Nordic whatchamacallit worked wonders. I feel 10 years younger."

"You look it, too," she said approvingly.

They lingered over coffee, enjoying one another's company and chatting about nothing of great importance. It was after 10 p.m. when they made their way back to their rooms. Before they parted, she turned and gave him a fierce hug.

"Thanks for doing this with me, Norman," she murmured, clinging to him. "I've loved introducing you to my favourite place."

"No, thank *you*. It's been terrific," he replied, exaggerating only slightly.

They said their good nights and retired to their respective rooms. Pugsley brushed his teeth, put on his pajamas and was about to climb into bed when he heard a tiny knock on the door between their adjoining rooms. When he opened it, Renata was there, wearing a diaphanous negligee and nothing else.

He stared at her, struck dumb by the vision before him. The silence lasted a few seconds before Renata broke it. "I think it's time, don't you?" she said. She grabbed him by his pajama lapels and gently, but firmly, pulled him into the room towards her. He offered no resistance, closing the door behind him with a foot.

Nineteen

OTTAWA, AUTUMN 1993

Norman Pugsley leaned back in his chair and surveyed his office. It had been his since his appointment as managing editor – the number two job in the newsroom – four months earlier but it still had that new-car feel.

As offices go, it was underwhelming. His desk, though large, was wood veneer. Recent editions of the *Daily Advocate* were stacked in a corner. A wall unit from IKEA held a few dozen reference books, mostly unread. The white vinyl walls were bare except for a poster that proclaimed the newspaper's rather prosaic mission statement – "to provide the information our readers need to live their lives" – along with its only two National Newspaper Awards, the most recent being for "spot news" photography in 1984.

After a roller-coaster 25-year career at the *Advocate*, Pugsley had finally ascended to the summit. Well, not quite the summit, but within a heartbeat. Only editor-in-chief James Reynolds stood above him in the newsroom hierarchy.

Reynolds had taken over the editorship a year earlier when his predecessor, Gordon Davis, had accepted a senior post in the office of Prime Minister Brian Mulroney, who was deeply unpopular after more than eight years in office. Davis's media savvy hadn't altered the prime minister's downward trajectory. Faced with certain defeat, Mulroney had recently announced his intention to resign and leave politics.

Reynolds, who'd been recruited by new publisher Reid Hartley, was seen as a crackerjack editor with lofty – some would argue unattainable – ambitions for the *Advocate*. To that end, he'd been methodically culling the deadwood.

Sports editor Casey Turnbull was shuffled off to a weekly affiliate newspaper and assistant managing editor Carl Dunning accepted a buyout. More importantly, Rob Sutherland's alcohol-fuelled reign as managing editor had abruptly ended when he was charged with public intoxication after urinating into a fountain on the Sparks Street Mall while whistling boisterously at passing women.

Through all the turmoil, Pugsley had kept his head down, his drinking reasonably discreet, and focused on his work. After five years as night news editor, he'd mastered the job and was widely seen as competent despite being one of Sutherland's drinking buddies.

Still, he was surprised when Reynolds called him into his office one Friday afternoon as he arrived for work.

"Have a seat, Norm," Reynolds said, glancing at his wristwatch. "It's only 2 o'clock. Doesn't your shift start at 3?"

Pugsley briefly wondered if he were somehow in trouble for starting work too early. "I like to get a jump on things – study the layout, read the stories, see if any of them need further work. I need the time."

"I've noticed," Reynolds said neutrally. "It's commendable."

Pugsley appreciated the compliment but felt obliged to add some context in the name of full disclosure.

"The other thing is – and I don't know whether you're aware of this, Jim – Rob Sutherland expected me to spend part of my shift with him at the Press Club. Coming in early helped make up for that."

A faint smile softened Reynolds' chiselled features. "I knew about Rob's drinking gang. He literally pissed his career away." He locked eyes with Pugsley. "What I need to know is what you think of Rob's … management style, let's call it."

Pugsley squirmed. He had disapproved but he'd also been part of Sutherland's cabal. "Rob didn't just blur the line between work and leisure," Pugsley replied slowly, "he erased it. I knew it wasn't right, but I went along. You do what you have to do."

"You did a lot of drinking on the job," Reynolds noted.

"I did." *No point in denying it*, Pugsley thought, bracing himself for the noose.

"Have you stopped?"

"The day Rob was fired."

"Good," Reynolds said, nodding briskly. "I can't have another drunkard as managing editor, can I?"

Pugsley's heart skipped a beat. "Are you saying what I think you're saying?" he asked.

"Depends. What do you *think* I'm saying?" Reynolds was smiling now.

"I think … I think you might be offering me the job of managing editor," Pugsley stammered.

"If I am, would you accept?"

Pugsley felt lighter than air, as if he were floating. "Christ!" he exclaimed. "You bet I would."

●●●

Less than a month after his big promotion, Pugsley's divorce from his estranged wife Maryanne was approved by the courts. It didn't come as a surprise. The two had been living apart for nearly five years, and she'd formally filed for divorce six months earlier.

Even so, the finality of it was a gut-punch. He'd met Maryanne when they were both in their early 20s. It was a whirlwind romance – love at first sight, they used to tell one another – and the idea that it might end had never occurred to him.

When she'd moved out – their daughter, Barbara, choosing to go with her – it seemed like a betrayal. The night work, the drinking, the strip-club visits – all the things Maryanne objected to – were necessary to salvage his career and provide for his family, he had repeatedly told himself. Why couldn't she see that?

That Barbara had sided with her mother made it even worse. Barbara, who'd snuggled up to him as he read bedtime stories, whose quick intelligence had regularly delighted him, who'd flowered into a graceful young woman. He was so proud of her. When Maryanne left, she was effectively erased from his life. It was a crushing blow.

He blamed Maryanne and his anger poisoned their relations. They went months without speaking. It wasn't until she filed for divorce that he began to accept that his marriage was truly over. When he was served the papers, he'd poured himself a Scotch, studied them carefully, then called her on the phone.

"I got your damn documents," he began before she cut him off.

"You should talk to my lawyer," she said tartly, "not to me."

"Jesus, Maryanne," he shot back. "I just wanted to say I won't fight you on this. Everything looks fine to me." That wasn't true, but by that point, his will to resist had evaporated. If it were really over, all he wanted was to make the pain stop.

"I'm happy to hear that, Norm. I think we both need to move on with our lives."

"Well … you know I never wanted this, Maryanne." There was silence on the line. "I still don't understand. But what's done is done. We're stuck with it now, I guess."

"Norm," she said, her tone softer but still firm, "I never expected this, either. We had some good years together, you and me. But then … I really don't want to rehash everything. It just stopped working for me."

"Whatever," he said gruffly. To his surprise, his eyes were watering. He didn't want her to know that.

"How long will this take?" he asked, pulling himself together.

"Since you're not contesting the terms, it shouldn't take long. Four to six months, I'm told."

"You get half of everything?"

"That's what I'm entitled to under the law, Norm."

"Right."

Silence again.

"How's Barbara?" he asked, the face of his now 24-year-old daughter flashing before his eyes.

"She's good. She has her own place, an apartment downtown. She can walk to work."

"I'd love to see her sometime."

"I'll let her know – or you could."

"Is there … you know … anyone special in her life?"

"She's been seeing someone for a few months now. He seems nice. His name's Ramesh. He works at the Department of Foreign Affairs."

"Do you think it's serious?"

"Maybe. Who knows? I'm probably not the best judge of that."

"Yeah. Well, say hello to her for me. Tell her I'm thinking about her, and I'll try to be in touch."

"I will. Sorry, but I have to go now. I'm expecting a call."

"Sure, no problem."

"Take care, Norm."

"You too, Maryanne."

•••

Bliss Browning rapped lightly on the half-closed door to Pugsley's office. "You wanted to see me, boss?" he said, an uneasy smile on his face.

"Yeah, come in Browning," Pugsley growled, waving at a chair across from his desk. "Sit."

The two had worked together on the night news desk after Rob Sutherland hired Browning to fill an opening. Pugsley, then still mired in his interminable tenure as night news editor, had opposed the hire, unimpressed by the introverted journalist. But Sutherland had warmed to him for unfathomable reasons – pity, maybe. So far, Browning's mediocre work on the night news desk had done nothing to alter Pugsley's low opinion.

Browning settled into the chair as instructed. "What's up?" he asked, left foot jiggling nervously as if on amphetamines.

Pugsley tossed a page from that day's newspaper across the table, the top headline circled in red. "Did you write this?"

Browning leaned forward and briefly studied the page. "Yes," he confirmed. "Is there a problem?"

"You tell me," Pugsley replied. "What does it say?"

Browning took a longer look, then paled. "Oh my God," he whispered.

"Oh my God indeed," Pugsley thundered. He snatched back the page and read the headline aloud. "Federal government calls pubic inquiry into sex abuse allegations." He glared at his crestfallen staffer. "Pubic? Pubic inquiry?" He tossed the page down in disgust. "I can't fucking believe it."

Browning's hangdog expression conveyed all he needed to know. "How the hell did this happen?" Pugsley demanded.

"Jesus, what an idiot I am," Browning blurted. "Obviously, I didn't mean to write that. It was a typo."

"Well, I'm glad to hear you didn't do it on purpose," Pugsley said sarcastically, "because if you had, you'd be out of here so fast you wouldn't know shit from Shinola." That made no real sense, but Pugsley's anger had clouded his faculties.

"I'm so, so sorry," Browning said miserably. "I always spellcheck but … pubic is a real word, so it wasn't highlighted."

"That's why we proofread pages," Pugsley glowered. "I can't accept such sloppiness. It's unprofessional and it makes the paper look ridiculous. I want you to write a correction …"

"Of course," Browning said quickly.

"… and I'm notifying your union that I'm giving you a reprimand." Pugsley glared at his cowering night news desker. "You're lucky I'm not suspending you, but we all deserve one mulligan. You just used yours up. Now, get out of here. And don't fuck up again or I'll make you edit, I dunno, the travel pages or something," he scowled, naming the most insignificant newsroom function he could imagine in the moment.

Browning scurried out of the office without another word.

Pugsley got no pleasure from disciplining errant employees, but it went with the territory. He regretted losing his temper with Browning, though. That shouldn't happen, particularly with such a milquetoast. He'd have to work on that.

That disagreeable duty discharged, he stood up, stretched his back, and headed for the newsroom. Pugsley had become a believer in what he called "Management by Walking Around." It made you visible to the newsroom and you picked up useful tidbits by chatting people up.

As he approached the news desk, Mick Mulligrew spotted him and hung up the phone, quickly turning to his desktop as if hard at work. Mulligrew was a talented editor and layout man, but he spent far too much of his shift talking to his broker about his investments.

"Hi Mick. Good to see you working for once," Pugsley teased.

"What do you mean, 'for once'?" Mulligrew said with feigned outrage. "I give my heart and soul to this bloody newspaper every single day."

Pugsley smiled. "Yeah, right." He kept walking until he reached the desk of the *Advocate*'s new books editor, Harrison Howard, whom he'd hired a month earlier. Since Howard was his first hire as managing editor, he felt a proprietary interest in the man's success.

The paper's former books editor, Huguette Burton, had recently retired and Howard struck Pugsley as a capable replacement. He had no daily newspaper experience but had edited a monthly book review magazine for four years.

"Hey there, Harry," he said. "How's it going? Starting to settle in?"

Howard looked up from behind the stacks of books colonizing his modest desk. "Oh hi, Mr. Pugsley– "

"Call me Norm. We're on the same team now." Pugsley craned his neck, trying to read the words on Howard's computer screen. "So, what are you working on?"

"I'm starting to put together my feature on the best books of 1993," Howard replied. "Most of the contenders have been released, so I thought I'd get a head start."

In the past year, Pugsley had managed to make it through a decent Robert Ludlum thriller, though he couldn't remember the title, and *Private Parts*, the smash bestseller by Howard Stern, which he'd thoroughly enjoyed. He was curious to know whether either book would make Howard's list.

"Can you give me a preview?" he asked.

"Well, there are a few obvious choices. *The Shipping News*, by Annie Proulx. Irvine Welsh's *Trainspotting. Paddy Clarke Ha Ha Ha* by Roddy Doyle. And of course, Vikram Seth's masterpiece, *A Suitable Boy.*"

Pugsley vaguely recalled hearing about *The Shipping News*, which had something to do with newspapers, but the others were Greek to him.

"*A Suitable Boy,* you say? Good title."

"Yes, but it is a bit of a commitment," Howard said.

"Why *is* that?"

"Well, it's 1,350 pages."

"Mother of Christ!" Pugsley exclaimed. "People actually read books that long?"

"They will if they're good."

"Are there any ... more popular books on your list?"

"You mean bestsellers?" Howard said. "Yes, a few. There's *The Client*, Grisham's latest, and *The Bridges of Madison County*, which was uber-popular. It wasn't my style, to be honest, but a lot of people loved it. And if you're into the *Outlander* series, you'd enjoy *Voyager*, Diana Gabaldon's latest instalment."

There was a brief silence while Pugsley digested what Howard had told him. "What about … *Private Parts*?"

"The Howard Stern book?" Howard asked, startled.

"Best book I read all year," Pugsley said.

"I wasn't considering it," Howard said carefully, "but since you liked it so much, I'll give it more thought."

"Good," Pugsley said. Howard was clearly a brilliant hire, he thought. A suitable boy, you might say, chuckling at his own jest. God, he loved his job.

Twenty

OTTAWA, OCTOBER 2006

For three days, Norman Pugsley had been searching fruitlessly for retired auditor and Jenny Birchmount murder suspect Günter Grunwald. He'd already placed calls to 54 Grunwalds in Canada and 112 Grunwalds in Florida without finding a single one named Günter, or anyone who even knew a Grunwald named Günter. He was sick of it. Grunwalded out.

It shouldn't be this difficult, he thought wearily. Grunwald was a relatively uncommon name in North America. Yet Günter's whereabouts remained a maddening mystery.

He had managed to track down someone who'd worked with Grunwald in the Office of the Auditor General who told him his former colleague was a misanthrope who routinely took winter vacations in the southern United States. While that didn't mean he was living there now, at least it was a lead.

Pugsley tossed his cordless phone on the dining room table and rose sluggishly to his feet. He was flagging and needed a boost. The situation called for beer, he told himself. He opened his fridge, extracted a frosty Molson Export, twisted off the cap and took a long, satisfying swallow. It was his fifth beer in the past three days – well above his recommended limit – but he reasoned that was justified under the trying circumstances.

"Where the hell are you, Günter Grunwald?" he asked the empty room. Unsurprisingly, there was no response.

If Grunwald had moved to a warm-weather U.S. state, Pugsley knew the likeliest places were Florida, California, Texas or Arizona. He'd struck out on Florida, at least so far. California and Texas were populous states that could harbour hundreds, if not thousands, of Grunwalds. Searching for Günter in those states would be a massive undertaking – one Pugsley was eager to avoid if possible.

That left Arizona, a state popular with Canadian retirees but one, he hoped, with a manageable Grunwaldian cohort. He resolved to look there next.

After draining his beer, Pugsley called up Arizona's online telephone directory. He looked first for Grunwalds precisely named Günter. Finding none, he phoned three whose first initial was G. Two Grahams and a Gerry. Sighing, he picked up his phone and began calling the remaining 43 Grunwalds in the directory.

At times, nobody answered, and he made a note to call again. More often, though, a person named Grunwald picked up the phone – just not the right Grunwald. It was beginning to look like another wasted day. Then everything changed in a heartbeat.

"Can I please speak to Günter Grunwald?" Pugsley said mechanically after placing his 37th call of the day.

"Speaking."

Pugsley wasn't sure he'd heard correctly.

"Sorry, are you Günter Grunwald?"

"*Speaking*," the man repeated more forcefully, a note of irritation creeping into his voice.

"Formerly of Ottawa?"

"Who the hell are *you*?" snapped the man claiming to be Günter Grunwald. "And what do you want?"

Now fully alert, Pugsley introduced himself and explained that he was calling from the Ottawa *Daily Advocate*.

"That rag," Grunwald sneered. "If you're trying to sell me a subscription..."

"No, nothing like that," Pugsley interrupted. "I'm actually working on a story about the murder of an Ottawa prostitute named Jenny Birchmount in 1985."

After a brief silence, Grunwald asked, "What's that got to do with me?"

"I've learned that you were on a police list of suspects," Pugsley replied. *Might as well hit him with it and see how he reacts.*

Another pause. "First I've heard of it," Grunwald said, a touch of exasperation in his voice. "The police interviewed me, but they never said I was a suspect."

"What *did* they say?"

"Apparently the young woman's killer drove a car like mine. They wanted to know where I was when she was killed."

"And where *were* you?"

"It was more than 20 years ago," Grunwald said gruffly. "I can't remember now what I told them. Why does it matter? You don't think I …" His voice trailed off.

"Did you?"

"Did I what?"

"Kill Jenny Birchmount?"

"Jesus! Is that what you think?"

"I honestly don't know what to think, Günter."

"For the love of God," Grunwald sputtered, "I'm a retired auditor, not some psycho killer. Look here, Mr. Puggins … Pug ... whatever your name is. I've got stage-four cancer and likely have only a few months to live. I just want to be left alone to enjoy the time I have left. The last thing I need is some bloody reporter stirring up unpleasant old memories."

"Then tell me where you were when Jenny was murdered," Pugsley pressed.

"I already told you, I can't ...." Grunwald made an odd, strangled sound – half-moan, half-sob – and the line went dead.

●●●

"I can't believe you found him!" Fawzia Hassan exclaimed as Norman Pugsley cautiously sipped from a mug of hot mint tea a day later in her apartment. He'd have asked for a beer, but as he'd learned months ago, Hassan wasn't a drinker. So he'd reluctantly accepted her offer of tea, a beverage that had rarely passed his lips in his 64 years.

"It wasn't easy," Pugsley acknowledged. "It felt like I called every Grunwald in North America. After all that, though, I'm not sure we're much farther ahead. He didn't have an alibi – not one he could remember, anyway – so he remains a suspect. But I'm still having trouble with the concept of a killer auditor."

"Yes," Hassan agreed, "there is some cognitive dissonance there, for sure."

Pugsley had another thought. "You haven't by chance found out who offered the $50,000 reward in Jenny's case?" he asked.

"Afraid not. I've asked my police sources about that several times, but they keep telling me the person wants to remain anonymous."

"Too bad. My gut tells me it might help us figure things out if we knew," Pugsley said. "What about the two dead suspects? Have you learned anything about them?"

"I've had some success," she said. "I wasn't able to find the widow of the lawyer, Bradley Gibson, but I did track down Laura Hendricks, the woman he was supposedly …" Hassan faltered.

"Having relations with?" Pugsley supplied, delicately.

"Yes."

"And what did she say?" he asked, gingerly ingesting a microscopic sip of tea.

"She said she still has nightmares about her husband shooting poor Bradley. That's what she called him, 'poor Bradley.' "

"So, they were on a first-name basis?"

"To put it mildly. She was infatuated with him, and would happily have slept with him, I think, but he wouldn't do it."

"Why not? Was he gay or what?"

Hassan shook her head. "He told her he didn't think an intimate relationship with a client was appropriate."

"Huh. So, the poor bastard was killed for something he didn't even do."

"Just more proof that life isn't fair," Hassan observed.

Pugsley stared at the young reporter. "How old are you again?"

"I'm 25."

"And you've already figured that out? I'm impressed. It took me until I was in my 40s."

"Well," Hassan noted, pointedly but not unkindly, "I suspect that's a lesson you learn at a younger age if you're from an immigrant family."

"Yeah," Pugsley conceded. "Anyway, it doesn't sound as if poor Bradley was the sex fiend we thought he might be."

"No. According to Laura, he was anything but. He had a wife and a couple of kids and from everything she observed, he was devoted to them."

"Almost sounds too good to be true," Pugsley mused. "But for now, based on what we know, I think we should eliminate him as a suspect." Briefly forgetting he was drinking tea, not beer, he chugged a mouthful of the steaming beverage, which traced a fiery passage down his esophagus.

Taking a large gulp of air to compensate, Pugsley managed to ask Hassan to fill him in on what she'd learned about the other deceased suspect, Laurent Dupont, the luckless dentist dispatched by an enraged hippopotamus.

"I spoke to his son, Louis. It's been five years, but he still seemed traumatized by the bizarre manner of his father's death. When he was telling me about it, he started sobbing."

"For real? They weren't crocodile tears?" Pugsley couldn't resist the wordplay. *Christ, I sound just like Jack Clifford*, he thought.

Hassan's brow furrowed. "If you're trying to make a joke, it's not very funny, not to mention grossly insensitive," she said.

Pugsley scrubbed the levity from his face. "You're right. I'm sorry. That was in very poor taste," he grovelled, reminded yet again that the irreverent humour that once flowed like mother's milk through newsrooms was no longer tolerated. How he missed those days!

"Let's move on," Hassan said. "I told his son the police once thought his father was a leading suspect in the murder of Jenny Birchmount. To my surprise, he was aware of that. He remembers the detectives coming to the house and grilling his dad for hours. Naturally, his father swore he was innocent, but it was a tense time for the family."

"The cops really must have thought he could be their man," Pugsley said.

"So it appears. But in the end, nothing came of it. He wasn't cleared but he wasn't charged, either. The whole thing just faded away."

"Did you ask the son … Louis, is it?" Hassan nodded. "Did you ask Louis whether there was anything unusual about his father's behaviour?"

"I did. He told me that dentists, as a profession, are much more prone to depression and suicide than the general population. His father wasn't immune to that. He was withdrawn, and his behaviour was sometimes erratic."

Pugsley considered this information for a moment. "Did that cause difficulties in the marriage?"

"Apparently. Louis said his parents often argued, and once the kids were grown, the couple separated."

"When did that happen?"

"In the mid-90s sometime."

"Long after Jenny was killed," Pugsley said. "Even so, if his marriage was rocky, Dupont might have looked for comfort in the arms of … sex workers."

"You think the late Laurent Dupont could be Jenny's killer?"

"He's near the top of the list, in my mind," said Pugsley. "Right up there with Jack frickin' Clifford."

●●●

"You sly dog!" Beauregard Fisher grinned. "I knew there was something happening when I saw the two of you together at that bloody Rape Crisis Centre benefit."

Pugsley had invited Fisher out for dinner, planning to inquire discreetly about the state of his marriage to Deirdre, as he had promised Renata. He knew it was a touchy subject, calling for tact and sensitivity, neither of which were his strengths. He decided to circle around the subject, approach it indirectly. The best way to do that, he reasoned, was to soften him up by telling his old friend about his own budding romance with Richter.

"The strange thing is, I couldn't stand the woman when she was my boss at the *Advocate*," Pugsley said, taking a bite of salmon. Fisher had nixed his proposed pizza dinner on health grounds, so they'd gone instead to a seafood restaurant that passed nutritional muster. "I guess that changed when she phoned the hotel in Greece while I was having a heart attack and more or less saved my life."

"It's hard to hate someone who does that," Fisher agreed.

"It started with a few restaurant meals," Pugsley continued. "Can't say I enjoyed the weird food. But I'd just retired and was still recovering. I craved human contact, and for some reason, she was willing. Things progressed from there. I'll admit, I didn't see it coming." Pugsley stabbed another piece of salmon and shovelled it into his mouth. "Guess we're like the characters in that old movie, *The Odd Couple*."

"Except Jack Lemmon and Walter Matthau were both guys," Fisher pointed out. "Next thing you know, she's inviting you to Mont-Tremblant for a dirty weekend."

Pugsley pursed his lips. "I wouldn't call it a dirty weekend exactly. She'd gone camping with me in Algonquin Park and I promised I'd go to her favourite spot in return."

"Let's cut to the chase," Fisher said, leaning in. "How was the sex?"

The sex had been good. Very good, in fact. But Pugsley was old-fashioned enough to think it was an inappropriate subject for discussion. It clearly would be disrespectful of Renata. At the same time, he recognized that Fisher's question, if parried properly, might provide an opening to probe the state of his friend's marriage.

"It wouldn't be gentlemanly of me to answer that question, Beau," Pugsley demurred. "Let's just say I have no complaints and leave it at that." He paused, searching for just the right words. "What about you and Deirdre? Everything … copacetic?"

The smile that had been on Fisher's lips faded. "You know how it is. We've been married 48 years. It's hard to keep the spark alive."

"I did notice a bit of tension between the two of you at the benefit," Pugsley said. "Nothing serious, I hope."

Fisher gazed into the middle distance before responding. "I'll be honest, Norm. Things aren't great. The goddamn Rape Crisis Centre has messed with Deirdre's mind. That's what I think, anyway."

"What do you mean?"

"It seems to have warped her view of men. She hears so many stories about abuse – horrible stories. It seems to have convinced her that many men are awful human beings, maybe even me. We used to mate like rabbits. Now, she never seems to want it. I have to plead and cajole to get anything. Even then, it feels as if she's just going through the motions."

"I can understand how working with rape victims could sour Deirdre's view," Pugsley said, "but I'd be surprised if she felt that way about you. You haven't done anything to piss her off, have you?"

Fisher heaved a sigh and shook his head. "To tell the truth, I don't know what pisses Deirdre off anymore."

"But you haven't, I dunno, had an affair or anything, have you?" Pugsley persisted.

Fisher's eyebrows shot up as if he'd stuck a finger in a light socket. "I'm 71 years old. I'm not going to risk everything at this stage of my life for a fling with another woman."

"I couldn't imagine you'd be unfaithful to Deirdre." Pugsley paused. "But you're still a healthy male. People like you and me, sure, we're getting on in years, but we still have urges, right? It's not like we're dead from the waist down."

Fisher gave Pugsley a sideways glance but said nothing.

"I don't know about you, Beau, but if I'm feeling … restless … I sometimes find relief, if you know what I mean, in a little porn. God knows, there's plenty to choose from these days," Pugsley ventured. Fisher looked uneasy, so he added: "I hope I haven't shocked you."

"I'm a doctor, Norm. It takes a lot to shock me," Fisher replied. "Porn's not my thing, but whatever turns you on, I guess."

"So, you're living like a monk? That's what you're telling me?"

Fisher shook his head. "You and I are friends, Norm, but should we really be talking about this?" he asked, just as his pager beeped. "Sorry, I need to look at this," he said, pulling the device from his pocket and scanning the text message.

"Shit. I'm afraid I have to go, Norm. Emergency at the hospital." He pulled out his wallet and extracted $100. "Can I give you this for my dinner?"

"No way," Pugsley said, waving off the proffered cash. "This is my treat."

"You sure? Thanks, pal." With that, Fisher rose and hustled out of the restaurant.

Twenty-one

OTTAWA, 2004

Managing editor Norman Pugsley glared balefully at the television in his *Daily Advocate* office. The Blue Jays were losing to the Yankees – again. It had been a trying season for his favourite baseball team, which was languishing near the bottom of the American League East standings.

The Blue Jays' struggles only amplified Pugsley's sense of grievance with a world that increasingly seemed aligned against him. For most of his 11 years as managing editor, he'd been reasonably content, even happy now and then. But that was before *she* arrived.

He preferred to use the third-person pronoun when referring to Renata Richter, the unhinged woman the paper's normally sensible publisher, Reid Hartley, had inexplicably plucked from academia a year earlier and installed as editor-in-chief.

Not only was Richter inept, unqualified, and quite possibly insane, but Pugsley had fully expected *he* would ascend to the top job when former editor James Reynolds retired in early 2003. He was, after all, the logical successor. He'd been managing editor since 1993 and, he liked to think, the paper had prospered on his watch.

It was he who'd hired the precocious Dylan Mosely fresh out of journalism school. Two years later, Mosely's beautifully crafted feature on poverty in the rural Ottawa Valley had won the *Advocate*'s first National Newspaper Award in a dozen years. Admittedly, there'd been no other wins, but the paper had snagged nominations almost every year.

Kimberly Taylor, the *Advocate*'s whip-smart medical reporter, was another Pugsley discovery. True, it was her glamorous looks that first attracted him, but somehow he'd known she'd be a brilliant reporter, or so he told himself.

The influx of talent he'd overseen had paid dividends, at least for a while. The paper's circulation had edged up in the late 1990s, though more recently it was eroding at an alarming rate. It was that decline Hartley cited when he informed Pugsley of Richter's hiring.

"Terrific news, Norm," the publisher had told him, in a discussion that still rankled a year later. "I've convinced Renata Richter to take a leave of absence from Harvard to become our new editor. She's just what we need to reverse our readership decline."

Pugsley was gobsmacked, both by the news and by Hartley's evident belief that he would celebrate it.

"Christ on a bicycle!" he blurted, scarlet-faced. "Does she know the first fucking thing about running a newspaper?"

That earned a startled frown from Hartley. "She'll have a steep learning curve, I imagine, but the woman is brilliant. With an experienced number two like you, I'm sure she'll pick it up quickly."

"That's just it, Reid. I've paid my dues. Why not appoint *me* as editor?"

A look of exasperation flitted across Hartley's usually unperturbable features. "To be blunt," he said, looking his managing editor squarely in the face, "I don't think you have the royal jelly. Don't get me wrong. You're a fine newsman, Norm. But you're too traditional. Our paper is in trouble. The whole damn newspaper industry is in trouble. Our readers are dying off or abandoning us and we're bleeding advertising. We need a new approach, fresh ideas. We can't keep doing the same old same old. It's not working."

Pugsley hadn't known how to respond to that. Royal jelly? What did *that* mean? Why wouldn't the publisher value someone with his experience and record of accomplishment? And even more puzzling, why would he think an ivory-tower egghead with zero newspaper experience would do a better job?

"It's because she's a woman, isn't it?" he grumbled, plunging recklessly into treacherous waters. "An old white guy like me doesn't stand a chance these days."

"That has nothing to do with it," Hartley snapped. "This paper is long overdue for a female editor, but I picked Renata for her brains, not her gender. She's creative, she's dynamic and she'll shake things up around here. That's what we need. That's what I want."

"And you don't think I could do that?" Pugsley pressed.

"You've been doing things the same way for 40 years. You're not going to change now."

It was hopeless. Pugsley could see that. Hartley's mind was made up. He stomped out of the publisher's office and headed straight for the newsroom, where he button-holed news editor Ryan Young, one of his most faithful acolytes.

"Young," he growled, "I need a drink. A lot of drinks. Join me, will ya?"

"Sure. What's the occasion?"

"Not a happy one," he said glumly. "I have big sorrows right now. You need to help me drown them."

•••

"Explain this to me like I'm a five-year-old, Norman," Renata Richter began, with a patient smile. "Why do we devote so many of our resources to coverage of crime and courts?"

A year into Richter's editorship of the *Advocate*, Pugsley had come to expect strange questions. But wondering why the paper covered cops and courts? That was off the Richter Scale of Crazy. (Pugsley had coined the smart-ass phrase in response to the flakiness of his boss's ideas.)

"I don't expect you to know this, Renata, given your academic background," he mansplained, barely concealing his disdain, "but crime and cop stories are popular with our readers. Very, very popular. They always get some of the highest readership in our surveys."

"Yes, but isn't that a sad commentary on human nature?" Richter said with her typical annoying obtuseness. "I mean, why do people want to read about the misfortunes of others? It's voyeuristic and pathetic. Shouldn't we as journalists aim higher than that?"

We as journalists. Coming from Richter, the words grated. Pugsley drew a deep breath, trying to maintain his composure in the face of the woman's boundless ignorance.

"Look here, Renata," he said. "It's not our job to judge our readers.

People read crime and court stories for all sorts of reasons. They want to know if their city is safe, whether the cops are protecting them and if the courts are holding the bad guys accountable. They look to us to tell them that, which is a good thing."

Richter waved a hand dismissively. "I know all that, Norman. I wasn't suggesting that we have no crime and court coverage at all. But do we need so much of it?" She rummaged through some papers on her desk until she found the sheet she was searching for.

"It says here," she said, brandishing the document, "we have five reporters covering police and three covering courts. That's nearly 20 per cent of our reporting staff. And the stories they write dominate our front page. We look like a tabloid instead of a serious newspaper."

"What are you suggesting?" Pugsley asked defensively. "That we should bury stories like that in the back of the bus?"

"What I'm suggesting," Richter said with exaggerated patience, as if Pugsley were the five-year-old in the room, "is that we redeploy some of the reporters now covering crime and courts and use them instead for more in-depth journalism."

"Like what? Give me some examples."

"More special sections on international topics, for one," Richter said.

Pugsley groaned. Richter had been obsessed with special sections from the moment she'd arrived at the paper. Most were arcane and impenetrable, in his opinion, a waste of resources.

"You think people would rather read about the roots of clan warfare in some African shithole than a murder in their own city?"

"If we choose the right topics and write about them intelligently, our readers will thank us and take us more seriously," she responded.

"All right, all right," Pugsley sputtered. "I'll shift one police reporter and one court reporter to general assignment."

"Let's make it two police and two court reporters, Norman. This is no time for half-measures. Also, let's take a hard look at some of our other newsroom talent to see if we can't deploy them better. Maybe some of the forgotten people on the night desk could do other things. Or our travel editor … what's his name again?"

"You mean Bliss Browning?" Pugsley said, summoning up the name of an employee he'd once had to discipline for sloppy work.

"Yes, that's him. I have a feeling he can do a lot more for us."

Pugsley gave a minuscule nod, mentally assigning the encounter a robust 7.8 on the Richter Scale of Crazy.

•••

Pugsley had to admit it: since Richter's arrival, his morale had cratered. Missing out on the top job had been a hard blow, not dissimilar to his unjust banishment to the night desk nearly two decades earlier. The fact that Richter was so culturally unsuited to traditional newspaper work only salted the wound.

He'd always been an early riser, eager to meet the day and its challenges. Now he lingered sluggishly in bed, unable to summon the motivation to face another vexing shift at the office. He straggled in, usually a few minutes late, and spent much of his day scanning his laptop for Blue Jays stories or watching sports highlights on his office TV.

When he could no longer avoid work, he was cranky and ill tempered, snapping at underlings whose mere presence seemed to annoy him. As ever, travel editor Bliss Browning was a favourite target, but more and more, his co-workers avoided him, which suited him just fine.

With only an empty house to return to at the end of the day, he regularly stopped by the Press Club for a drink or five after work, often with Ryan Young in tow. Young had been reluctant at first, protesting that his wife expected him home for dinner. But Pugsley, who'd promoted Young to news editor two years earlier, leaned on him until he agreed. The parallels with Rob Sutherland's behaviour were obvious even to him, but he brushed that aside.

After a beer or two to loosen their tongues, their Press Club talk usually shifted to Renata Richter and her latest nonsensical ideas for the newspaper.

"You won't believe what she said today," Pugsley told Young one evening, rolling his eyes. "She wants to give Harrison Howard his own weekly section for books – 16 pages no less!"

"What the fuck?" Young said, playing his lackey role to perfection. "Is she insane?"

"Wait, there's more," Pugsley said, warming to his rant, a cold beer in hand. "She doesn't want to review the popular books our readers enjoy – too 'downscale,' she says. She wants to focus on history books, poetry and what she calls literary fiction."

"She *is* insane," Young chimed in on cue.

Pugsley drained his glass. "The incredible thing is the publisher is on-side with her plan. He thinks it's brilliant, believe it or not."

"Insane," Young chanted.

Pugsley signalled the barman for another beer. "Ya know, Young," he said, "seems like I spend my days trying to skate Richter into the boards when she has one of her brainwaves."

"Thank God. I'd hate to think where we'd be without you," said Young, hurdling over the line into outright obsequiousness.

Pugsley grunted. "I know, but it's not very rewarding, know what I'm saying? I should be running this bloody newspaper, not playing defence against a goddamn rookie who shouldn't even be in the league."

"Nice metaphor," Young noted, well beyond shame.

"There are days when I think I should just quit and let this ship sink," Pugsley said gloomily, switching metaphorical gears.

"Christ, no, don't do that, Norm," Young said, his face full of alarm. "Think of all the people in the newsroom who count on you to be a voice of sanity." *Think of me*, Young thought, but did not say.

"Yeah, you're right. The paper needs me, even if Reid Hartley doesn't know it, the bastard."

Pugsley yawned and checked his watch. "Getting late. Let's call it a night. Day game tomorrow between the Jays and the damn Yankees," he told Young. "Pop by my office and watch a few innings with me."

"Wouldn't miss it," Young said.

Part Three
Pugsley's Progress

Twenty-two

OTTAWA, NOVEMBER 2006

Breakfast coffee in hand, Pugsley sat at his kitchen table, mulling his recent dinner conversation with Beauregard Fisher about the state of the doctor's marriage to Deirdre. He didn't know what to make of the news that their 48-year union might be in trouble. Why was this happening? He had no answers, only questions.

The telephone jangled, interrupting his brooding thoughts.

"Are you sitting down, Norm? Because I think you need to." Fawzia was on the phone, breathless and speaking too quickly. "I have amazing news. The Ottawa police have just charged Liberal Senator James Brody with sexual assault!"

What! Her words were so dumbfounding that, at first, Pugsley couldn't believe he'd heard correctly. His pounding heart signalled it had no such doubts.

"Say again?" he croaked.

"Senator Brody has been charged with sexual assault," she repeated, more slowly this time. "He's accused of assaulting half a dozen women between 1988 and 2003. He's denying it, of course, but the police say there may be more victims and are encouraging anyone with further information to come forward."

"Christ!" Pugsley whispered.

Fawzia cleared her throat. "I never told you this, but when I was first researching the Jenny Birchmount case, I read that 1985 story you wrote about Brody on our library's microfilm. I saw the retraction and apology, too."

There was silence for a few seconds.

"Then I guess you know that wasn't my finest hour," Pugsley said.

"I can only imagine what you must have gone through," she said. "I even wondered whether you'd be willing to help me. That's why I called as soon as I heard that Brody had been charged. The police aren't releasing many details, other than that the victims ranged in age from 18 to 25 at the time of the alleged assaults. As usual in these cases, the women aren't being identified." She paused before continuing. "I just got off the phone with one of my police sources. She told me something else, but I had to promise I wouldn't report it until it comes up in court."

"What?" Pugsley asked.

"OK, here it is: One of the victims alleges that Brody choked her while they were having sex. Apparently, it's called erotic asphyxiation." Fawzia's disgust was audible over the phone. "Some people get their kicks from it, I understand, but the victim told police she feared for her life."

Pugsley felt his heart literally skip a beat. *Erotic asphyxiation. Jenny had been strangled. Was it possible that James Brody had killed Jenny Birchmount after all?*

Fawzia continued. "It looks like we might have a new – or rather, old – suspect in the Birchmount case," she said.

Pugsley slumped in his kitchen chair. This wasn't possible. Everyone back in 1985 – police, politicians, the senator – had denied it. Brody had successfully sued the newspaper over it. A tempest of emotions: astonishment, confusion, anger, even horror flooded over him. But his instinctive reaction was denial. *You've been here before, Norm. It can't be the case. Don't be an idiot.*

"Norm?" Fawzia's voice on the phone cut through the trance clouding his faculties. "What do you think?"

"I'm not sure what to think," he replied, still dazed. "The last time I worked on a story about James Brody, it ruined lives."

Then he straightened up in his chair. "These charges raise questions we can't ignore. I had a feeling Brody was a slimeball the first time I met him – on a canoe trip in the Northwest Territories, believe it or not. This only confirms that. Has the Liberal party said anything?"

"I've put out some calls," Fawzia said. "Not surprisingly, they haven't returned them. But the Harper government is already urging the Senate to suspend Brody until his case has been heard."

Pugsley drew a deep breath and spoke with what he hoped the young reporter would interpret as a resolute voice. "We need to pursue this. Based on what you've told me, James Brody could well be Jenny's killer. We can't let it drop."

"No," Fawzia agreed. "I'll go back to my sources and see if anyone will tell me whether they now consider Brody a suspect in our cold case. Why don't you have a word with Detective Lachance? Then let's get together and compare notes."

"Right, boss," Pugsley said, his legs still wobbly. "I'm on it. We're going to open some old wounds."

•••

That same afternoon, Pugsley emailed Bernard Lachance, asking if he had a few minutes to talk. The detective called back within the hour.

"Thanks Bernie. Sorry for the short notice," Pugsley said.

"I live in a world of short notice," said Lachance. "What can I do for you, Norm?"

"I'm calling about the charges announced today involving Senator Brody," Pugsley said.

There was a brief silence on the other end of the line. "I'm sorry, Norm, but I'm not on that case. You probably know as much as I do."

"That's not the case I'm interested in," Pugsley said.

"OK, now I'm confused. What *are* you calling about, then?"

"The Jenny Birchmount case."

This time the silence lasted nearly10 seconds before Lachance spoke. "You're not … you don't mean … Jesus, Norm! Are you suggesting …?"

"Yes."

"Fuck me sideways," Lachance gasped. "Are you insane?"

"Probably. But I need to know. In light of these new charges, will the cops investigate Brody for the murder of Jenny Birchmount?"

"Tabarnac!" Lachance muttered, lapsing into French. "You know better than anyone what happened the last time Brody's name was linked to that murder. Do you really want an encore?"

"Not an encore," Pugsley said. "A do-over of the investigation."

"Look, Norm. Anything's possible, but I wouldn't hold your breath. Jenny Birchmount was killed a long time ago. I worked on that case, and as far as I can recall, we never had any evidence linking her to Senator Brody," Lachance said. "This is dangerous, dangerous territory for you."

"Brody would have been in his late 40s when Jenny died – the age of her suspected killer," Pugsley said, brushing aside Lachance's concerns. "Did he drive a black luxury car too? It wouldn't surprise me, given his position."

"We checked out hundreds of men who fit that profile," Lachance reminded him. "I don't think Brody was one of them, though I could be wrong."

"Could you find out?"

"At this late date, probably not. You've got to remember, Norm, Brody was a senator in 1985. A powerful and respected man. Cops don't usually go after people like that for murder."

"He's *still* a senator," Pugsley pointed out, "and he's just been charged with sexually assaulting multiple women. There's every reason to investigate him now."

There was a sigh on the other end of the phone line. "I'll talk to my bosses," Lachance said. "But like I told you, don't hold your breath."

•••

The following day, Pugsley rose before the sun, prepared a simple breakfast of cornflakes, milk and sliced bananas, fired up his Ford Explorer and set out for the offices of the *Daily Advocate* in downtown Ottawa.

He hadn't set foot in the place since his retirement 13 months earlier, but he wanted to meet with Fawzia Hassan and figure out what to do about Senator James Brody.

The rush-hour traffic on Highway 417 was much as he remembered it from his working days: jammed with vehicles moving at the pace of a glacier in winter. The only positive was that it gave him ample time to think about what he should say to Fawzia.

Most of the paper's reporters and editors hadn't started their shifts when he arrived, so there was none of the hubbub that had greeted him after his return from Greece. He took a moment to scan the newsroom that had been his second home for 37 years. On the surface, it was as familiar as a favourite sweater, yet something felt different, as if somehow he no longer belonged there.

Pugsley knew Fawzia worked an early shift. When he spotted her, she was on the phone at her desk, so he hung back for a couple of minutes. She looked surprised when he approached.

"Norm! You're here!"

"I wanted to tell you about my conversation with Bernie Lachance and find out if you'd learned anything more from your sources," he said. "Is this a bad time?"

"I'm just finishing my morning cop checks," she said. "I won't be long. Pull up a chair."

After two more calls to area police services elicited the usual "nothing happening here" response, she hung up and turned to him.

"Why don't you tell me what you heard from Lachance first," she suggested.

"He wasn't very encouraging," Pugsley said. "After I badgered him a bit, he agreed to raise the idea of investigating Brody for Jenny's murder with his bosses. He didn't hold out much hope they'd actually do it, though."

"That's not quite the message I got," Fawzia said. "My source told me Brody's charges might prompt police to take a closer look at him with respect to Jenny. She also told me Brody wasn't one of the men police checked out after Jenny's death."

"He didn't own a black car?" Pugsley said.

"She didn't know. But she told me they may have given him a pass because he was a senator."

"Yeah, Lachance said something like that, too," Pugsley said. "But times change. I think we need to keep pushing the cops on this. And let's try to speak to people in Brody's circle, see if these new charges have loosened any tongues."

Fawzia nodded. "What about Renata?" she said. "Shouldn't we brief her on what we're doing?"

Pugsley blanched. "This whole thing went off the rails last time because

I brought up Brody's name with my editors prematurely. We don't have any evidence, just our suspicions based on the way Jenny died and what we know of Brody's character and the charges. Let's wait until we have more."

Twenty-three

OTTAWA, DECEMBER 2006

There was a hint of snow in the air when Norman Pugsley joined a growing crowd, predominantly of women, gathering in Minto Park to mark a black day in Canada's history. It was December 6, the anniversary of the 1989 massacre at Montreal's École Polytechnique, the day a man with a toxic hatred for feminists shot and killed 14 women at the school. In memory of that horrific event, vigils had been held in Ottawa and other Canadian cities every year since.

Pugsley had attended none of the previous vigils. Yes, he'd been sickened by the gunman's murderous rampage. But something – perhaps the tough-guy persona he'd taken on that disguised any feelings of empathy– had always kept him away.

Now he was at the Ottawa Women's Monument, erected in 1992 in response to the Montreal Massacre and, more broadly, all violence against women. Even he couldn't fully explain why he was present. Partly it was because he wanted to talk to Deirdre Fisher, and he was pretty sure she'd be present. But it wasn't only that. Jenny Birchmount had something to do with it, along with the stunning thought that they might be closer to catching her killer. So did Renata Richter if he were being honest. Getting to know her since Greece – *really* getting to know her – was changing him in unexpected ways, leading him to question his stereotypical view of women. At times, he even wondered if he might be turning into the type of person he used to ridicule. A SNAM: a sensitive new-age male.

Feeling a bit like an interloper, Pugsley hung back on the edge of the crowd, taking in the scene. Many vigil participants held candles and he berated himself for failing to bring one. A young woman approached and offered him hers.

"Don't *you* need it?" he asked.

She smiled. "We need more men to raise a light against the darkness. Will you do that?"

"Of course," he said, accepting the candle and shuffling forward into the silent sea of women and men, faces illuminated by flickering light. He was struck by the connection he felt to these people, gathered in the early December gloom. For someone who'd always held himself apart, it was a new and somewhat disconcerting experience.

When the speeches started, he listened intently, swept along by the passionate calls for change. He thought about Jenny Birchmount and the ravenous men – including, perhaps, Senator James Brody – who'd used her without a thought to the consequences. He thought about his daughter, Barbara, who had become a disconnected voice on the telephone every few months. His eyes misted and he wiped them with the back of a hand.

When the speeches were over and the vigil was winding down, many seemed reluctant to leave. Pugsley lingered as well, regaining his composure. Though he'd expected she would be there, he was startled when Deirdre suddenly appeared at his side.

"Norman Pugsley! What brings you here? Are you covering this for the newspaper?" she asked. "I thought you were retired."

"No," he replied. "I just thought it was time for me to attend one of these vigils."

She raised an eyebrow. "That's good. Why now?"

He hesitated. "Let's just say I'm pissed at the way a lot of men treat women. We need to clean up our act."

Deirdre studied him. "You *are* Norman Pugsley, aren't you? Not some imposter?"

"Believe it or not, it's really me," Pugsley smiled, adding: "Do you have time for a coffee?"

She looked at her watch. "I've got about an hour."

They walked the few short blocks to a coffee bar on Elgin Street. Pugsley ordered a decaf skim milk latte for her and a caffe Americano for himself. They found an empty table in a corner and settled in.

"So, Norm," Deirdre said, taking a sip of her latte, "how are things?"

"I actually have a question," he said. "I hope you won't be offended."

"Try me."

He took a deep breath. "I had dinner with Beau a few weeks ago and he told me the two of you are having … some problems."

She snorted. "Oh, he told you that, did he? What else did my husband say?"

Pugsley shifted uncomfortably. "He seems to think your work with sexually abused women has somehow altered your view of men. For the worse," he added, in case that was unclear.

A look of irritation flashed over Deirdre Fisher's face. "Did he try to tell you our marriage is on the rocks because I think all men are beasts and rapists?"

"Something like that," he acknowledged.

A mirthless laugh. "He wouldn't tell you the real reason – of course not."

"What do you mean?"

She hesitated. "Frankly, it's none of your business," she said. "But … what the hell, you and Beau are friends, so: A couple of months ago, my so-called husband was caught trying to solicit sex from an undercover policewoman posing as a street prostitute."

Pugsley heard the words but found himself struggling to process them. *Did Deirdre just say Beau was caught trying to solicit sex?*

"There must be some mistake," he blurted. This man was his doctor, his friend, a person he'd long admired. "How do you know that?"

"Well, I didn't hear it from Beau. He didn't say a word. One of the women who works at the Rape Crisis Centre has a good police contact. She told her about it, and she told me."

"My God," Pugsley whispered. "Did you ask *him* about it?"

"Of course."

"And what did he say?"

She shook her head. "He tried to tell me the police officer misunderstood what he'd said. That it was all a big mistake. He'd just offered her a ride home because she was alone."

"But …" Pugsley prompted.

"Eventually he admitted it. He called it a lapse of judgment in a moment of weakness. Said he was overworked. Swore he'd never done anything like it before. I want to believe that. I really do." She looked away for a moment. "Beau and I have been drifting apart for a long time. Maybe it's because we never had kids. Maybe something was missing as a result. I don't know … his work always seemed more important to him than I was. He was never home."

Pugsley was astonished. Beau and Deirdre had always struck him as a perfect couple. Until his recent conversation with Fisher, there'd been no hint of trouble in the marriage – not that he'd noticed, at least.

"What's going to happen to Beau?" he asked when he was again capable of speech. "Is he being charged?"

"To avoid charges, he's agreed to go to 'john school.' He and a bunch of other first-time offenders have to go through a program run by the police and Salvation Army that highlights the harms caused when men try to buy sex. It's supposed to educate them, so they don't do it again."

"I'm sure Beau will get the message," Pugsley said. "He won't make that mistake twice."

Deirdre looked at him, her expression defeated. Her eyes were filling with tears.

"I hope you're right, Norm," she said. "The thing is, I'm not sure I can forgive him."

Pugsley patted her arm but said nothing. There was nothing he could say.

Deirdre sighed and glanced at her watch. "I have to go," she said. "I didn't mean to mess up your friendship, but I suppose you should know. And," she added, "this off the record, OK? Nothing in the newspaper."

"I'm so sorry this is happening to you," he said, "but I want you to know I'm here for you."

That drew a wan smile. "I really don't know what that means. But never mind."

"Let me walk you to your car," he offered, extending an arm. They exchanged few words as they walked to her car, parked on a nearby street. It was, Pugsley noted, a jet-black Mercedes E-350 sedan.

"Nice car," he murmured, to break the silence.

"Yes. Beau has always loved his Mercs. They're all he's ever owned. Always black. He thinks that's classy."

•••

The morning after his disturbing conversation with Deirdre, Pugsley sent another email to Detective Lachance. "We need to talk – again," was all he wrote.

The seed of an idea had taken root. An idea so preposterous, so unimaginable, that he could scarcely acknowledge it. Was it possible that Beauregard Fisher had something to do with Jenny Birchmount's death?

Every fibre railed against the idea, but what he'd learned from Deirdre had shaken him. The news that Beau had been caught trying to solicit sex was troubling enough. But what if it wasn't an isolated act? What if it was part of a pattern of behaviour? Could he have been seeking out the company of prostitutes when Jenny was killed? It didn't fit with what he knew about Beau, but Pugsley couldn't dismiss the idea.

If Deirdre's throw-away comment was right, Beau had owned a black Mercedes at the time of Jenny's death. If he'd been cruising the ByWard Market for sex in the mid-1980s, perhaps his was the elusive black luxury car police were seeking.

When Lachance messaged that he was available, Pugsley quickly telephoned.

"I just found out that Beauregard Fisher, my family doctor, recently tried to solicit sex from an undercover cop. He's in john school now," Pugsley said.

Lachance let out a low whistle. "*Merde!* Didn't see that one coming. Isn't he a friend of yours?"

"Indeed. There's something else. Beau owned a black Mercedes when Jenny Birchmount was murdered."

Lachance said nothing for a moment. "What are you suggesting, Norm?"

"Just doing my due diligence. Was he one of the people you spoke to when you and your team were checking out the owners of black luxury cars?"

"Fuck me, Norm. I'm still trying to get you an answer about Senator Brody."

"I know. I want to know about him, too. But if you interviewed a prominent citizen like Beauregard Fisher, someone might remember. If you tell me you spoke to him and he wasn't a suspect, that's all I need to know. I can drop it."

"OK, Norm," Lachance said, "I'll see if anyone here remembers. I will say this, though: If we did check him out, he must have had a solid alibi. Otherwise, he'd be on our suspects list."

"And he wasn't?"

"Definitely not."

●●●

Pugsley met with Fawzia later that day.

"I have great difficulty believing Beau had anything to do with Jenny's death," he told her. "I've known the guy for decades. He's always been a Boy Scout."

Hassan nodded slowly, but Pugsley could tell something was troubling her. "You don't agree?" he asked.

"You're probably right," she said. "It's just that when it comes to sex, often it's the people who appear to be above suspicion who are the guilty ones. I mean, think about all the sex abuse scandals in the Catholic Church. The men molesting those boys were mostly priests – holy men. Until the stories started coming out, who would have believed that?"

"Fair point," Pugsley said. "Sex can make people do terrible things. But if Beau were capable of murder, I'd know that. Anyway, let's see what Lachance finds out. What about you, Fawzia? Anything to report?"

"Nothing new about Senator Brody," she said, "but I did learn something interesting yesterday about your friend Jack Clifford. It seems a former girlfriend lodged a complaint with Ottawa police in 1991, accusing him of sexual assault."

"That *is* interesting. What happened?"

"Apparently the police investigated but there wasn't enough evidence to lay charges. He denied it, and it was her word against his."

"Typical," Pugsley said, shaking his head. "Unless there are witnesses, the justice system rarely believes women who say a partner assaulted them – especially if the man's rich and powerful, like Clifford. I think that's a problem."

"Me too," Hassan agreed. "Can we do anything with this information?"

"We can dig further," Pugsley said. "At the very least, it reinforces my suspicion that Clifford might be capable of murder. I think I should pay him a surprise call and see what he has to say."

"OK," said Hassan. "But be careful."

Twenty-four

OTTAWA, DECEMBER 2006

Though he was wearing gloves and thick woollen socks, Pugsley's fingers and feet were numb with cold. He'd been on the sidewalk outside Jack Clifford's house on the Queen Elizabeth Driveway, one of the city's toniest addresses, for nearly an hour. It was a frigid mid-December morning and the wind chill had taken up residence in his extremities.

His plan seemed sound when he'd hatched it the previous evening: stake out Clifford's home before dawn and confront him about his former girlfriend's sexual assault complaint when he emerged. But with no sign of his quarry, his strategy seemed more ill-advised with every shivery second.

He removed a glove from one hand and blew on his frost-bitten fingers. The relief was fleeting – a few seconds of tepid thawing before the Arctic air reasserted its dominion over his digits.

Abandoning his fingers to their fate, Pugsley focused on his feet, stamping them to kick-start blood flow. When that didn't help, he tried brief bursts of rapid walking, accelerating at times to a sluggish jog.

So focused was he on his frozen feet that at first, he didn't notice Clifford emerge from his house, wrapped in furs, to embark on a lumbering promenade along the Rideau Canal. By the time he spotted him, Clifford was half a block away.

Pugsley set out in hot pursuit, though "hot" wasn't the right adjective under the circumstances. He hobbled after him until he calculated his quarry was within hailing distance.

"Jack!" he yelled. "Jack! Wait up!"

At first, it appeared Clifford, whose head was swaddled in a black balaclava topped with lime-green earmuffs, hadn't heard him. As Pugsley edged closer, still bellowing his name, he stopped, turned, and registered Pugsley moving towards him like an arthritic penguin.

"Norm Pugsley! What in the name of frosty foreskin are *you* doing here?" Clifford demanded, peering at him through the balaclava's narrow eye-slit. "And why are you walking like that?"

Pugsley limped forward until he was a few feet from Clifford. "Christ, Jack," he wheezed, puffing noticeably, "I can't feel my toes. It's a miracle I can walk at all."

"OK. But why are you chasing after me at" – Clifford checked his watch – "7:32 a.m. on the coldest morning of the season?"

"Believe me, I'd rather be at home, sipping coffee in front of a crackling fire," Pugsley said. "But I came into some information yesterday and I need to ask you about it."

Clifford's eyes narrowed. "Information? What information?" A wary expression flashed across his face. "This better not be about that hooker you think I murdered."

"No, it's about another woman."

"Who?"

"Your former girlfriend. The one who accused you of sexual assault in 1991."

"You mean … Trixie?"

"I don't know her name," Pugsley admitted, momentarily flustered. "But she made a formal complaint to the cops."

"Her name was Trixie," Clifford said, his scowl almost visible beneath the balaclava. "A stripper I dated a few times. We had some laughs, but she knew I had money and wanted more. When I told her no, she went to the cops with a bullshit story."

"Really?" Pugsley said, making no effort to disguise his skepticism. "The cops thought there was enough there to investigate."

"It wasn't much of an investigation. They could see she was just trying to shake me down," Clifford said.

To Pugsley, it seemed the police often dismissed allegations of sexual assault too easily. He was beginning to think it was time men started believing women.

Clifford's eyes hardened in their balaclava frames. "Why are you asking me about this now? It's ancient history."

Though Pugsley doubted Clifford's story, it had raised questions about the narrative playing in his head. If Clifford had sexually assaulted his girlfriend, it was easy to imagine him as Jenny's killer. But if, as he claimed, he'd been falsely accused, well, that was something else altogether.

"I dunno, Jack. Guess I just wanted to know if you were capable of … sexual violence."

"What's it to you?" Clifford demanded. He'd moved forward and was now just a stride away from Pugsley.

"It's just … dammit Jack … if you could do something like *that*, maybe Jenny Birchmount" – he could feel how clumsy his words were.

"Her again!" Clifford interrupted, eyes flashing. "So, you *still* think I killed the bitch?"

"I don't know," Pugsley said, still flustered. "But the police *did* think you were a leading suspect …"

"You don't learn, do you?" Clifford snarled. Without warning, he lashed out with a fist, striking Pugsley squarely on the jaw and knocking him to the ground. It took Pugsley a minute or so to recover from the blow. When he staggered to his feet, Jack Clifford was nowhere to be seen.

●●●

Pugsley was at home, nursing his swollen jaw with an icepack, when Lachance called later that day. "Still nothing to report about Senator Brody, but I have some news about Beauregard Fisher," he began. "One of my colleagues told me we did check him out at the time of the Birchmount homicide – and he had a solid alibi."

"That's terrific news," Pugsley said, a smile jousting with his damaged jaw for dominance. The relief he felt was overwhelming. The slim possibility that Beau had something to do with Jenny's death had been hanging over him like a menacing thundercloud. Now, the sun could emerge again.

"Bernie, what *was* his alibi?"

"His wife explained that he was with her. They went to see some movie called … let me check my notes … *Amadeus* or something."

"Never heard of it," Pugsley confessed. "But that's good, right? If his wife said he was with her, he's in the clear."

"Yeah, pretty much," Lachance said. "By the way, Norm. I also confirmed what you told me. Fisher *was* arrested for soliciting recently and is now in the john program."

"Good to hear it officially," Pugsley said. "I presume someone like Beau isn't a typical john school student."

Lachance snorted. "You'd be surprised. We've had lawyers, businessmen, politicians, church ministers – even a judge or two. Guys thinking with their dicks. When they get caught, they're desperate to keep it quiet. A few hours in john school isn't such a high price to pay."

"I guess not. Thanks, Bernie. You've been a big help."

"You know me. I live to serve."

•••

A couple of days later, his jaw still tender, Pugsley placed a call to Deirdre Fisher. She'd been understandably upset when they'd talked after the vigil, and it was time to see how she was doing. So far, he had avoided calling Beauregard Fisher.

"Deirdre, it's Norm," he said. "I've been worrying about you ever since our chat. Just checking in to make sure you're OK."

"Oh, that's thoughtful, Norm – and unexpected coming from you. I've been on a bit of an emotional roller-coaster, to be honest. Sometimes I think I'm fine, but then it hits me and I'm back in a dark place. I'll survive, one way or another."

"I'm so sorry you're going through this, Deirdre. Never thought I'd say this, but Beau has been a real prick. What was he thinking?"

"Who knows what makes men do things like that?" she replied. "When I'm feeling generous, I think maybe it's his job. People like Beau – skilled medical professionals – are always under pressure. They're almost like gods, with power over life and death. Perhaps they don't feel like they're worthy and they do something self-destructive in response." A brief, bitter laugh. "Listen to me. Sounds like psychology 101 claptrap, right?"

"A bit," Pugsley answered. "Beau has always seemed totally together to me, but one thing I've learned is that everyone has a hidden side, a part of them they don't want anyone else to see – not even their own family. Whatever it is, at some level, they feel ashamed."

"So," Deirdre asked hesitantly, "you think Beau's hidden side conceals an attraction to prostitutes?"

"No, no. More likely, it was just a lapse in judgment, like he told you." Pugsley paused, wondering whether he should share what he'd learned from Lachance. He decided he would. It was good news, after all.

"Deirdre, I think you know I've been working with Fawzia Hassan, the *Advocate*'s police reporter, on a story about an unsolved crime – the 1985 murder of a young prostitute named Jenny Birchmount."

"You mentioned it at the fundraiser, I think," she said.

"That's right. Anyway, one of the very few clues in the case is that her killer, who police think was in his 40s or 50s, was driving a black luxury car. The cops screened hundreds of cars that matched that description. So, when you told me Beau owned a black Mercedes at the time, well … I wondered if they'd checked on him, too."

There was an audible gasp on the phone line. "What are you implying?"

"Nothing. But my old reporter instincts kicked in. You know, never assume, always verify. I was relieved when they told me he had an ironclad alibi – that he'd been with you that night, watching a movie."

There was a long silence on the line. Pugsley briefly wondered if they'd been disconnected.

"Deirdre? Are you there? Are you all right?"

"Oh God, Norm. My God," she whispered. "Beau wasn't with me that night. I told the police he was, but I lied."

Now the silence was at Pugsley's end of the phone line. "You … lied?" he sputtered. "Why?"

"Beau told me he'd spent the evening at an underground casino. This was before casinos were legal, and he was afraid police would charge him if he told them where he'd really been."

"And you believed him?"

"I was scared. I didn't want Beau to face some sort of charges for a simple spin of a roulette wheel."

Pugsley's own mind was whirling. Could Beau really have been gambling illegally the night Jenny was killed? Or was there another, more sinister, possibility?

"You never thought he might be seeing prostitutes?'

"Never, never, never. We had a good sex life for most of our marriage, and he was a highly respected professional. Why would he do that?"

"I don't know," Pugsley said grimly. "Only he can answer that question. All I can do is ask."

"Or I can," she said. "God, I don't know what to do."

"Let me," Pugsley said. "Your marriage doesn't need the extra strain."

•••

The waiting room at Dr. Beauregard Fisher's medical office was nearly full when Pugsley arrived for his 4 p.m. appointment. He'd been able to book it on short notice by claiming that he'd suffered a dizzy spell. "You might have to wait a bit, but we'll squeeze you in," Fisher's receptionist had assured him.

There'd been no dizzy spell. That was a ruse to secure some private time with Fisher. Once they were together, he planned to ask about the phoney alibi Fisher had cooked up for his whereabouts on the night Jenny Birchmount was killed. The idea that his friend could be involved in her death was inconceivable, but Deirdre's admission that she'd lied now had him questioning everything.

He grabbed a two-month-old issue of *Time* magazine from a table and settled into a padded chair in the waiting room. The cover story was about a young Black senator named Barack Obama, exploring the improbable notion that he could be America's next president. Pugsley read the whole article and several others before his name was called, nearly an hour late.

A nurse led him into an examination room. "Just slip off your shirt and have a seat," she told him as she left the room. "The doctor will be with you shortly."

Pugsley sat down but left his shirt on. This wouldn't be that sort of examination. He'd be the one asking the questions, praying that his doctor had the right answers.

Fisher burst into the room a couple of minutes later, looking agitated. "Thank God, a friendly face," he said when he saw Pugsley, his harried expression softening slightly. "You wouldn't believe the day I'm having. Seems like every patient I see is giving me grief."

He shook his head apologetically. "Sorry, Norm. You're not here to listen to me bellyache. You've got worries of your own. What's this about a dizzy spell?"

Pugsley drew a deep breath, trying to steady his jangled nerves. He was about to embark on what might well be the most difficult conversation of his life. He wasn't looking forward to it.

"The good news is I didn't have a dizzy spell," he began.

"No dizzy spell?" Fisher said, puzzled. "Then why are you here?"

"That's the bad news." Pugsley motioned to an empty chair. "Maybe you should sit down, Beau."

"Just tell me!" Fisher said. "Has someone died? Is Deirdre all right?"

"Deirdre's fine, but I wouldn't say she's all right. She's pretty devastated by what you've done."

Fisher stared at him. "I don't know what you're talking about."

"Come on, Beau. You know exactly what I mean. You tried to solicit sex from a prostitute. Unfortunately for you, she was an undercover cop."

"Did Deirdre tell you that?" Fisher glowered. "That fucking rape centre has really messed with her head. To her, every man is a potential sexual predator. Even me."

"You're saying you didn't try to solicit sex?" Pugsley asked.

"Of course not! I thought you knew me better than that, Norm."

"I thought I did too, Beau. But I guess not." He paused before proceeding. "It gives me no pleasure to tell you the police confirmed you were arrested for soliciting. They told me you're now in john school."

Fisher said nothing at first, then erupted. "Those bastards! They told me there'd be no charges or publicity if I went to john school," he raged. "Obviously, that was a lie."

"They only confirmed what Deirdre had already told me."

Fisher grimaced. "Deirdre! Why can't she keep her mouth shut?"

Pugsley was disturbed by his friend's outburst. This wasn't the Beauregard Fisher he knew. He stiffened his spine for the hard questions yet to come.

"Forget about Deirdre. I want to focus on you, Beau. A few moments ago, you denied that you'd been arrested. Now, you're admitting it. Do I have that right?"

Fisher nodded curtly. "Not that it's any of your business."

"So you lied to me," Pugsley said. "Why?"

Fisher scowled. "It's embarrassing. And it would ruin me if people knew."

"I'm not 'people,' Beau," Pugsley pointed out. "I'm a friend as well as a patient. If you can't be honest with me, who can you be honest with?"

Fisher ran his fingers through his thinning hair. "You're right. Forgive me. I'm sort of a mess right now." An apprehensive expression crept over his face. "You aren't planning to put this in the newspaper, are you?"

"The fact that you're in john school? It would be a juicy story," Pugsley said, "but no, I wouldn't do that."

"Thanks, pal," said Fisher, visibly relieved. "I knew I could count on you."

"However," Pugsley continued, "I do have *other* questions."

"What questions?" Fisher asked.

"For starters, how long have you been seeing prostitutes?"

"I'd only just started when I got caught," Fisher declared.

Pugsley wasn't buying that. Why would an eminent citizen like Beau start seeking out the company of prostitutes at age 71?

"So you're telling me that after a successful life and an enviable marriage, the urge to buy sex from strangers suddenly became irresistible?"

"When you put it that way, it *does* sound implausible," Fisher admitted. "But Deirdre and I have had our ups and downs over the years. We aren't the picture-perfect couple we appear to be. For whatever reason, she lost interest in sex in recent years – with me, or anyone else, for that matter. Even so, I wanted to save our marriage. We'd spent a lifetime together, after all. You don't just throw that away. I thought it might help if I could satisfy my sexual needs in … other ways. Outsource them to a neutral third party, so to speak."

Pugsley listened with astonishment. Was Fisher really trying to blame his wife for his recourse to paid sex? And was he seriously trying to cast it in a positive light – as a sort of extracurricular marital therapy?

"I don't buy it, Beau," he said. "A leopard doesn't change his spots, especially so late in life." He tried to collect his thoughts, knowing that his next few words would be crucial. "You've already lied to me once today. I think you're doing it again. You need to come clean. When did you *really* start seeing prostitutes?"

Fisher looked like a deer dazzled by onrushing headlights. He raised his hands in surrender. "OK, Norm. You got me. I have paid for sex before. But it was a very long time ago."

"When?"

"A couple of decades ago. Since then, I swear, I've been a good boy. Until recently," he added, now appearing sheepish.

"Was Jenny Birchmount one of the prostitutes you saw?" Pugsley asked, fearing the answer.

Fisher was very still. He didn't meet Pugsley's gaze. "I don't know. She never told me her real name."

"She? There was only one?"

"Yes. Only one."

Pugsley struggled to rein in his racing thoughts. "You owned a black Mercedes in 1985, right?"

Fisher nodded.

"The man who killed Jenny was in his late 40s or early 50s – as you would have been at the time – and was driving a black luxury car – just like you."

"The police checked me out," Fisher protested. "I had a solid alibi."

"So I understand. Deirdre told them you were at the movies with her."

"That's right!"

"That was another lie, though, wasn't it, Beau?" Pugsley said softly.

Fisher's head jerked up. "Why would you say that?" he asked.

"Because Deirdre told me. You asked her to cover for you. You said you were at an underground casino that night. But that's not true, is it? You don't like to gamble. I should know – you always turned down my poker game invitations." He drew a deep breath. "You were with Jenny, weren't you?"

Fisher stared at him for a full 10 seconds, his face turning an alarming shade of magenta. "We're supposed to be friends," he said at last, voice rising. "And you come to my place of work and accuse me of murder?"

He was shouting now. "I don't believe it. Get out! Get out or I'll throw you out myself!" He took a menacing step towards Pugsley, brandishing his stethoscope like a weapon.

Stunned by Fisher's fury, Pugsley retreated, keeping a wary eye on the enraged doctor. When he reached the door, he gave him a sorrowful look. "Sorry, Beau," he said, and quickly left. He wasn't sure what he was sorry about, but he knew things would never be the same.

•••

At home that evening, a shaken Norman Pugsley replayed his confrontation with Fisher. He couldn't decide whether his volcanic response signalled innocence or guilt. If Fisher had played no role in Jenny's death, wouldn't his accusations seem like a terrible betrayal? But if he *were* involved, might not that also trigger his fury?

Pugsley was wrestling with these thoughts when he heard a faint knock on his front door. It was nearly midnight. The door had no peephole, so he cautiously opened it a crack and peered out.

It was Fisher. "Let me in, Norm," he said, his voice subdued. "We need to talk."

"If I let you in, you won't hurt me, will you?" Pugsley asked, not sure what to expect.

"No, Norm. I won't hurt you."

Pugsley slowly opened the door and ushered the doctor into his living room. They remained on their feet. Fisher's shoulders were slumped and his face was a mask of misery.

"I never meant to harm her. I swear," he whispered, eyes rimmed with tears. His normally strapping body seemed diminished, as if depleted by his admission.

As he steadied himself, the words came tumbling out. Between sobs, he told Pugsley about Jenny. How at first, they just talked, how things escalated from there, how in the end everything went horribly wrong.

"I know it sounds crazy, but I loved her," he said, tears staining his face. "Maybe she loved me too, in her way. There was a real bond between us." His anguish was unlike anything Pugsley had ever seen. "It was impossible, of course. We were from different worlds. She was young enough to be my daughter."

Pugsley was speechless. He'd clung to the belief that his friend could somehow demonstrate his innocence. That had been shattered.

He'd always expected to feel triumphant if he discovered who killed Jenny. Instead, all he felt was heartache and regret – for Jenny, for Beau, for Deirdre and for himself.

"I'll have to report on this, you know," Pugsley told Fisher, when he was finally able to speak. "You need to turn yourself in to the police. You did a terrible thing. It was wrong to exploit her like that. But I don't think you meant to kill her. I might even believe you cared for her."

Fisher managed a tiny, pained smile. "I'll turn myself in tomorrow morning. Will you come with me?" he asked. "I could use a friend."

Twenty-five

OTTAWA, THE FOLLOWING DAY

With Fisher safely delivered to police that morning, Pugsley urgently called Hassan. "We've got work to do," he said. Then he phoned Richter. "You'll want to clear Page One. This story is worth it."

"My God, Norm!" she exclaimed when he told her about Fisher. "This is the story of the – oh hell, I'm going to swear – f-f-f-fucking century! Take as much time as you need. We'll hold the press run if necessary."

It was nearly 10 a.m. when Pugsley and Hassan arrived in the *Advocate*'s newsroom and began to write. Pugsley was at the keyboard with Fawzia crouched behind him, tossing out clarifying phrases and helpful suggestions.

Their first stab at a lede was a bit clunky. "Beauregard Fisher, one of Ottawa's most prominent family physicians, turned himself in to police Thursday and confessed to killing prostitute Jenny Birchmount in 1985, resolving one of the city's longest-standing cold-case homicides."

After further discussion, they settled on: "Ottawa doctor Beauregard Fisher confessed on Thursday to killing teenaged prostitute Jenny Birchmount in 1985 but tearfully insisted her death was accidental."

The story went on to recount Jenny's fleeting life and tragic death, the police search for a middle-aged suspect in a black luxury car and the dogged investigation by Pugsley and Hassan that had ultimately unravelled the mystery.

They worked on the story all day and finished their 2,500-word epic with minutes to spare before deadline. Their story ran the next morning across Page One under the banner headline, "*Advocate* solves cold-case homicide." A secondary headline added further details – Jenny's death,

Fisher's confession. Main art was a four-column file portrait of Fisher alongside a smaller, poor-quality shot of Jenny, taken a couple of years before her death.

Within a day or two, the story of the prominent physician who killed the teenaged prostitute was reprinted by news media across Canada and around the world. Tabloid-TV shows pored over the salacious details for weeks. Pugsley and Fawzia fielded dozens of requests for interviews from places as distant as Australia.

The plaudits seemed endless – there was even talk of newspaper awards to come – but Pugsley was unable to savour the acclaim. He felt satisfied at having played a role in bringing Jenny's killer to justice. But the fact her killer was his friend and doctor tortured him, as did his own early blindness. Why hadn't he kept at it, he asked himself, even after being exiled to the night news desk all those years ago? He'd worried more about his own dignity than the fate of the young victim.

He also had to endure jeers from Jack Clifford, who made a point of calling him the day the story appeared.

"Glad you finally got the right guy," Clifford taunted. "He was right there, under your nose, the whole time, but you wouldn't see it."

Pugsley choked back his exasperation, recognizing he'd allowed his distaste for Clifford to colour his view of him. He offered a mumbled apology, but Jack Clifford didn't appear to be taking it well.

"Fuck you, Pugsley," Clifford barked. "You think a few words will make things right? I should have sued you. Maybe I still will."

Then he laughed long and hard. "Just fucking with you, Pugs!" he chortled. "Let's have a beer sometime."

True to form, Pugsley thought – Clifford still has his twisted, in-your-face sense of humour.

•••

His most difficult conversation was with Deirdre Fisher. Though he telephoned her as soon as he finished writing, he'd intentionally allowed time for Beau to call her first from the police station.

When Pugsley phoned, she greeted him with silence – seemingly endless but probably lasting less than five seconds. "Norman Pugsley," she finally said, enunciating each syllable with measured calm. "You've got a lot of nerve calling me."

Pugsley stumbled to find the right words. "I know you're upset, Deirdre," he began, but she cut him off.

"Before you started stirring the pot, I had a husband. He had flaws, God knows, but at least I had him. Now, thanks to you, he's likely going to prison," she said. "I'll be 65 next year. What am I going to do?" He heard what sounded like a sob.

"Believe me, Deirdre, I never dreamed this would happen. Not only have I lost a friend, in a very real sense, I was his executioner. I'm heartbroken."

Hearing nothing from Deirdre, he plunged on. "I'm sure Beau didn't mean to kill Jenny, but the fact is, he did. She was a young woman. She made some terrible choices, but she didn't deserve to die. If there's any good to come from this mess, it's that there'll be justice for Jenny at last."

A shuddering sigh from Deirdre. "If only I hadn't offered that reward," she said. "None of this would have happened."

"Wait," Pugsley gasped. "You're the one who offered the reward?"

"I was angry that no one had ever been held accountable for her death. I'd seen that too often at the Rape Crisis Centre. I wanted the killer found. But I never thought …" Her voice trailed off.

Pugsley struggled to digest what Deirdre had told him. Beauregard Fisher, it appeared, had been laid low by the two unlikeliest of people: his wife and his friend.

Richter was right, Pugsley marvelled. It *was* the story of the fucking century.

•••

On Christmas Day, Pugsley got a phone call. Her voice was instantly recognizable, though they hadn't seen one another in person for nearly five years.

"Merry Christmas, dad," she said.

"Barbara!" Pugsley's heart was thumping, and his mouth felt Kalahari dry, abruptly dehydrated by the unexpected call. "It's … so lovely to hear from you."

"Well," she replied, "it's Christmas, after all."

"I know, but …"

She interrupted him before he could complete the thought. "I read your story about that young woman's murder on the *Advocate*'s website. I thought it was excellent and so important. Just wanted to tell you that. And wish you Merry Christmas, of course."

The lump forming in Pugsley's throat made speech temporarily impossible. The tears in his eyes didn't help, either. It took three or four throat-clearing hacks before he was able to respond.

"You have no idea what that means to me," he said, struggling to rein in his surging emotions. "I haven't seen you for so long. Then to hear from you like this …" He paused to wipe his coursing eyes.

"It must have been hard," Barbara said. "Turning in your friend, I mean."

"One of the hardest things I've ever had to do. But not nearly as hard as losing you, daughter," Pugsley said. "That was … unbearable."

Neither spoke for a moment, savouring the unfamiliar but comforting sensation of connection. Then Barbara broke the silence, saying words he'd never expected to hear.

"I've missed you, dad."

That triggered another round of joyful tears, this time from them both.

"Oh Barbara. I don't have the words to express how much I've missed you."

"I'm so sorry," she said.

"Don't be," he said. "I lost myself for a while before your mom and I split. She was right to leave me. And you were right to be with her."

"But now," Barbara asked, "you've what – found yourself again?"

Pugsley smiled. "I think so."

"I want to tell you something. Don't be mad," she said.

"I won't," he promised, bracing for something dreadful.

"Mom told me to call you. I wanted to after I read your story, but I was scared. I didn't know how you'd react. But mom said, 'Just do it.' "

"Your mother always was a wise woman. How's she doing?"

"Really well. She and Clarence were made for each other. She couldn't have found a better husband."

"You see her often?"

"Sunday dinner. Every bloody week since she moved to Toronto." She laughed. "I'm joking. It's lovely, really. I just wish she'd graduate from the Mateus."

"That's always been her drink, for better or for worse." His heart felt full – fuller than it had been in a very long time. "We've got a lot of catching up to do, you and I," he said.

"What are you doing today?" she asked.

"Just hanging out at home with my Christmas tree."

"Would you like to come for dinner?"

"Today? Aren't you in Richmond Hill?"

"Yes, but the weather's good. You could drive here in five hours or so. You wouldn't even have to speed."

"I don't know … I don't want to horn in on your family Christmas."

"It's OK. I already talked to Ramesh," she said. "And besides, you could finally meet your new grandson."

"Grandson?" he gasped. "I have another grandson?"

"You do. Grayson. Cutest four-week-old kid in the universe."

"Christ on a bicycle! That's fantastic! But … I don't have a present for him. For any of you."

"Don't worry, dad," Barbara said. "You're the present. But please, try not to swear around the kids."

Twenty-six

OTTAWA, 2007

The months following publication of the Jenny Birchmount story were eventful.

Within days, Fawzia had tracked down one of Jenny's aunts, along with two cousins, and had written a poignant follow-up story. Pugsley was impressed. "That young woman is a crackerjack," he told Richter during one of their frequent dinners. "I can't believe I ever doubted her."

Their story was nominated for a National Newspaper Award but lost to a *Globe and Mail* team's eight-part series on questionable conduct in the office of the Ontario Securities Commission.

After discussions with his lawyer, Beauregard Fisher pleaded guilty to manslaughter and was awaiting sentencing. He was widely expected to do time in prison, though his decision to admit guilt, along with his evident remorse, weighed in his favour.

Senator James Brody pleaded not guilty to sexual assault and was suspended by his Senate colleagues pending the outcome of his trial, set for the spring of 2008.

After Pugsley declined her $50,000 reward, Deirdre donated it to a local shelter for sexually abused women. But she couldn't easily forgive her husband's betrayals and ugly crime. Most days, she was ready to sever all ties with him. Pugsley understood her anger, though part of him hoped her decades-long bond with Fisher might prove durable enough to endure.

Jack Clifford never did sue Pugsley, perhaps because the construction magnate was caught having sex with his 25-year-old receptionist in a Tim Hortons washroom. The tabloid press and a new social media site called Twitter had a field day.

For Pugsley, it was the best of times. His Christmas visit with Barbara and her family had gone well. His older grandchildren – 10-year-old Jeremy and eight-year-old Sarah – were distant at first, but soon warmed to their rediscovered grandpa and his occasionally colourful vocabulary. As for newborn Grayson, cradling him in his arms melted Pugsley's flinty heart.

Since then, they'd talked periodically on the phone, slowing rebuilding their fractured relationship. Pugsley had invited Barbara, Ramesh and their children to camp with him in a provincial park in the summer. They were considering it.

Within the journalistic community, the story he and Fawzia had written was widely admired. Harrison Howard, Pugsley's successor as the *Advocate*'s managing editor, made it clear he'd welcome further contributions. "I know you're supposedly retired, Norm," Howard said, "but you still have the fire in your belly. The paper could use a reporter like you right now."

Pugsley was flattered, but politely declined. "A wise man knows when to leave," he replied. "Not saying I'm wise, but I'm smart enough to recognize I should quit while I'm ahead."

In his mind, the Jenny Birchmount story was one of a kind: an unsolved mystery that had long tugged at his heart. He doubted he'd encounter another like it.

Besides, retirement wasn't so bad now that Renata was part of his life. Though her job as editor consumed huge chunks of her time, they saw each other regularly, sharing romantic dinners and sometimes more.

They enjoyed movies, even if their tastes were far from aligned. To please him, she sat through the heist comedy *Ocean's Thirteen*. He, in turn, endured Deepa Mehta's Hindi film, *Water*, nominated for a best foreign film Oscar. Renata was moved to tears. Pugsley struggled to stay awake.

One afternoon in mid-June, Renata telephoned in a state of high excitement.

"I've got the most amazing news," she began. "Bliss and Matina are getting married!"

It took a moment for Pugsley to absorb what she was saying. "Bliss Browning is … getting married? Our Bliss Browning?" he asked, dumbfounded by the notion that the once pusillanimous former travel editor would take the plunge.

"Next April! And guess what, Norman?"

"What?" he asked cautiously.

"We're invited to the wedding!"

"We are?"

"Harrison too. We're all invited."

"That's … incredible," Pugsley blurted, finally shedding the interrogative voice. In truth, it didn't sound unpleasant. Weddings could be fun, especially the receptions. *We'll have to take a cab*, he thought. *Renata wouldn't want me to drive after I've been drinking.*

"There's no rush," she interjected, "but at some point, we'll have to look into getting tickets."

"They're selling tickets to the wedding?" he asked, lapsing back into the interrogative.

"No, my silly darling. Airline tickets. The wedding's in Greece, of course."

Pugsley's heart nearly stopped. "Greece? Perhaps you've forgotten, but the last time I was in Greece I almost died."

"Yes," she acknowledged, "but this time I'll be there with you." He could sense her dazzling smile through the phone line. "Don't worry. I won't let you die on my watch. And you never know," she added, "it might end up being a double wedding."

Double? What was she suggesting? Pugsley struggled for a response, but words failed him. *Christ on a bicycle!*

Acknowledgements

When my first novel, *A Life of Bliss*, was unleashed on an unsuspecting public in 2021, it was a Kindle e-book. You could buy print-on-demand copies from Amazon but only a handful of independent bookstores in the Ottawa Valley sold the print version. Though *A Life of Bliss* garnered favourable reviews and was read by several book clubs, I quickly learned about the Herculean challenges first-time authors face in drawing attention to their literary babies. Even so, my début novel did well enough to convince Ron Corbett, the talented owner of Ottawa Press and Publishing, to order a modest print run in 2022. That got *Bliss* into bookstores across the National Capital Region and introduced it to a wider audience. It also encouraged me to dream about a sequel (or two).

Norman's Conquest is the result. One lesson I've learned is that seeking feedback on your work-in-progress from discerning readers is an excellent idea. It usually produces a better book. For reasons I can't explain, these individuals are known as beta readers. I had none for *A Life of Bliss*, an error I was determined to avoid with the sequel. I approached eight people and asked them to read my manuscript and offer feedback.

To my astonishment, they all said yes. Many of their responses were positive. But there were pointed critiques as well, usually accompanied by suggested remedies. I cannot overstate how invaluable their input was. These beta readers (the Magnificent Eight, as I think of them) were novelists Amy Tector, Mark Richardson and Joy Ferguson, and journalists Ros Guggi, John King, Janice Kennedy, Bruce Ward and former Montreal Gazette editor Lucinda Chodan. Thank you, thank you, thank you!

The person who had the greatest influence on *Norman's Conquest* was my wife, Christina (Tina) Spencer. In a very real sense, she was my co-author, suggesting plot twists and fiercely wielding her editor's pencil to tighten flabby writing or improve word choices. Even after I thought the novel was finished, she did one final edit that made it better. I couldn't have asked for a more splendid collaborator.

I'd also like to thank Ron Corbett, who agreed to publish *Norman's Conquest* even though non-fiction books on local subjects are more typically the bread and butter of Ottawa Press and Publishing. I'm very grateful.

And as it customary, but necessary to add, any mistakes, typos, infelicities or muddles in the book are mine alone.

About the Author

Don Butler, an award-winning journalist, worked for the *Ottawa Citizen* for more than four decades, including six years as executive editor. He has the good fortune to be married to another exceptional journalist, Christina (Tina) Spencer, whose guidance and support have been pivotal to any success he's enjoyed as an author. His first novel, *A Life of Bliss*, was released in 2021. His second novel, *Norman's Conquest*, is the sequel to that book. If all goes well, there may be more.

Praise for Don Butler's first novel, *A Life of Bliss*

"*A Life of Bliss* is a hilarious and moving novel with a mystery at its heart. Life-changing opportunity can be a dangerous thing; this novel reminds us of why risks are worth taking. Don Butler has taken a place on my shelf alongside past masters of funny Canadian literature, and I'm grateful for his deft portrait of the rapidly changing culture of a newsroom, a place that was an important part of my life for many years."

– **Kate Heartfield**, author of *The Embroidered Book*

"When it comes to the novel's endearing central figure, Bliss Browning, you find perhaps the most bumbling foreign correspondent to emerge in a work of fiction since renowned satirist Evelyn Waugh dispatched William Boot to East Africa in his 1939 classic, *Scoop*."

– **Jamie Portman**, Postmedia News

"Part mystery, part romance, part ghost story, and wholly entertaining. This brisk story carries us from the raucous newsroom of an aging fictional newspaper to Greek locales still haunted by entities of myth and legend. It's about finding the courage to have hope and to take a leap of faith, in yourself most of all, even if the odds are 50/50 between it going horribly wrong … or liberating you to live the life you were always meant to have. I highly recommend it."

– **Leo Valiquette**, author of *Bane of All Things*

"*A Life of Bliss* has whiffs of Richler and Amis about it. Yet author Don Butler has fashioned something unique. He retains a veteran journalist's readability, along with the depth of soul required to tell a moving story. Highly recommended with a glass of ouzo and a vinyl recording of Maria Callas."

– **Richard Schwindt**, contributor to
The Magnolia Bluff Crime Chronicles series

